Alaskan
BRIDE

D Jordan Redhawk

BELLA
BOOKS

2016

Bella Books, Inc.
P.O. Box 10543
Tallahassee, FL 32302

First Bella Books Edition 2016

Editor: Shelly Rafferty
Cover Designer: Judith Fellows

ISBN: 978-1-59493-501-5

Dedication

To Nene Adams. Her loss diminishes the world and all that is in it.

And always to Anna Redhawk, my partner in multiple crimes.

Acknowledgment

I'd like to thank Anna Redhawk—without her sacrifice (of my time, of her sanity, of...) this book would never have been written. She's the one who becomes glassy-eyed as I ping weird ideas off her. She deserves an award!

Nene Adams was a dynamo when it came to writing, whether historical romance or science fiction. Though ailing she still had time to answer questions that I had regarding property rights in the late eighteen hundreds. I miss her wicked humor and tales of the sweet life she built in the Netherlands. (She's probably up there right now discussing medieval fashion with royalty!) Thank you, Nene!

Many years ago, a friend gave me an album by K.T. Tunstall. Man, that was some awesome music! When I created the soundtrack for writing this book, that album became the top choice. Thank you, Katie Anderson, for sharing.

Thanks to Shelly Rafferty and Jackie Eddy of Crossfield Writers for their editing prowess. Editing a manuscript is such a chore, but I learn something new every time. I promise never to get hung up on the "Ing Thing" again! And what about that cover, huh? Judith Fellows created a great piece with little input from me. Thank you!

And my hat's off to Bella Books and all the wonderful people who worked so hard to get this book into your hands. They're a spectacular group of people.

CHAPTER ONE

"Are you cutting a shine with me?" The young woman rattled the section of newspaper across the table at her companion. Her cheeks dimpled as she smiled. "You? A mail-order bride?"

Clara Stapleton felt the skin of her face and throat heat. Her eyes darted about the cafe, and she prayed to God that the nearest patrons hadn't overheard Emma Whitman's loud proclamation. None of the half-dozen other habitués paid their table any mind, either having missed the implications of Emma's words or perhaps being too polite to exhibit a response. Clara's stomach quivered with a mixture of relief, excitement and quiet audacity that she even considered this controversial topic. The idea of searching for a husband via matrimonial agencies smacked of desperation. Confident that the occupants of neighboring tables remained oblivious, she snatched the newspaper from Emma's hand. "Hush!" She leaned over the table to scold her best friend. "Keep your voice down!"

Emma glanced around the small establishment, the impish joy on her round face extinguished by sudden concern. The expression didn't last long as she too judged there had been no witnesses to her outburst. A familiar mischievous light returned to her brown eyes, and her bow mouth creased to allow the dimples a speedy return. She mimicked Clara and leaned close across the detritus of their afternoon tea. "Are you serious? Searching the advertisements for a husband?"

Clara's butterflies intensified. The revelation of her intentions to her dearest friend somehow brought her purpose into sharper focus. Her scheme was no longer an amorphous wondering in her mind now that she'd dared speak the words aloud. For a brief moment she entertained the notion of naysaying herself, of capitulating to Emma's delighted question with a negative. To do so would conjure a prevarication between them, something to which they'd promised one another as children they would never fall prey. Such a lie would chip away at the foundation of their closeness and eventually destroy that which Clara held so dear. She pressed her hand against her trembling stomach. "Yes Em. I'm serious."

Emma flounced backward in her chair, eyes wide, smile turned incredulous. Her fingers worried her napkin ring, the silver flashing reflections from the sunlight that splayed across the tablecloth. She studied Clara for a long moment. "I must say, Clara, the idea never occurred to me." She gazed at the newspaper clutched in Clara's hand and lowered her voice. "But it sounds positively wicked!"

Relief briefly overrode all other concerns, and Clara wondered why. She and Emma had supported one another through dozens of escapades throughout their shared childhood, some undertakings more questionable than not. Why wouldn't Emma throw her full support behind Clara for this cockamamie idea? She returned Emma's smile. "It does sound wicked, doesn't it?"

Emma reached across the table and wiggled her fingers at the newspaper until Clara returned it. She carefully straightened out the wrinkled pages, shuffling through them until she found the one with the title "Matrimonial News." Her eyebrows rose as she noted Clara's careful selections marked on the newsprint. "I see you've found some creditable entries."

Clara's cheeks burned. She used her napkin to fan herself. "There are a few that seemed...appropriate." Her discomposure wilted under a stronger sense of exhilaration, and she scooted her chair closer to Emma's. They both perused the advertisements, and Clara pointed at a circled entry as she spoke. "This gentleman seems nice enough. Landowner, successful farmer and relatively young." Another. "And this one is a widower with a pub here in Boston."

Emma scowled at the adverts. "Yes, but the landowner is in Georgia. His property is no doubt still war-torn even after all these years. Do you want to marry a man whose family may have been slave owners? He'll probably have you singing the 'Bonnie Blue Flag' at your wedding." Before Clara could respond, Emma skipped to the second example. "And a pub owner? Really?" She glared with stern intent at her best friend. "You don't know the first thing about running a tavern. What he needs is a workmate as well as a wife. Do you believe you're capable of pouring busthead and ale for hundreds of drunken men?"

"I'm not certain," Clara said, more unsettled by Emma's use of the slang for whiskey than by her argument.

"I am certain. Neither of these men is suitable." Emma returned her brisk attention to the paper, rapidly scanning the pencil marks her friend had used to accentuate possibilities. "And this one? Alaska? There's nothing there except smelly old miners and snow!"

Clara eyed the advertisement as she groped for the proper words. "To be honest, that one is my favorite."

Emma gaped at her. "Your favorite?" She read the advert aloud, ducking her head closer to the newsprint and lowering her voice when Clara hissed. "Matrimonial - A worthy man, age 34, seeking a well-educated younger woman for marriage in the Alaskan District. A trapper by trade, I am industrious, clean and even-tempered with thirteen hundred acres of homestead and need a help-mate and loving wife." She let the paper fall to the table and rounded on Clara. "A trapper? In the mountains of the Alaskan territory? Are you moonstruck? When was the last time you spent a night out-of-doors?"

A little riled, Clara returned Emma's unrelenting gaze. "He has a homestead."

"A hovel, perhaps." Emma sniffed disdain as she retrieved the advertisements once more. "It would be easier to learn how to sling drinks in a pub." She peered at the trapper's advert. With an air of disgruntled reluctance, she pursed her lips. "Thirteen hundred acres isn't something to sneeze at, I suppose. It's a wonder he claims to be a trapper rather than a gold miner. And thirty-four seems a bit old." She turned the paper, as if looking for more information on the backside. "It doesn't say he's a widower. Why hasn't he been married before now?"

"He's no older than some of the layabouts rooting around for companionship here," Clara argued. She and Emma had both had their fill of the local men who had taken it upon themselves to woo them. The majority of those allegedly eligible bachelors were too old, too young or had neither the stability nor financial fortitude to begin families. Those men that would have been acceptable already had wives or had located connubial prospects far away. The last thing Clara wanted was to succumb to the sublimely wearisome businessmen who'd come knocking at her father's door. She craved something different, something provocative. She tapped the Alaskan's advert. "And he's already an accomplished tradesman and landowner."

"Both excellent points."

Emboldened, Clara continued. "I've also heard that the countryside there is absolutely stunning. Crisp freshwater springs, Olympian mountains and deep forests." She stared into the distance, inadvertently falling into a daydream. "Fish fairly jumping out of the rivers and lakes, elk and moose wandering right up to your home. Pristine air…"

Emma cocked her head at Clara. "But…Alaska. We'd never see one another."

Clara's fantasy popped. Aghast, she snatched Emma's hand, holding tight. "Yes we will! I'll come visit and bring my family. My children must meet their godmother, of course. And my best friend." She smiled. "And you must come visit me as well. Perhaps I can convince you and your future husband to join us there."

"Perhaps." It was Emma's turn to blush, her dimples turning a delightful shade of red. The man she'd always wanted for her future husband was no secret to either of them. Clara's brother, Bradford Stapleton, currently attended Harvard University as a student of law. Emma had become enamored of his gallant good looks and bright blue eyes when they were children.

The vision expanded in Clara's mind. She and her jaunty husband stood on their porch, overlooking the majestic scenery of Alaska while their children played in the yard. Emma and Bradford, arm in arm, coming abreast of a slight rise, waved greeting as they led Clara's many nieces and nephews to their new home.

"Will there be anything else, young ladies?"

Flustered by the interruption, Clara blinked up at the new arrival at their table.

The proprietor of Huckleberry Above Persimmon, Mr. Tally, hovered at her elbow. His pronounced girth was swathed in a pristine apron, and he grinned at the two young women as he wiped his hands on a towel.

Emma was quicker to her senses, folding the newspaper with alacrity in order to block the nosy restaurant owner from discerning the topic of their interest. "I believe not, sir. Thank you."

Faint disappointment brushed across Mr. Tally's face. Clara didn't know if it was due to his inability to learn what they'd discussed or the realization that they were finished with their meal. Gossip about town suggested that he had wandering hands.

Taking Emma's cue, Clara located her handbag. "How much do we owe, Mr. Tally?"

The owner's dissatisfaction faded, replaced with rapacity. "The 'tally,' if you will," he chuckled at the oft-repeated play on his name, "is twenty cents. Unless I may interest you in a serving of baked apples? They're hot out of the oven and most delicious."

Clara extracted a coin purse, and carefully selected a quarter. "Thank you, but that won't be necessary, Mr. Tally." She proffered the coin. "The beefsteak was quite filling." Mr. Tally bobbed his head as he accepted payment. While he fished in a pocket for change, she smiled and patted his forearm. "Please keep the remainder."

"As always, the service was excellent," Emma cut in, preparing to rise.

Mr. Tally hastened to assist them from their chairs. He peppered them with inconsequential chitchat until the women found themselves on the front step of the restaurant.

"Next time it's my turn." Emma used the reflection in the front window to adjust the gray felt sailor hat she'd donned for their outing. When all was to her satisfaction, she turned to her friend.

"Certainly." Clara linked her arm through Emma's and they strolled down the busy sidewalk.

"So, you're certain then?"

Clara squeezed Emma's arm. "Yes, I am." She watched the bustle of horse-drawn carriages and trolleys rumble past, the clouds of dust left in their wake. Freshly cut wood lashed to a cart went by, the scent of pine drifting through the air. The sidewalk was crowded with people—mostly men on business—but the occasional woman or two had chosen this fine day to shop or enjoy their afternoon tea in style. Clara would miss the flurry of activity in which she'd been raised, the cosmopolitan atmosphere of her hometown.

"And you're set on the Alaskan?"

"Yes." Clara smiled.

Emma made a moue. "I can't change your mind?"

Clara stiffened. "I must confess that I've already written him."

"What?" Emma pulled back, mouth and eyes wide. "You did not!"

Unable to speak, Clara nodded. She didn't know whether Emma would take her precipitous action as daring or a betrayal of their friendship. Emma's quicksilver emotions could sway in either direction.

Emma's expression teetered between dismay and awe, finally settling on grudging admiration. "You are a little hussy, aren't you?" she asked in a whisper, a puckish grin upon her face.

Her acceptance nearly caused Clara to swoon as relief flooded through every muscle and nerve. Her eyes stung with the unshed tears of uncertain stress. The one constant in her life had been Emma. Hurting her was akin to hurting herself. Now that Clara had vaulted the obstacle of Emma's opinion in this matter, she realized how foolish she'd been. Of course Emma would support her in this endeavor, foolhardy or no. Such had been the way of their friendship throughout their lives. They loved each other more than their own siblings and parents. Clara doubted she'd ever be able to discover that depth of adoration with a man. If such was the case, she could at least live a life surrounded by natural beauty.

CHAPTER TWO

The ropes dug into Callie Glass's shoulders, a familiar sensation after a half-dozen years on the trapline. Behind her she heard the wooden rails of the sledge grate against rock and hardpack. Occasionally she'd hit a patch of ice and snow from the last storm, and the sledge would lurch forward, its load of carcasses swaying with the abrupt change in speed. Though she sweated from the exertion, she wore her jacket. She hated the fact that she'd taken after her mother, inheriting a frail-looking and feminine body that belied her sinewy strength. To counteract the initial impression of being a lightweight, a pretty little thing with a tendency toward hysteria, she wore bulky clothing to appear physically larger. The tactic didn't always work.

A wisp of golden hair fell from beneath her slouch hat, tickling her nose. She puffed a breath to dislodge it from her face. The stubborn lock drifted back into place. As much as she wanted to stop and tuck it back under the brim, she refrained. The cabin was ahead on an uphill incline. If she halted now, she might not be able to get the heavy sledge back into motion for the last hundred feet. It would be mortifying to wait for her brother to return from Skagway with their only horse because she'd foundered the sledge this close to home.

The scent of rich loam and pine trees gave way to the smell of wood smoke and the sea. About a quarter mile away from the cabin, the waves along the Taiya Inlet slapped loud against the shoreline. Another steamer full of miners must have recently passed en route to Skagway. To distract herself from her recalcitrant tresses and the burn of exertion in her thighs and back, Callie gazed over the water toward the fold of land that hid the Chilkoot Inlet. Another ship had rounded the corner and was headed landward, smoke and steam emitting from its stacks as it neared.

She sneered at the ship, stilling her face as the action brought another annoying tickle to her nose. Every ne'er-do-well and blowhard had turned up with gold in his or her eyes these last few months. Skagway hadn't been her most favorite place in the world to start with, but now it had swelled to bursting with the influx of Johnny Newcomes and muckmen who thought they could make it rich in the northern goldfields.

Callie put her back into the effort as the sledge hit a rough patch of ground. Not for the first time did she thank God above that her brother, Jasper, hadn't fallen sway to gold fever. Rather than drop everything in her lap and head north with the rest of the hopeful miners, he'd extended their trapline and sold the extra meat and hides to Skagway butchers. As the town's population bloated beyond its borders, more mouths needed feeding and more bodies needed furs to keep warm. Up in the Yukon, optimistic men grabbed up mining claims. South of Skagway and in the opposite direction of the goldfields, Jasper Glass had extended his property to thirteen hundred acres so as not to completely trap it out. The Glasses did excellent business without overtrapping their land or having to worry about trespassers and squatters. No one gave the passing hillsides a moment's thought as they sailed past to Skagway with their fever-dreams of glory and wealth.

With a grunt, Callie pulled the sledge the last few feet into the yard, a cleared area at the edge of the shore pine forest. The land here transformed from trees to scrub and meadow as it rolled down to the inlet's edge. In the past she'd go down to the rocky shore and watch the occasional ship come through, and wave at the curiosity seekers and sailors on the deck, but not anymore. There were too damned many of them.

She shrugged the ropes off her shoulders and swung her arms back and forth to ease the muscles. Removing the wide-brimmed hat from her head, she shoved the noncooperative hair back up onto her scalp and wiped her forehead with a handkerchief she fished from a pocket.

Three buildings squatted around the yard. Smoke drifted from the largest one's chimney and the front door stood open, a packhorse tied to the railing. The roof peak was barely six feet tall, and the roof jutted out four feet past the threshold to create a dirt-packed porch. The low ceiling inside was uncomfortable to Callie who stood only two inches shorter. Jasper was forced to duck his head while inside, being somewhat taller than she. The oilskin that normally covered the two windows had been rolled up and the shutters thrown wide. An assortment of tools and accouterments for day-to-day living in the wilderness cluttered the rudimentary porch—two wooden stools, a pair of snowshoes that needed repair, chains of different sized metal traps and two canteens hung from hooks, Jasper's leather pack and about a cord of firewood. Moose antlers adorned the top of the forward roof peak, high enough so as not to impale anyone attempting to enter.

The smallest building was the smokehouse. It doubled as a place to store and prepare meat and furs to be sold in town. A cord of mostly cedar wood was stacked to one side. Between the two stood a sturdy shed just large enough to house their one packhorse, with thick walls and a single door to protect against the carnivorous wildlife. Deep gouges had been dug into one corner, white against the weathered logs, where a hungry bear had attempted entry. Callie had received three hundred dollars and a healthy respect for charging grizzlies from that skin.

"Ho! Jasper!" Callie called. "I'm back!"

She saw movement out of the corner of her eye; her brother ducked out into the late afternoon sunlight. Like her he was tall and slender, his blond hair cut short and thinning at the temples. He smiled welcome from beneath a meticulously shaped mustache that curled ever-so-slightly at the ends; he looked more and more like their father every day. "Looks like a fine haul." His trousers were stained but serviceable and the top three buttons of his butternut shirt were open. Brown suspenders dangled from his waist.

"Not a bad 'un." Callie untied the tarp and pulled it free. "Mostly marmot and hares, but we had a lynx and a couple of red foxes on the line."

"Bully." Jasper circled the sledge and helped her sort through the day's catch. "Supper's almost ready. I can put this up in the shed if you want to go eat."

As much as she desired to do exactly that, Callie shook her head. She prided herself in not shirking her responsibilities. Most men fell into two categories. The worst one by far was the "little woman" syndrome where she received pats on the head and advice to return to the house where she belonged. The less ammunition she gave anyone for that opinion the better. "Naw. It'll take less time if we both work."

Jasper knew better than to argue. They unloaded the sledge and hanged the carcasses inside the smoke shed. As they toiled, he kept up conversation, filling her in with news from his trip to Skagway.

"And can you believe that lily-livered Billy Quinn? Sucking up to every skirt that sways past like God Himself has put him on this earth for all womankind?" Jasper shook his head in disgust. "It's a wonder he ain't been shot. He doesn't care if a woman is married or not. He just barges right in with his innuendo."

"Billy Quinn's a deadbeat. I don't think he's worked a day in his life." Callie folded the tarp from the sledge as her brother bundled the rope. "Besides, he hangs with Jamie Perkins. You need to stay away from them. Rumor has it that all them are running from the law."

Jasper shrugged, tied off the rope and tossed it onto the already disordered porch. "I know. I ran into him at the post."

Neither of them had family to speak of so why would her brother check the mail? He hadn't mentioned contacting the government about expanding their property again. Not that she'd mind if he did, but he normally discussed business propositions with her. She hauled the now empty sledge to the side of the shed and grunted as she hoisted it up. Jasper came to help and they tipped it over to rest at an angle against the side wall.

Callie dusted off her hands. "What's at the post?"

A blush spread across Jasper's fair face, alarming in its brilliance. "I—I got a letter." He pulled the trimmed but long edges of his bushy mustache into his mouth, hands on his hips as he stared out over the water.

Her suspicions grew and she cocked her head. For the life of her she couldn't think of anyone who'd send Jasper a letter. All their family had been dead and gone for years. *Unless there's something about the property in Oregon. But he sold that, didn't he?* "Who's it from?"

If anything, Jasper became more flustered. He gave a half shrug and rubbed at his mouth and chin, muttering into his palm as he answered.

"What?" Callie stepped closer. "What'd you say?"

"A woman." He dropped his hand, the gesture sharp as it resumed its place at his hip. "I got a letter from a woman in Boston who wants to come marry me."

Callie stared, unable to comprehend his words. She puzzled over them, repeating them in her head in an effort to make sense of it. A woman? Marry Jasper? "Wait…what?"

"Jesus, Mary and Joseph! I ain't getting any younger, Callie! If I want to start a family, I need to be getting on with it."

His irritation sparked the same emotion in her. She mirrored his stance and glared back. "How'd she know to write to you? Huh?" He looked away and she shifted to recapture his gaze. "That newspaper man three months ago, right?"

Jasper nodded. "Yes. When I sent you to pick up the beans from Hank Sheraton."

She recalled the man they'd met during a supply run, thinking him a slimy weasel at the time. "Did you pay him money?"

He rolled his eyes. "You know I did. How else could I get an advertisement?"

Scoffing, she threw her hands up in the air before slapping her thighs. She turned away. "You had no way of knowing if he was on the up-and-up. He could have been lying. Didn't I say I saw him talking to Soapy?" She referred to Skagway's local crime boss. If there was a shady way to make a dollar off an unsuspecting soul, the con man Soapy Smith could find it.

"But he wasn't lying. See?" An envelope crackled in Jasper's hand as he reached over Callie's shoulder from behind and waved it in her face.

She snatched it from his grasp, twisting with long practice to avoid his immediate grab to get it back. Two quick steps took her out of his reach, and she checked to make certain he didn't follow. They'd had years of keep-away though he was a full twelve years older than her. When he didn't chase her down, she relaxed and opened the envelope, the scent of lilac wafting from the paper. She paused as she inhaled the aroma, experiencing both enjoyment and scorn for the hussy's use of perfume as a lure. Another quick peek back showed Jasper resigned as he stood with his hands in his pockets. Callie unfolded the letter.

Dear Sir,

I confess I am nervous as I pen this missive for it has never before occurred to me to seek matrimony from the pages of a newspaper. I hope I do not portray myself as a shameless harridan—I do not even have the pleasure of knowing your name. Nevertheless, I have found your entry most intriguing.

My name is Clara Stapleton. I am aged twenty-two and seeking a husband. I live in Boston, Massachusetts, but do not let my metropolitan origins sway your rudimentary opinion of me. Though I am born and bred a city girl, I have had the opportunity to spend summers out of doors, fishing and camping with my family in the Green Mountains. I imagine your property must be splendid beyond words. Grand mountains, forests and rivers... Living in such magnificent beauty every day must seem a gift from God Himself!

Though I have no experience with the trapping lifestyle, I'm more than willing to learn. I would like to provisionally accept your offer of matrimony if you'll have me. I only ask that any marriage will be annulled should we discover that we are unable to coexist.

Please contact me posthaste with your answer. I breathlessly await your response.

Sincerely Yours,

Clara Stapleton

The penmanship flowed with delicate lines, and the letter was dated a month ago. Callie picked out the details, already disliking the woman who wrote it. "Boston? Really?" She handed the letter and envelope to Jasper who snatched it quickly from her hand. As he carefully returned the letter to its envelope, she crossed her arms over her chest. "You want to bring a city girl here?"

"She's been camping and fishing during the summers."

It was Callie's turn to roll her eyes. "Well, so had I before Ma and Pop passed on. That didn't mean I was experienced enough to live up here in the bush."

"You've done well enough." Jasper tucked the folded envelope into his pants pocket.

"Because I'm not a normal girl." Callie shook her head. "You really want to do this?"

Jasper gusted out a sigh. "Look. I know you don't want children or a husband. That ain't your way." He held his hands up to stop her as she opened her mouth to argue. "This isn't about you, Callie! It's about me. I want a wife, children. Can't you just imagine a passel of young'uns playing out here in the yard? You'd have nieces and nephews to spoil rotten."

A sense of loss fought with wistful yearning. She'd always liked children, just didn't want to have her own. The idea of bedding down with any man disgusted her. "There's not enough room for three in the cabin, let alone a bunch of kids."

"I know that, silly!" Jasper laughed and jerked a thumb behind him. "I thought we could build another place over there, a bigger one for me and the missus." He pointed to the cabin. "You can keep the original homestead."

Callie brought both hands up to her head, knocked her hat back and scrubbed at her temples. Things were going to change, and all Jasper could see were his imaginary children frolicking in the yard. She couldn't blame him—he was right that it was past time for him to get started on a family if he was of a mind. He was strong-willed, handsome and a decent man. He'd make a fine husband to some lucky woman. That didn't mean Callie wanted to be around to watch it happen.

She hated change with a blind passion.

Jasper sighed. He grimaced at the ground. "Look. If you're that dead set against it, I'll tell her no. In fact, I just won't answer the letter." He punctuated his words by kicking at the dirt with a toe.

"You'd do that?"

He shrugged. "You're the only family I've got, Callie. I don't want to lose you over a woman I don't even know."

Damn it. She hated it when he capitulated like this. His reasonable reaction always made her feel like a cad. She was jealous, plain and simple; she had no right to interefere with him finding someone with whom to settle down. Just because she didn't feel the urge to get hitched to a disgusting hairy bastard who'd make the rest of her life miserable didn't mean Jasper couldn't get married.

Jasper had already turned away, taking her silence as agreement. He trudged toward the cabin.

"Wait." Callie closed the distance between them. She took his hand in hers. The bones of their fingers and their fingernails were identical despite the difference in size, echoing their familial ties as strongly as the shared blood beneath their skins. "You're right. I'm the only family you've got, but that's because you need to get to work on it." She squeezed his hand. "Write her back. Tell her to come."

His face lit up. "Are you sure? I don't want to—"

Scoffing, she released his hand and pushed him away. "I said it, didn't I? What more do I have to do? Write her a letter myself?"

Jasper's smile faded. "About that…"

Immediate suspicion leeched the forced levity from Callie's spirits. "What?"

"Your writing is much better than mine," he began.

"Aw, you're joking! You want me to write the letter?" Callie punched him in the arm.

Jasper grunted with the force of the strike. He stepped out of reach and rubbed the injured area. "Would you? Please? I don't want to frighten her with my chicken scratches."

Callie didn't like the brassy woman as the situation already stood. That dislike wouldn't take much to tip over into active hatred.

When Callie didn't answer, Jasper wiggled his eyebrows. "I'll run your trapline all week," he offered, his expression one of hopefulness.

Callie pointed a finger at him. "You're damned lucky I love you."

Jasper laughed with relief, knowing that this was his sister's way of saying she conceded. "Come on. I have a pot of blackstrap on the stove. I know just what I want to tell her."

Callie allowed herself to be dragged into the cabin, half pleased by Jasper's high spirits and half disgusted by the cause of them. Whoever this woman was, she'd better be the best thing in the world for her brother. If she wasn't, Callie was prepared to make her life a living hell.

CHAPTER THREE

Clara sat on a bench in the Common overlooking the clearing where the Great Elm had once stood in all its glory. Many a Bostonian still visited the spot of Boston's "oldest inhabitant." Her brother and parents had told Clara that she'd played as a toddler beneath its century-old shade. But the tree had fallen three months prior to her fourth birthday, ravaged by time and disease. Though mourned by her father who, upon occasion, would wax philosophic over the loss, Clara had scant recollection of the tree. Regardless, the Common was a marvelous park in which to pass the time, either with friends and family or simply to ruminate over life's vagaries.

The spring sun warmed her, making her wish the Great Elm still stood to cast its shade. Though sweat trickled down her spine, she remained. She'd asked Emma to meet her and couldn't leave until her friend had arrived. She entertained herself with thoughts of the District of Alaska, wondering what her potential husband was doing right this very moment. Did he march across the frozen tundra in search of game? No, it was

May. Spring would have already made an appearance up north, wouldn't it? In any case, she imagined him stern of eye with a cleft chin, cutting a heroic profile as he braved the magnificent wilds of his domain. It was a daydream that oft-occurred since she'd taken the audacious leap of writing him, one that filled her with both anticipation and trepidation.

A drawstring purse rested in her lap, clutched in her fingers. If she flexed her hands she heard the crinkle of the envelope tucked inside. She'd spent every day of the past three weeks hovering near her home's front door to intercept the postman. Today had finally yielded the letter she'd sought...but she couldn't bring herself to open it. Instead she'd sent word to Emma and fled the house, letter in hand.

Clara stared at her purse, the envelope's presence interrupting her fanciful calculations. *What if he's declined? And why shouldn't he? I was far too bold. No man wants that sort of woman as a wife!* Her heart fluttered in her chest, and she searched the park for a method to quell her uncertainties.

Nannies and their charges played in the grass; childish laughter floated through the air. Businessmen took brisk constitutionals as they continued office discussions as they meandered the pathways. A couple strolled past, arm in arm, enjoying both the sunny weather and each other's company.

Clara's gaze fell upon the young lovers, placing herself in the woman's position, walking along with her future husband. His name was Jasper Glass; she'd received that much from the address on the envelope. *Mrs. Jasper Glass.* Jasper was a nice name. She'd known a boy named Jasper in school, and he'd been kind and friendly. Did people become like their names? Were all the Claras in the world like her? Would Mr. Glass be as pleasant as the Jasper of her youth?

"Here you are!"

Emma's whirlwind arrival startled Clara from her thoughts. "Goodness!" she gasped aloud. She patted one hand on her chest though the action didn't ease her beating heart.

"My apologies." Emma gave her a remorseful pout. "I didn't mean to frighten you. It appeared that you were looking right at me when I came up." She settled herself onto the bench, expanded an Oriental fan with a flick and busily waved it.

Clara leaned in for a welcome kiss. "My mind was elsewhere."

"As it's been for months." Emma smiled with a wink. "One doesn't need a gypsy fortune-teller to know what's been on your mind these last weeks."

The bright sunlight had nothing to do with the heat on Clara's face. She searched the middle distance for something to distract her from the burgeoning fear of rejection. "I've had word."

Emma dropped the fan into her lap, mouth open in surprise. She seized Clara's hand. "You have? When? Where? What did he say?" Each question was punctuated with a squeeze as her volume increased.

Miserable and partially thankful for their separation from the other park denizens, Clara struggled past the alarming knot developing in her throat. "I don't know."

"You don't know?" Clara studied Emma. The fan remained in Emma's lap, and the little line between her eyebrows bespoke confusion. "If you've had word, Clara, that would mean you've received an answer," Emma said, her tone that of a nanny correcting a rather slow child.

With clumsy fingers, Clara opened her purse and withdrew Mr. Glass's unopened letter. "I received this by post this morning." She laid it in her lap, and ran her palm across its surface to straighten the folds it had received in transit.

Emma's voice became soft. "But you couldn't open it."

Clara shook her head, feeling a sting in her eyes and wishing she could show more courage and fortitude. It wasn't as if Mr. Glass's declination of her offer meant the end of the world. Matrimonial advertisements were everywhere. If Mr. Glass didn't want to marry her, she'd find someone who did, someone both kind and adventurous enough with whom to share a life.

The letter slid from beneath her fingertips. "Mr. Jasper Glass," Emma read. "That's a nice name. A strong name."

Clara clutched her hands rather than submit to the urge of snatching the letter back. She had to clear her throat before she could answer. "Do you think so?"

"Oh, yes. I'm an authority on these things you know."

Emma's absolute and cheerful certainty caused Clara to smile. "Are you?"

"Of course. Did I never tell you that I suggested my cousin name her son Peter? Instead she's called him Ignatius." Emma's pretty nose wrinkled in distaste. "The poor child will grow up being called 'Iggy' by his friends. How horrid."

Clara laughed. "Thank you."

Emma smiled back; she needed no clarification. She patted Clara's hand. "Shall we be about it then?" Before Clara could respond, Emma peeled aside one corner of the envelope, stuck her finger inside and ripped it fully open.

Closing her eyes, Clara braced herself.

"My, he certainly has exquisite penmanship." There was a pause. "And quite a flair for words, if I do say so myself."

Clara squinted one eye open to glance at the letter, noting Mr. Glass's excellent handwriting before squeezing it closed once more. "I can't look!" After many years of shenanigans with her friend, she easily imagined Emma's jovial amusement over her discomfort. Clara reached over and pinched Emma's thigh in blind retribution, ignoring the slight yelp. "Just read it."

"Yes, ma'am." Emma cleared her throat with great theatrics before she began to read.

> Dear Clara,
>
> I may call you Clara, mayn't I? I apologize if my salutation seems too forward, but I cannot help myself. Clara is such a beautiful name, and I cannot help speaking it aloud over and over. I look forward to speaking your name in friendship and—dare I say it? —in love as well. And you must call me Jasper. I cannot abide a woman who is not allowed to use her husband's given name in conversation, public or private."

Clara's hands shot up to her mouth, covering the gasp as her eyes opened wide. *"In love?"* *He's accepting me?* She plucked the letter from Emma's hand, and scanned the masculine scrawl for herself. She hardly noticed Emma jostling closer to continue reading his words aloud as Clara's eyes followed them on the page.

Your letter was most intriguing. I have never had the pleasure of visiting Boston. You must tell me everything about it. My family hails from Oregon, though none are left there, and before that from Iowa. Despite my long association with that state I have only had the pleasure of visiting Portland twice. The hustle and bustle there would no doubt seem a small village in comparison to one of our country's oldest founding cities! I've sojourned the majority of my life in the wilderness of one forest or another, whether in the Oregon and Washington rain forests or the frigid northern territories. I have made my home in the great north for the last twelve years.

The District of Alaska is exactly as you have imagined and more. It is magnificent! The air is so crisp and clear that you will never understand why you have lived so long in your large city. Birdsong greets you every morning and the deer have been known to walk right up to the cabin in search of sustenance. I reside south of Skagway on a spit of land between the Taiyasanka and Taiya Inlets. The bounty of the ocean is but a short hike away from my homestead. Every morning I awake and look out over the mountain forests, smelling sea air and pole pine as I take my daily constitutional. I believe you will love your new home as much as I.

The life of a trapper's wife will be no different than a shopkeeper's or farmer's wife. It requires hard work on both our parts. It is rare that I am away from home longer than a day. As I run the traplines, you will keep our home. (If you consent to come to me, I will begin building a palatial cabin for our future family.) Occasionally we will venture into town to sell my merchandise and purchase goods. As you settle into your new home, I will be more than happy to teach you how to trap or fish or hunt as you please. You need only ask.

Indeed, yes, I will have you for my wife if you but agree. Send me your travel itinerary as soon as you have it so that I may make plans on my end for your timely arrival. If we choose not to marry due to incompatibility, I will of course help pay your passage home.

I look forward to meeting you.

With Sincerest Affection,

Jasper Glass

Clara stared at the second to last paragraph. "I will have you for my wife if you but agree." How could she not? This is what she'd hoped for since she'd dropped her initial letter in the post.

"With sincerest affection," Emma repeated, tapping the letter. "And he writes so familiarly. Your letter must have turned his head!"

"I'm going to the District of Alaska," Clara whispered.

Emma's eyes brimmed with tears of joy and sadness. "You're going to be married."

It suddenly occurred to Clara that this was no longer an intellectual exercise. There were no more castles to spin from thin air. This was reality. Not only did she have to make arrangements to travel west and north but she'd also have to consider the imminent separation from all she'd ever known— her home, her family and her best friend. Loss and soaring joy fought equally in her heart, and she started to weep, clutching at Emma. Handkerchiefs were produced from their purses as they held each other, crying tears of celebration and mourning. Some time passed before Clara extricated herself, dabbed at her eyes and blew her nose with a proper modicum of delicacy.

Beside her, Emma did the same, adjusting her hat that had been knocked askew. "How do I look?"

Clara gave the hat brim a twitch. "Acceptable. And me?"

"A blushing beauty." Emma chucked Clara's chin. "I'm so happy for you."

"I'll miss you." Another round of tears threatened, but Clara held them off with a tremulous smile. "You must marry Bradley and follow. Jasper," and she paused a moment to savor the taste of her fiancé's name, "Jasper and I will build you a cabin as well."

Emma laughed aloud, sniffling. "Be certain to inform your brother of your plans for him. He might have other ideas, Miss Bossy Pants."

"That's Missus Bossy Pants to you." Clara evaded the reflexive swat.

"Not yet, young lady. First you must arrange passage for yourself and your belongings. And you mustn't go empty-handed, you know. It would be most despicable to arrive at your destination without a dowry."

A dowry. Clara blinked, the thought having never occurred to her. "Do you think Jasper will expect one?" She looked at the letter, turning it over in search of an answer.

Emma placed her hand on Clara's. "I saw nothing in his letter to indicate he required a dowry. He's rich in land and probably doesn't need recompense." She squeezed. "But that doesn't mean you shouldn't consider bringing more than yourself and your baggage along. I've read some news articles about the gold rush; to arrive with a load of foodstuffs as well as a full selection of winter clothing for yourself wouldn't be amiss."

Clara had considered her wardrobe. Boston winters were severe upon occasion, so she wasn't a complete novice. Finding a heavier mackinaw or arctic mittens wouldn't be remiss. Newspaper articles about the gold rush always had lists of food and equipment, most of which could be purchased in Seattle before she boarded a steamer north. "You're right. I shouldn't set ashore empty-handed. I'll be burden enough at first simply from lack of experience. I'll need to have money on hand to purchase supplies to bring along with me."

Emma's next words were hesitant. "Have you yet broached the subject with your father?"

A flash of lightning raced through Clara's spine, not fear exactly but apprehension nevertheless. "No. I wanted to wait until I had a definitive answer before discussing it with him." Clara felt Emma's hand tighten on hers.

"Fortunately you are the apple of his eye."

Clara scoffed. "And unfortunately that may be my downfall. It's debatable whether Father will accept this proposal because he wishes me to be happy or deny me the opportunity out of fear for my safety."

Emma nodded in commiseration. "If you should need anything—a shoulder to cry upon, a place to stay—come to me. I even have money to lend if you have need."

Warm love filled Clara's heart. She brought Emma into an embrace, upsetting both their hats once more. "Thank you," she whispered. "You're without a doubt the most wonderful friend I can ever have."

* * *

Clara fussed before the mirror that stood in the corner of her bedroom, smoothing the material of her dress for the hundredth time. She paused and took stock of herself. Dark hair, almost black, had been artfully pinned up, no longer in disarray from the afternoon's joyful weeping with Emma. Eyes of hazel scanned the lavender tea gown she'd donned, her favorite dress with its leg o'mutton sleeves and an ivory splash of lace at the high collar. The deeper-colored caftan contrasted well with her alabaster skin.

Despite her alleged beauty, at twenty-four years of age she was considered a spinster in many social circles. There'd been a boy in her youth—handsome and dashing—but his family had moved to Paris before his age of majority. Though Clara had shared multiple-paged letters over the first year of his absence, their contact eventually dwindled to a halt. She'd heard that he'd recently married and had a baby boy. Heartbreak manifests a hundred fold in adolescence. After she'd received the devastating news, Clara would have nothing to do with the suitors that her parents had paraded through the house. Her months had passed in misery, brightened only by visits with Emma and outings forced upon her by her elder brother Bradford. When Clara's heart had finally healed enough to begin her search anew, no man seemed worthy. None were as jaunty as her Clem had been, none as good-looking. The young men of her generation now attended college or learned a trade; they scarcely had the time or resources to court a well-to-do young woman. Those moneyed gentlemen who were interested in marriage were of an age with and of similar business background as her father. She'd never been able to abide their sly smiles and coquetry, their behavior oddly causing her to feel shame more than desire.

"Not any longer." Clara's reflection stood taller, more confident. "Soon I'll be Mrs. Jasper Glass of the Alaskan District." *At least once I tell Father.*

Her image slightly wilted at the thought.

"Clara! Come down to supper!"

Clara whirled, wide-eyed and panting as if she'd run all the way home from the Common. She calmed herself with an iron will. "Coming Mamma!" At least her voice didn't sound as washed out as she felt. She gathered her arguments and confidence, mentally wrapping them around herself as she prepared for the impending battle. A last look in the mirror revealed a steely glint in her eyes that reminded her of her father when his dander was up. Pleased by the comparison, she felt the worst of her trepidation fade to a more manageable level as she marched out of her bedroom.

All meals were held in the formal dining room. Clara hadn't eaten in the kitchen since she was four years old. Other than two servants to deliver food to the table and a visit from Cook to receive critique and accolades for this evening's presentation, only Clara and her parents dined. Bradford was at Harvard for spring classes, which meant his attendance at family suppers was often sporadic. Clara had hoped he'd be present for her announcement. She knew she could count on him for support regardless of the apparent preposterousness of her intentions.

Eventually the last course was removed and the crumbs swiftly brushed away. A serving of mince pie was placed before her with a tiny porcelain cup of coffee. Her father was poured a glass of brandy. Supper conversation had been about his work at the store, a small grocery that he'd expanded into four stores that all bore the same name. Mamma interjected appropriate commentary and suggestions while Clara sat quiet through the meal.

Father finally turned to Clara. "And how was your day, pumpkin?"

Clara blinked, startled from her thoughts of frosty Alaskan mornings and the delicious smell of mincemeat pie and coffee filling a small cabin. "W—what? I beg your pardon." She patted her mouth with her napkin. "What was it you said?"

"I asked how your day was." Father cast a wry grin at his wife. "Considering the depth of your thoughts, I imagine it was most entertaining."

"Oh, goodness. She must have met with Emma." Mamma filled her fork with a delicate bite of pie. "The constable hasn't darkened my door so whatever trouble they've gotten into today hasn't been met with official authority."

"Yet," Father added, raising his brandy in toast.

Clara felt her cheeks heat with a blush. There were times when she still felt like an awkward teenager in her parents' presence. Her youth had been one of multiple infractions, both of family rules and a healthy flirtation with the edges of legal propriety. Her only saving grace had been that she was born a girl rather than a boy. She hadn't suffered sterner penalties for her brash actions for that reason alone.

Knowing there was no better time to bring up her plans, Clara lost her appetite. She dropped her fork with a *clink*, and pushed the plate away. "I've made a decision." She forced herself to look Father in the eye, fighting the fluttery urge to turn her gaze away, to flee the table.

A knowing spark flashed in the hazel eyes so like her own. "Do tell, pumpkin."

His expression was one of amusement and faint concern that he'd have another mess to clean. He thought she'd gotten into some sort of frivolous trouble and needed him to cover the cost of her indiscretions. Piqued, Clara frowned. She was an adult, for goodness sakes! It had been some years since she'd gotten into a scrap that required his assistance, either influential or monetary. Her annoyance bolstered her confidence. "I've an offer of marriage by Mr. Jasper Glass of the Alaskan District."

Father's face melted from vague amusement into serious concern. It was his turn to sputter, "W—what?" His glass thunked to the table, splashing the alcohol over the rim. The smell of brandy overpowered the scent of mince pie.

"An offer of marriage," Clara said, tilting her chin in practiced defiance. "It will take approximately a month to gather the necessary supplies and make travel arrangements. I plan to leave town by the beginning of June."

Father stared, perplexed, unable to speak. It was Mamma who interjected herself into the conversation. "And who is Mr. Jasper Glass? Have we met this young man?"

Clara refused to give in to the sudden return of her uncertainty. "No, you haven't. I...I answered a matrimonial advertisement last month and he responded with his proposal."

"A matrimonial—!" Father clamped his mouth closed, and his face became ruddy with the effort to not swear.

Clara had seen the signs before and knew what words would spill from his lips if he didn't control himself. She suffered from the same condition. She felt a hand on her right forearm and turned to her mother, grateful for the distraction.

"What can you tell us about him?"

Clara briefly dropped her gaze. There wasn't much to tell. She swallowed and met her mother's eyes. "He's thirty-four years old and lived in Oregon. He owns thirteen hundred acres of land south of Skagway."

"A no account muckman?" Father demanded. "Dropping everything to scour the territory for bits of gold?"

"No Father!" Clara hastened to clarify. "He's a trapper with property. The Klondike is thirty-some miles north along the Chilkoot and White passes. I've been reading the newspaper accounts."

"A trapper?" Relief and distaste fought for dominance on Father's face.

Clara empathized with him. "I assure you, Father, I'm not the least bit interested in throwing my future into the hands of a man chasing fleeting fortune. Should Jasper decide he wishes to pursue such foolishness, I'll be on the first transport home."

Though mollified, Father shook his head. "And if he decides to stop you from leaving?"

Frowning, Clara considered his question. "How would he do that?"

Father snorted exasperated laughter. "Clara, pumpkin, you've had a sheltered childhood, and we've used a gentle hand with you despite your youthful infractions. There are men in the world who will not take no for an answer."

Clara puzzled over his words, unable to recall a single instance where she'd been overridden by anyone but people in authority and the occasional disagreement with Emma.

"Your father is right, sweetheart. We've done our best to protect you from the...baser elements of society. Without meeting Mr. Glass in person, you have no way of knowing if he can be trusted." Mamma patted Clara's forearm again. "What if he misrepresented himself to you? You are our most precious treasure. We want you to be safe."

Though the sentiment warmed Clara, years of experience had taught her this was a prelude to their denying her what she wanted. Her parents always brought up her safety as the primary reason to follow their rules. "While I do appreciate your concern, I am a woman grown. I simply cannot live under your roof for the rest of my days!" She pulled away from her mother's touch. "I'm not seeking permission. I have enough money saved for the train and to book passage to Skagway. The decision is mine to make. Alone."

Her father growled. "Then why tell us? Why not leave a note and run away to a life of strife and misery?"

Clara studied the thunderclouds on her father's face. "Because I love you." She watched the clouds break, and the bleak anger at her apparent desertion collapse. "Because you've raised me to be strong. Because I want your blessing." She left her chair to kneel by his, taking a brandy-stained hand in hers. "You've always told me that happiness is a choice, and I choose to seek it in Alaska. Jasper is a kind, well-worded man. He's not a barely literate cretin digging into creek beds for a hint of riches. He's a landowner, runs a trapping business and lives in the wilds of Alaska. I want to see if I'll be happy there." She sighed. "And if I'm not, I'll return home. I promise. But I have to try."

Several minutes passed as her father considered her words. "You'll book round-trip passage from Seattle. If you require it, you can wire me for the return train fare," he said at last.

Exuberance swept through Clara's body, the strength of it almost causing her to reel and fall over. She clutched her father's hand and heard her mother's soft gasp of surprise. "Thank you!"

Father held up a finger of admonishment. "Don't thank me yet." He clasped both hands over hers, and leaned forward. "You'll write at least once a month to keep us posted on your life. Should you fail to do so, I'll be on the first train out of Boston."

"We both will." Mamma rose, coming round the other side of the table to place a hand on Father's shoulder.

Mamma received a stern wink from Father as he continued. "You'll need arctic weather clothing for the winters there, and I'll cover the cost of both that and a year's provisions. I'll not have you reach Skagway and discover a shortage of food." He glared at Clara. "Those are the terms of this contract. Do you accept them?"

Clara stared at her parents, astonished at their generous offer. The most she'd hoped for was to leave without fully destroying their relationship. Now she would have a year's provisions to offer as dowry upon her arrival in Skagway. "Yes! Yes, I accept." Unable to stop herself, she burst into tears. "Thank you."

She was urged into her father's lap where she cried into his jacket, an experience she hadn't had since the loss of the family dog when she was eight. Her mother's hands stroked her hair as her father cuddled her. "I don't love the idea of you haring off to parts unknown with a stranger, but you're welcome, pumpkin."

CHAPTER FOUR

Callie cradled the tin cup in her hands. Her bared forearms rested against the rough grain of the dining table. Jasper had built it from the wood of a yellow cedar she'd discovered her first year in Alaska. She caressed the familiar grooves with one hand, exploring the warp and weave of tree fibers slowly growing dark with age. The burnt ring where Jasper had set a hot fry pan down without a cloth, the scratches from that time he'd cut strips of leather to repair snow shoes, the gouge when he'd dropped the hammer while fixing the roof last year. Though its existence as a table was mighty short in tree years, it had certainly seen its fair share of excitement. The smooth surface felt cool beneath her fingers, as cool as the tin cup she still held. She frowned at the cup, and inspected her dented and scarred reflection. Why was the coffee cold? She'd just poured it, hadn't she? She tipped it, and the cool liquid slopped over the rim to splash her thumb, confirming that she hadn't unwittingly drained its contents. Her reflection shifted into sepia tones for an instant before coffee puddled on the tabletop.

She straightened, surprised by the sharp ache in her neck and shoulders as she looked at the stove. From this distance she should have felt the heat of it, but it seemed the fire had gone out. How long had she sat here? It had still been dark when she'd put the coffee on and now light tumbled through the cracks in the shutters and door. A jolt of fear brought her to her feet, the stool crashing to the floor. She needed to rebuild the fire! Jasper needed the warmth. Jasper needed—

Memory sliced through the fear. The iron smell of blood blending with a growing putrid scent, the doctor's sorrowful gaze at his last visit, Jasper's last rattled breath as it passed through his lips. Jasper only needed burying now.

As wooden as the table, Callie picked up the stool and sat back down. Her eyes were drawn to the large bed in the corner, the mound of blankets that hid her older brother from view.

There'd been no warning that day, no indication of danger as they'd checked the traplines. Callie had pointlessly gone over and over her recollections, searching for anything that she could point to and say, "Yes, this! I should have seen this! I could have stopped it!"

But even Jasper had said as she hauled him home on the sledge that he'd been as shocked as her when the grizzly bore down upon them. The ursine had been poaching their trapline from the opposite direction and upwind. The only notification they'd had was the sudden roar of challenge as a thousand pounds of grizzly charged them. Jasper had been on point, unable to bring his Winchester up quick enough. He'd suffered the full brunt of the attack. It had been Callie who'd put the bear down, firing multiple rounds into its fat-layered hide as her brother screamed beneath it. Jasper had insisted later that it had been bad luck alone that had put him in the bear's path.

She'd gotten Jasper home and patched up as best she could. By nightfall he'd developed wound fever. She'd wanted to leave immediately for Skagway to get the doctor, but Jasper had talked her into waiting until morning. She'd be stumbling in the dark, rousing nocturnal predators in her wake. No sense in both of them getting seriously injured when a few hours wouldn't make a difference. *Maybe he'd still be alive if I hadn't listened to him, if I'd gone to get the doc that night.*

It was early afternoon of the next day when she'd finally returned from town with the doctor. The scraggly man had assured her that Jasper had been right. Mr. Bear had done a fine job on her brother's internal organs and broken several of Jasper's bones. There was nothing the doctor could do except ease Jasper's passing. He'd left her a bottle of laudanum with instructions on its use—just a few drops in a cup of sugar water to be administered four times a day. If Jasper was given a full day's dose at one go…well, he'd sleep with the angels.

Callie reached for the cup again. It was Jasper's cup, identified by the crudely etched "J" on the handle. Hers still dangled from a hook under the shelves that held their cooking kit. She pulled Jasper's cup close, and peered inside. Though the coffee was cold, she imagined the bitterness of the laudanum mixing with the bitterness of the blackjack. Normally she didn't drink her coffee with sugar, but she'd made an exception this time. She didn't want to gag from the taste. Just a few swallows and she could climb into Jasper's bed and fall into blissful sleep, never to awaken.

Jasper needs burying.

She frowned. Though she didn't particularly give a damn what happened to her mortal remains, the thought of leaving Jasper to the vagaries of Mother Nature didn't appeal much. While the location of the Glass homestead wasn't a complete secret, most folks didn't travel south from Skagway. Months would pass before someone would recall that fella Jasper Glass and his odd sister. Callie had to admit that it only seemed right; a rather fitting end that she and Jasper become food for the animals from which they'd earned their livelihood. Several minutes passed as she wrestled with her desire to yield immediately to Death's whisper or do the proper Christian thing. Jasper might not see the black humor in being left to the elements. Eventually she pushed Jasper's cup away. *I'll drink it later. Maybe tonight.*

She stood with effort. She'd only been bruised in the bear attack as the monster had brushed her aside to focus on Jasper, its tiny brain associating the pain of multiple gunshot wounds with the screaming man at its feet. Several days of inactivity as she cared for Jasper had taken its toll. Her joints creaked with disuse as she stomped into her boots. She couldn't remember when she'd last changed her clothes or eaten.

At the door, she turned to look back at her brother's bed. If she unfocused her vision she could almost see the blankets rise and fall with his breath, hear his familiar snore—the one he'd always denied—as he napped. But his was the slumber of eternity. There'd be no more mornings of his waking with corkscrewed hair and squinted, sleep-encrusted eyes. The back of Callie's throat burned along with her eyes. She fought to control her sorrow as she threw open the door. Jasper needed burying and no amount of sniveling could keep her from the task.

* * *

Dirt and dried tears streaked Callie's face, and exhaustion leeched the energy from her body. Time had no meaning. It had been hours, minutes, days since she'd left the cabin that morning intent on Jasper's grave. Hours, minutes, days of selecting his final resting place, of digging a deep enough hole that overlooked the Taiya Inlet, of carefully bundling his body, still wrapped in blankets, and hauling him to his burial. Spent, she sat in the dirt at the foot of Jasper's grave, enveloped in darkness as she listened to distant water splash the shore, the rustle of nocturnal rodents and the flurry and flap of wings as birds of prey hunted.

She lay back onto the soft dirt that separated her from Jasper, ignoring the chill as the cool night breeze caressed her sweat-soaked body. Jasper had picked a beautiful night for a trip to heaven. She studied the cloud of the Milky Way stretched across the sky. The entire thing looked like a river or canyon seen from above. Was Jasper somewhere up there, his spirit riding the ethereal rapids like a leaf tossed into a fast-moving stream? Did he shoot forward, pausing as the celestial currents veered past obstacles and eddies before rushing onward to

Heaven? Callie had no doubt that Jasper would arrive at St. Peter's gates, hair blown out of place by the brisk journey as he brushed self-consciously at his bushy mustache. Her brother was too kind and generous a man to ever fall prey to the Devil's temptations. Hell would never hold him.

She wasn't too sure about her own chances at the Pearly Gates. Church people saw the taking of one's own life as a sin. Surely God didn't think that, did He? All Callie wanted was to be by her brother's side. That was a worthy goal, not something of which to be ashamed. Desperately missing a part of her life, unable to find cause to continue this painful existence, that seemed a valid reason to follow the choice she'd made. She didn't think God would deny her entry to Heaven for such a sacrifice. Her parents had taught her that He was a loving God. He wouldn't want to see her suffer. To stay here would be agony.

"What do I do, Jasper?" she whispered. "I don't think I can do this without you."

Jasper's coffee cup beckoned in the silence. She began to make a list of chores—tidy the cabin, make Jasper's bed, start a fire, change into her nightshirt. The coffee would be very cold by now. Perhaps it wouldn't taste as bitter this way. The fire would warm her after she drank it. Then she'd crawl into bed and sleep forever.

Just as Callie made up her mind, just as she began to push away from the gelidity of Jasper's grave soil, a flash of movement caught her eye. She paused, leaning on her elbows as she stared into the sky. A tiny point of brilliant orange flame traversed across the Milky Way. A stream of light trailed behind it until it faded from sight. She stared, mouth open in awe. "Did you see that, Jas?" At the moment she registered that her brother would never see anything as magnificent as what she'd just witnessed, two more streaks crossed her vision, following the first's trajectory. They too disappeared as they burnt out.

Callie studied the star field above for more, mind working furiously for the first time since Jasper had succumbed. She'd asked him what to do and he'd sent her a meteor. Then he'd sent two more. A distant part of her, the one that had never fallen sway to portents and omens, scowled at the idea of Jasper responding from beyond the veil. She mentally shushed it. The doubting voice didn't matter. What mattered was that Callie searched beyond the sorrow that had gripped her for several days.

With Jasper gone, the Glass line would end. There were no other siblings, no cousins that could carry on their family name. Jasper had wanted to have a family, to have children. He'd already begun to clear ground for the future cabin he'd planned to build for his wife. The wife that had no idea her groom was gone.

Callie imagined the poor woman arriving at the homestead, finding Callie's body in the cabin and having no idea where Jasper had gone. No doubt it would appear that he'd done Callie in and run from the law. His name would be ruined, his future wife bereft. The thought occurred to her that Skagway's doctor would know the reality, but rumor had a way of ignoring truth. In any case, Jasper wouldn't want that city woman to make the trip seeing as how he wasn't available any more.

Callie had to write a letter. She mentally clutched at the task, uncertain why it had become all-important to complete when her opinion of the brazen hussy had always been low. The survivor in her—the girl who'd watched her parents die in the house fire, who learned to hunt and trap and fish at her brother's side, to clean and skin her kills, to live the life that her brother had given her—that survivor felt an odd sense of relief at having something to do which didn't entail death in one form or another. The survivor wasn't ready to lie down, to give up. Callie stared at her hands. Jasper wasn't ready for her to give up either. He'd sent those meteors to wake her up from her stupor.

"I'll write her," she promised Jasper. "And I'll keep up the homestead. I promise." She turned onto her knees, facing the soft ground upon which she'd reclined, facing the crude cross she'd lashed together. "I don't know how long I can do this, but I'll try." Her voice cracked and tears burned the back of her throat. "I'll try, I swear."

CHAPTER FIVE

Clara stood on the deck of the steamer ship *S.S. Queen*, head held high. The coastal city of Seattle, Washington was blanketed in gray skies and surrounded by emerald green forests. It slid by, picking up pace as the steamer got under way. Clara clutched the souvenir passenger manifest, a list of four hundred men and women taking the same leap of faith as she, daring to brave the unknown and uncertainty of the far north. How many of her fellow travelers would stay the course, stick to their guns and every other verbal cliché of which she could conjure?

She smothered a giggle, and scanned those that had remained on deck to watch the wet greenery of the Puget Sound islands glide along, pleased to note she wasn't the only woman to have dared this journey. That had been what had made her most nervous as she traversed Seattle, to set up passage to and from the Alaskan District and purchase the requisite one thousand pounds of supplies. Her tenuous hope had been that she wasn't the only woman on board a ship of hundreds.

In retrospect, her fears had been absurd. Female passengers were as plentiful as their male counterparts. Many were relations following husbands and brothers and fathers into the wilderness, bringing much-needed supplies and feminine stability to a new homestead. But there were also a handful of hard-looking women that Clara had noticed smoking cheroots in front of the shipping office as everyone waited to board. New Women, they were called. She'd secretly read books about them with Emma, illicit novels of romance and tragedy where women eschewed men and strove to build lives for themselves. These women that shared the ship with Clara evinced such a masculine aura that she was both appalled and intrigued, unable to keep from staring at their obvious confidence and wise-cracking laughter. She didn't know whether to be scandalized by or to emulate their outrageous behavior. She wished Emma had come with her. No doubt her friend would say something shocking about the rough women, and cause Clara to laugh.

Due to the current popularity of the Canadian Yukon, single staterooms were not available. Clara shared hers with a mother and daughter, the Perys, who were en route to meet with Mr. Pery. It was quite a satisfactory arrangement. Mrs. Pery was in her late twenties and of an age with Clara. Her daughter, Julia, was an even-tempered child of eight or nine years and not inclined toward temper tantrums. At least Clara hadn't been assigned one of those hard women as a rooming partner. Regardless of the apparent safety and security of her short-term roommates, Clara kept her money and return passage voucher pinned inside her dress. "Lead us not into temptation," the good book always said.

Clara turned away from the temperate rain forest and made her way toward the front of the boat. *Ship*, she reminded herself. The wind here was stronger, and the mist that these people called rain kissed her cheeks with ice. The temperature was cooler than Boston, more from the higher levels of precipitation than anything else. She'd been forced to don her heavy wool stockings to combat the chill. She expected another five- to ten-degree drop by the time the ship reached its destination in Skagway.

Smiling, she stood with legs wide to retain balance as the *Queen* pushed through the sound, slicing through the ocean water. In a scant few days she'd meet her future husband in person and present him with the load of goods her father had purchased. She'd written Jasper prior to her departure from Boston two weeks earlier, and informed him of her estimated date of arrival. There was no telegraph in Skagway yet, so she had no way of updating him now that she'd booked passage. The sporadic contact made her a little nervous. She didn't know what she'd do if he wasn't there to meet her. Though she'd seen smaller towns in her rail travels to the Pacific coast, she imagined Skagway as large and as busy as Boston but without the social amenities of a well-established metropolis. How would she get around when there? Did they have boarding houses? She only had the vaguest of notions of Jasper's location—south of Skagway. How would she get a message to him?

With effort Clara pushed away her worries, falling into the recurrent reverie of life in the wilderness with a husband and children. Skagway wasn't as large as Boston. Someone would know who Jasper Glass was, and she had the necessary funds to hire a messenger. If there was a persistent dread that Mr. Jasper Glass wasn't the gentleman he purported to be, she smothered it, imagining herself smoking a cheroot and laughing with confidence as had those admirable women she'd seen aboard the ship. Certainly, if they could make their own way in Alaska without a man or marriage prospects in the future, so could she.

* * *

Callie sat Turkish-style beside Jasper's headstone. It had taken her a week, but she'd finally chiseled his name and dates into a slab of granite to replace the hastily erected cross. The lettering was crude, but she didn't feel right not having a hand in her brother's memorial. Maybe she'd have a headstone professionally done in a year or two. This was enough for now.

She came out every morning and evening, rain or shine, to sit with him. Sitting alone in the cabin had been torturous. At first she'd brought out a stool, but that hadn't lasted long. She needed to be as close to her brother as possible; seated on a stool so far above him made her feel like a judge squatting on a bench, looking down his fault-finding nose at the accused. The only concession she'd made to the vagaries of weather and comfort was to bring a folded canvas tarp to pad her backside.

"It's warming up good now. I expect the skeeters are going to be pretty prevalent this year. I'll have to get some more sodium bicarbonate from town to deal with the bites. At least you won't miss that, will you?" She unconsciously rubbed her arm, and remembered her initial experience with the veritable swarm of mosquitoes that made Alaska home. That first year she'd looked more pink than tan, her skin pebbled by multiple bites. Jasper had called her a skeeter lodestone, shortening it to Lode. He'd called her that every summer without fail since. A faint smile curved her lips as she remembered his laugh, a smile that quickly faded with the knowledge that she'd never hear his laughter again, never hear the nickname he'd given her.

A month had passed since she'd interred him, a month of everyday struggles with that bottle of laudanum that still sat on the table. Getting past the urge to follow her brother in death hadn't been her first hurdle. It was a daily fight to get out of bed, ignore the lethargy that had crept into her soul and do what needed doing. There were plenty of people who had fallen sway to the peace of laudanum, just like there were plenty who drank themselves into oblivion every day of their adult lives. It would be easy to follow suit, but Jasper had never cared for opium and morphine addicts. While not a teetotaler, he didn't think it right to cloud the mind like that. It was for that reason alone that Callie hadn't chosen to take a dose or two to in an effort to allay her bone-deep sorrow.

The sound of a ship's bell in the distance interrupted her one-sided conversation. Her eyes drifted past the scrub pushing green shoots from the ground down to the Taiya Inlet. Another steamer rumbled past, its motor muffled by the distance. A crowd of excited passengers mingled while the deckhands prepared for their arrival in Skagway. So many crackbrained people thought they could pull up stakes and come here to strike the red, rolling in money for the rest of their days. When would those idiots realize that the only thing of value was family and blood, acceptance and companionship? All this fuss for a rare metal would never bring back lost loved ones. It couldn't buy happiness or satisfaction or a sense of well-being. Callie almost felt sorry for the several hundred strangers on that ship.

She watched until it drew even with her and then took a deep breath. Patting the grave stone, she told Jasper, "I've gotta go. There's been wolves raiding the eastern trapline. I set up some traps for them and I need to see if I've been able to catch any." Callie stood, brushed the butt of her trousers, then picked up the tarp and folded it. "I'll see you tonight when I get home."

She heard her brother's whisper in her head. *"Be safe."*

"You know I will be," she said to the emptiness.

* * *

Clara leaned against the rails on the port side of the ship as it entered another inlet. According to the crew, this was the Taiya Inlet, the one that Jasper had mentioned in his letter. She'd been told that the Taiyasanka Inlet was farther west, which meant the finger of land in front of her was the location of her future home. She scanned the rocky coast with eager eyes, following the stretch of new-growth scrub until it transformed from meadow to forest. Was that smoke she saw on the distant rise there? Could that be the Glass cabin, her new home? If there had been any way to jump ship and march up that hillside, she'd have done so in an instant. Contrary to her desire, the ship continued on its course for another fifteen miles or more. Reluctant, she turned to the prow, her groom's possible homestead passing from sight.

A haze heralded the settlement known as Skagway. Curious, Clara edged forward, ignoring the busy crew and excited passengers. Skagway seemed a sprawling ramshackle town from this vantage. A sea of off-white covered the immediate foreground; a mass of canvas tents that had been erected to temporarily house transient miners as they prepared for their trips along the mountain passes to hopeful riches. The water along the beach teemed with carts and horses, the floor of the wagons just high enough to avoid being drenched. No docks reached out to sea, the water shallow enough to allow the horse-drawn carts to unload the ships. Deckhands, passengers and teamsters swarmed over the few ships already anchored in port as they offloaded tens of thousands of pounds of goods onto carts or pole rafts.

Clara frowned at the industrious activity. It had been almost a year since the first news of gold had reached the nation. *You'd think they'd have built piers by now. Goodness!* She wondered if she'd be required to slog through a mile of water and muck before reaching the shoreline or if there was some sort of ferry for passengers. Many men waded, hip deep in some cases, but she wasn't sure if they were new arrivals. She took stock of the fashionable boots she'd donned this morning. They'd be ruined if immersed in salt water.

The palaver of the crowd faded as others began reckoning their ability to disembark with their baggage and loads. As the *S.S. Queen* closed the distance to the shore, the sound of teamsters and haulers calling back and forth became louder, punctuated by the slap and splash of water, the shouts of alarm as an unwieldy load toppled and the general buzz of a large crowd gathered in this pocket between two tall hills. For the first time in several days, the smell of water gave way to that of dense human habitation—smoke, horse and human manure, stale beer and sweat fighting for dominance with every kind of cooking food imaginable drifting across the bay from Skagway.

When the ship dropped anchor, Clara chewed her upper lip in consternation. Several carts had altered direction, water breaking past the horse's chests as they each vied to be the first to attain legitimate drayage. She raised her chin and mentally kissed her boots goodbye. Footwear would not get between her and her destiny. Besides, she had money enough. Surely in that mass of humanity someone would be an experienced cobbler.

With an assurance she didn't feel, she marched across the deck in search of a purser.

CHAPTER SIX

Clara leaned uncertainly against the canvas sacks that bore the food she'd had shipped north. Her trunks peeked from beneath one corner. Several hundred pounds of potatoes, onions, sugar, coffee, cornmeal…the list she'd created from her research had been precise and exhaustive. The wait for a cart to unload her goods had been tedious, but the work was quick once it started. She'd asked among the workers about Jasper Glass and had received responses ranging from common ignorance to amusement and actual disgust. When questioned about his location, none who said they knew him could say where he lived. The whole affair caused Clara to wonder if she'd made a mistake. Why would Jasper's name engender such an assortment of reactions?

She fretted silently until a man with the Pacific Freight Company arrived at her side, a sheaf of papers in hand and three men at his heels. He wore overalls and a Scottish cap that had seen much better days. "Miss Stapleton?"

"Yes, sir." Clara put on her most pleasant expression.

"I'm Mr. Lutkins, the foreman." He studied her bill of lading. "Have you examined your belongings, miss? Was anything damaged or missing?"

Clara looked at the large pile of goods. "Everything appears to be accounted for, Mr. Lutkins, thank you."

He nodded a grizzled head and proffered the papers. "Sign here please." Once she did so, he smiled, revealing a gap where his front teeth should have been. "Very good. And will you be taking immediate possession?"

She stared at him for a brief moment of befuddlement. "I'm not certain. I find myself at a slight loss as I need to locate my… party before I can make arrangements for delivery."

"Very good." Lutkins scribbled something on her paperwork. "I'll have my men keep an eye on things for a nominal fee of one nickel. If you haven't returned by nightfall, we'll secure your inventory at a rate of twenty-five cents a day, payment upon return. Is that acceptable?"

Clara calculated the prices, weighing the cost of storage against the difficulty of locating Jasper in this unfamiliar town. Her father had given her more than enough to rent a room at a boarding house—should she be able to find one in any case—for a month. A dollar for four nights of security and storage seemed most satisfactory, and she told Lutkins so.

"Very good." He wrote the additional charges on her paperwork. "Your merchandise is safe here for the next ten days. If you haven't checked in with the office after that time, we'll be forced to sell the goods to cover our costs."

She refrained from a wry snort. If she couldn't find Jasper in ten days, she'd no doubt be on her way back to Boston. They could have the load without argument. Rather than make such a bald statement she agreed to his terms, signed the papers again and watched him trundle off to the next person awaiting his attention.

Now what? She adjusted her hat, unsure if it was crooked and unable to confirm or deny the possibility. The ground remained damp from the horse that had pulled her goods to shore, and she picked carefully along the path heading inland.

At least her boots had survived the trip to land. In Seattle she'd only purchased foodstuffs, which had lightened her load considerably compared to those who planned to continue on to Dawson. Without the additional mining equipment, there had been plenty of room in the wagon for her to ride.

It had been early morning when the *S.S. Queen* had arrived in the bay. The sun sat lower in the sky than Clara was accustomed to, but the delicate pocket watch she carried proclaimed that it neared the midday meal. Her stomach agreed with the assessment as she left the loading area for the ramshackle bustle of a bursting frontier town.

Feed stores and saloons, mining outfitters and packing companies, land assayers and hardware stores advertised their services and goods with placards that jutted out into the street. Wooden plank walkways lined both sides of the busy lane, allowing pedestrian access without the dangers of encountering horse manure. Clara eyed the soft dirt that comprised the avenue, and realized that a good rain would turn the dusty road into a veritable quagmire. She counted herself lucky that she'd come during a dry spell. Her boots may have survived her landing but they certainly wouldn't last long in mud up to her calves.

She explored this last bastion of civilization, and asked after Jasper, giving the scant information she had to any who would listen. Most people she approached didn't know him, small wonder with the heavy influx of strangers into the area. Those that did find his name familiar either didn't know him well or couldn't give her any more specifics than that his property lay south of Skagway.

A petite-looking man with a slender triangular face was the exception. He smiled at his rough companions, stroking a beard that he'd grown in two tufts from his chin. "Are you a tom as well then?" He scrutinized Clara from head to toe. "You certainly don't look it. I doubt he'll be interested." He and his friends burst into laughter. "Come looking for me, Jamie Perkins, when you want a real man, sweetheart." He sauntered away, leading his vulgar pack down the street.

Clara stared after him, not sure if his words had been meant as insult to her or Jasper. She was half-tempted to chase after him for more information regardless of the repugnance oozing from his pores. If he knew Jasper, then he could at least give her some idea of where to search for him or who could run a message. She watched the slender man shove one of his comrades into a bystander, and the bystander cringed aside. No. Better not to engage that gentleman any more than necessary. He was bad news whoever he was.

She put the altercation from her mind, and considered that the first order of business was to find something to eat. Despite the rough appearance of this predominantly male crowd, the majority of the men she encountered were solicitous. One directed her to a hotel that boasted an attached restaurant. Upon her arrival she was dismayed to discover a line of folk awaiting a table. She realized that she had no luxury to be picky. It was here or the saloon across the street and, regardless of those assertive women she'd seen on board the ship, she didn't have the courage to brave that particular establishment quite yet. She joined the back of the restaurant line, the closest men doffing their hats in her direction as she attempted to mentally calm her stomach's growing demands.

Half an hour later, the line had moved a few steps closer to the door. The passage of time gave the people in the queue a sense of casual acquaintanceship, and one of the men in front of Clara glanced back at her. "Newcomer, eh?"

"Is it so obvious?" she asked with a faint smile.

"Yes, ma'am. There ain't no way I'd miss a girl as pretty as you walking about town." He grinned at the chuckles from his companions.

Clara felt her skin heat, but ignored the compliment. She wasn't an uneducated rube; she'd spent years fending off the polite advances of interested men. *At least this one is polite.* The smile remained upon her face, neither waxing nor waning as she regarded him with a cool eye. "I'm here to meet my fiancé. Perhaps you've heard of him? His name is Jasper Glass."

Her impending nuptials dashed the overly familiar smile from his bearded face, in favor of a thoughtful expression. "Glass. I reckon I've heard that name."

"He's a trapper by trade," Clara offered, inching closer in her eagerness for word.

The man stepped out of line, and peered at those in front of them. "Ho! Daryl! Daryl McKenzie! You know a Jasper Glass, dontcha?"

An elderly gentleman turned and looked back at them. His hair and beard were snow white, framing a gaunt face and deep-set eyes. "I do. He's a trapper. Lives south of here with his sister."

Sister? Jasper hadn't mentioned a sibling. Clara filed that tidbit away as the men's conversation continued.

"This little lady says she's here to marry him."

Daryl McKenzie raised an eyebrow. "I haven't heard anything about that." His gaze was stern as he studied her. "Come here, young lady. Join me."

Clara demurred, not wanting to cut the line, but the man who'd started the conversation took her by the arm and guided her forward. "Go ahead, missy. A half hour between us and a meal ain't gonna make that much of a difference."

"Says you, Al," someone grumbled as Clara walked past. She thought she heard the *thwap* of someone's head being smacked. The others all gave her respectful nods.

"Marriage, eh?" McKenzie asked. He gestured for her to step into line ahead of him. "I don't recognize you and I know Jasper hasn't been south in years. How'd that happen?"

Clara stood proud, refusing to fall beneath his critical eye. She'd faced down her parents; the opinion of a stranger in the middle of nowhere hardly mattered. "A matrimonial advertisement in the *Boston Herald*." She held out her hand. "I'm Clara Stapleton, Mr. McKenzie. It's a pleasure to meet you."

His lips twitched in a smile. "My apologies, Miss Stapleton. In my defense, I've just returned to town after two months in the hills." He gestured down at his disheveled clothing and appearance. "I've not yet had time to find a room or a bath, let alone recall the social niceties of cultured civilization."

Though he still radiated a sternness that reminded her of a fiery preacher, his grin eased the formidable lines of his face. She returned his smile. "Apology accepted."

The line moved forward, putting the pair of them at the door. A delicious aroma of meaty stew distracted her, and her stomach gurgled in anticipation. She felt a blush, pleased that McKenzie didn't call attention to her audible gastrointestinal yearnings.

"How long have you known Jasper?"

Clara regarded McKenzie. "To be honest, I can't say that I know him at all. I've never had the pleasure of making his acquaintance in person having only corresponded via post."

"You're a braver person than I, uprooting yourself on nothing more than a mere promise." McKenzie chuckled. "I assume that his advertisement was most satisfactory?"

"It was." Clara decided she liked the old man. "I know he owns land south of here and that he traps for a living. His letter presented him as a pleasant and honest man. I hope to find it true."

McKenzie nodded with nary a twitch of eyelid or sidelong glance. "Indeed he is. Patient and hardworking too. You could do much worse for a husband."

His immediate endorsement did much to ease Clara's heart. She thought herself a decent judge of character, and Daryl McKenzie didn't seem the type of man to lie or make light of the topic. "Would you consider yourself a friend of Mr. Glass?"

He cocked his head. "I do. We share many attributes—the love of this great wilderness, an interest in nature's wonders." Something crossed his mind, and his smile widened. "When the first load of newcomes came last year, he was so relieved that they continued northward. The last thing he wanted was to have miners mucking up his property and disrupting the game."

"When the ship traversed Taiya Inlet en route to here, I saw a finger of land to the west. That's Jasper's land, yes?" At McKenzie's affirmation, Clara clapped once and cupped her face in delight. "I thought it so! There was cabin smoke just out of sight!"

"That entire area is Glass property." Again the line moved. "So indeed, it had to have been the cabin you spotted."

For a moment Clara had the urge to run from the restaurant, stomach be damned, and leave town for Jasper's property. She glanced up at the sky, unable to measure when night would fall in these northern environs. "How long would it take to reach his cabin?"

McKenzie craned his neck to follow her gaze, pursing his lips in thought. "No more than two hours by horseback. His homestead is near fifteen miles from here on a decent enough track."

Clara studied his profile, noting laugh lines at the corners of his eyes. "Would it be possible...?" She dropped her eyes to avoid his, mentally kicking herself for the action. Forcing herself to look at him, she said, "I don't mean to be forward, Mr. McKenzie. I realize you've just arrived in town yourself but I've yet to find anyone who knows where Jasper lives. Would it be possible for you to guide me there?"

He studied her as the line moved forward once more and put them just inside the restaurant.

Distracted by the vision of industry as men shoveled food into their mouths, Clara scanned the room. Five small tables, each with four chairs, sat in the tiny room. A sideboard held an assortment of bowls and plates from which an untidy man in an apron served. Though concerned about the cleanliness of the establishment, Clara almost swooned at the meaty smell of savory stew.

"I can take you."

Clara blinked, her request briefly forgotten in her ravenous hunger. "You will?"

"Yes." McKenzie's full smile transformed his severe expression, erasing the unforgiving cast he normally wore. "I'll hire a wagon. It shouldn't take too long to deliver you to Jasper."

"Oh, thank you, Mr. McKenzie!" In her excitement, Clara grabbed his forearm and squeezed. "Thank you! I don't know how to repay you."

He patted her hand with laughter. "No worries, Miss Stapleton. I'm certain I'll wheedle a dinner or two out of you when I visit Jasper." Chairs scraped the floor, and three miners rose to leave. "In the meantime, would you care to join me for lunch?"

Smiling, Clara took his offered arm and strolled to the available chairs. She'd be with Jasper before the sun set. She could hardly wait!

* * *

McKenzie had been correct in his estimation of travel time. According to Clara's watch, two hours had passed since they'd left town in the cart she'd rented from the same company that had warehoused her foodstuffs. Though barely midafternoon, the sun brushed the tops of the trees and cast its golden light across the clearing. It felt much later than it was.

"Ho, the cabin!" McKenzie called as he pulled the single horse up short in the clearing. Silence was his answer. He wrapped the reins about the brake handle and climbed down. "Must be out on the line."

Clara eagerly took in her environment, pausing only long enough for McKenzie to help her from the wagon. Three buildings took up space here, two on the far side and one closer. The closer one was a rustic cabin with a smokeless chimney. She had no idea what function the other two buildings served and ignored them for the moment. Jasper had said in his letter that he planned a larger cabin for them, and she searched for evidence of such construction.

"What are you looking for?" McKenzie circled the wagon to unload Clara's baggage.

She eyed the cramped little cabin with the low-hanging roof. "Jasper mentioned he would build a larger cabin for us, but it doesn't appear that he's started it yet."

McKenzie grunted as he lifted a trunk. "Not surprising. March and April are the worst for soggy ground. That's spring break up." He set the trunk at his feet, and reached for another. "Too wet to build until May or June. He'll probably start soon though."

Clara absently nodded. The mean little cabin aside, Jasper hadn't lied when he'd informed her of the beauty of his home. The pole pine forest began directly behind the cabin. A breeze caused the trees to sway, timber groaning and leaves whispering. She saw the distant edge of the Chilkoot Inlet that fed into the Taiya Inlet on which she'd sailed that very morning. A few steps in that direction and she was certain she'd have an excellent view of the steamer ships that navigated to and from Skagway.

The silence had faded as McKenzie worked. The forest denizens took voice once more. Birds and insects made their presence known, filling the fresh, clean air with their song. Clara closed her eyes to listen, amazed at the lack of man-made sound. She'd lived her whole life in Boston where even the quiet of her neighborhood was broken by civilization. Here she heard nothing beyond McKenzie unpacking her luggage to indicate humanity existed. *How novel!* This solitude must have been what Thoreau had experienced during his two-year experiment on Walden Pond.

"Want I should bring your things inside?"

Clara turned back to McKenzie. He'd placed her baggage and trunks next to the cabin on the hard packed dirt floor of a rudimentary porch. The collection of tools and other items gathered there fascinated her—chains and contraptions, hammers, axes and a wooden hoop with a skin stretched across it. Half the porch was given over to a woodpile. Her eyes alighted on a woven contrivance, and she squinted at it. *Snowshoes!* She ducked her head to avoid the low roof though it wasn't necessary, reaching out to finger the wood and leather contraption. She wondered what it felt like to walk upon the deepest snows in them.

"Miss Stapleton?"

She blushed at her discourtesy. "No, Mr. McKenzie. Thank you but you've already done so much for me. I cannot tell you how much I appreciate your assistance!"

"I'm glad to have been a help, miss." He touched the brim of his hat. "Now you're sure you don't need me to stay until Jasper returns?"

"No." Clara took in her surroundings. "Jasper said in his letter that he's rarely out overnight. I expect he'll be home soon."

McKenzie nodded. "All right then. I'll head back and turn in the wagon. If you'd like, I can make arrangements for your supplies to be delivered tomorrow."

"That would be most acceptable." She went to him and shook his hand. "Thank you so much. Expect an invitation to dinner when next we meet."

He chuckled. "I'll hold you to that, miss." He backed away, and formally tipped his wide-brimmed hat. "Take care."

"And you, Mr. McKenzie." She waited under the overhang of the porch as he climbed onto the wagon and clucked a tongue at the horse, waited long after the sound of his passage faded before turning to her new home.

When she opened the door, she stepped into darkness. Unlike outside, the air here was stale and musty, the shutters tightly closed. Once her eyes became accustomed to the dim light from the door, Clara eased past the noticeable furniture, stubbed a toe against a low stool and reached the nearest window to throw it open.

With better lighting she opened a second and third shutter, revealing an interior as cluttered as the front porch. An iron stove squatted in one corner, its faint warmth an indication that it had been used that day though the fire had long grown cold. She found a box of matches in the kindling bucket and proceeded to build a fresh fire. When the flames cheerily licked at the wood, she set a pot of water to boil. Half a pot of beans still sat on the stove. She gave it a sniff, decided it was still viable and added some water. Until she had the opportunity to see what stores were on hand here, she'd have to make do with what was available. Thankfully she'd insisted on bringing along sacks of dried corn and flour. She wasn't completely helpless in the cooking department.

The interior of the coffeepot looked horrendous with crusted-on coffee grounds. It needed a serious scrubbing. She spun around, hands on her hips, and allowed as the entire cabin needed a decent scouring. Dust layered on much of the sturdy furniture, with the exception of one chair and the dining table.

Cobwebs sprouted from the upper corners, and draped across the wooden beamed ceiling. They fluttered in the gentle breeze that now flushed the musty smell from the interior.

"No time like the present." She rolled up her sleeves and got to work.

CHAPTER SEVEN

Callie lugged the loaded sledge along the trail. There hadn't been much on the trapline but a couple of beavers and a hare, but she'd stumbled across a young bull caribou that had gotten entangled in the dead undergrowth between three trees. The sharp branches had pierced him in a number of places, the smell of blood enriching the air. She couldn't get close enough to safely free him, and the longer he remained trapped the less likely he'd survive the predators that would inevitably gather for a free meal. And it had been awhile since she'd had a taste of good venison, not since before Jasper…

Once she'd slaughtered the caribou, it had taken her most the afternoon to free it from the nest of branches. She missed Jasper at the best of times; she sorely regretted his loss when it came to matters of sheer strength. After suffering a number of scratches as she chopped and tugged at the lifeless carcass, she finally towed it from its bloody trap. She gutted and field stripped it before loading it onto the sledge. As she dragged the caribou home, she considered the day's work. The hide would be worthless with all the holes in it though the bones, teeth and sinew would be of interest to some. She decided to keep the hide for herself along with half the meat. That would sit her pretty for a month as well as give her decent leather for a new pair of boots.

She'd only been to town once since Jasper's... Her mind shied away from the thought. The town trip had been about as bad as she'd expected. The people there had never cared much for her, seeing her as unnatural and strange in her men's clothes. Jasper had been the friendly one, the one who joked with folks and put them at their ease. Callie had never had the knack, seeming to rub people wrong at first encounter. She knew that the butcher had taken a good ten percent off the worth of the meat on her last delivery, but there was nothing she could do without Jasper around to call the bastard out on his cheating ways. Though a boon, the caribou meat was also an albatross. She'd have to head into town before it spoiled, and she didn't look forward to dealing with people that soon again.

Wood smoke tickled her nose and she looked at the horizon with a frown. A trickle of smoke puffed into the sky, smoke that obviously came from her cabin. Immediate fear stabbed her heart. *Did the cabin catch fire?* But no, the smoke was an innocuous white, typical for a wood stove that had been enkindled and belched exhaust. Had the homestead been on fire, the smoke would be a dense black and she would have caught wind of it some time ago.

Someone was there. Someone had trespassed and invaded her privacy. Who the hell would have the audacity to barge into her cabin and start up the stove? Callie knew a number of people who didn't like her, but most wouldn't have made the effort. It took two hours on a mediocre track to reach the cabin. Besides if anyone meant her harm, they wouldn't warn her, would they? Those few lowlifes that had it out for her would wait in the woods until they had her in their sights and shoot her.

She glanced back at her sledge. She'd imagined a thick venison steak, maybe with some eggs on the side. If she abandoned the load to investigate the cabin, she might lose the meat to predators before she could return. Better to bring it along even if it made a sitting duck out of her. Maybe Daryl McKenzie had come down from the hills; he was about due and was the only person she knew who would make himself at home. Mind made up, she put her back to the task at hand.

Another half hour passed before Callie hauled the sled into the yard. She hadn't seen any evidence of prowlers in the brush. The cabin windows and door had all been thrown open. Several trunks and bags were stacked on the porch, and her frown deepened to a scowl. That wasn't Daryl's gear. Did she have a squatter who thought her property was free for the taking now that Jasper was gone? Maybe some no-account from town had scammed a new arrival, selling land that wasn't his to some rube fresh off the steamer. Callie knew her rights in the case of property law—this land and all the buildings on it were hers now, and no muggins could take it from her. Though she usually shied away from confrontation, she'd be damned if she'd roll over for this blatant thievery.

With a growl, she let the sledge straps fall as she marched toward her home, rifle in hand. Nearing the door, she smelled beans and cornbread. *Cornbread?* She'd used the last of her cornmeal a week ago. A glance at the bags and trunks revealed that the baker had brought their own staples. There was a strange sound too, a humming coming through the window. It wasn't until she burst into the cabin that she realized that what she heard was music.

A young woman stood in one corner of the cabin, a broom in her hands as she swept vigorously at the ceiling. Her dark hair had been pinned up but was in disarray. She'd rolled up the sleeves of her dress, and Callie registered a proper feminine hat on the freshly scrubbed dining table.

"Who in the hell are you?" Callie demanded.

The woman stopped humming and gasped as the broom dropped to the floor. Stray cobwebs drifted away from her industry as she stared at Callie with large hazel eyes, one hand on her chest as if to physically calm her heart. "Oh, my! You nearly scared the life out of me!"

A quick scan of the interior showed no one else present. Emboldened, Callie leaned the rifle against the table and crossed her arms over her chest. "I asked you a question. Who are you and what are you doing in my cabin?"

"You're Jasper's…sister?" The woman's voice was hesitant. "I believe Mr. McKenzie mentioned he had a sister, though Jasper never informed me."

"McKenzie? Daryl?" Callie looked over her shoulder at the door, expecting the old man to appear. When he didn't, she turned back to the stranger. "Who are you again?"

The woman blushed prettily. Dusting her hands on an apron tied about her waist, she closed the distance between them. "My name is Clara Stapleton." She held out her hand. "It's a pleasure to make your acquaintance."

Callie stared at the hand, the name rattling in her head. Where had she heard it before? Clara Stapleton… She recalled the crackle of paper, the smell of lilac perfume. "You! What are you doing here? Didn't you get my letter?"

Clara cocked her head, hand slowly pulling away from Callie's distaste. She clasped her hands together before her, her stance reminiscent of Callie's mother the moment before she began a serious dressing down. "I'm afraid you have me at a loss. I've told you my name and it's only polite that you return the favor in kind."

Heat raced up Callie's cheeks. She struggled not to drop her gaze. "I'm Callie Glass. And yes, I m Jasper's sister. And you," she pointed a finger at Clara's face, "shouldn't be here! I sent you a letter calling it off weeks ago."

For a brief instance it appeared that Clara planned to bite the offensive finger, but it passed as dismay washed across her face. "Calling it off? The wedding? But why?"

Callie groaned. She pulled out a chair and collapsed into it, planting an elbow on the table and rubbing her forehead. Apparently she hadn't taken Miss Stapleton's eagerness into account when she'd written to tell her of Jasper's…

"Where's Jasper?" Clara demanded, her voice catching.

Surprised, Callie looked up. Clara's hands now wrung each other, her pleasant countenance having given away to outright worry. It occurred to Callie that even though this woman had never met her brother, she'd had a head full of dreams that were spoiled as surely as Callie's own. Had Clara seemed more callous over the matter, Callie would have delightfully used the information to cause her pain. Callie fought with an irrational urge to let the woman down easy. She stood and offered the chair. "You need to sit down."

Clara grasped her elbows, her ivory skin bleaching. "Why? What happened to him? Where is he?" Hazel eyes darkened as they darted about the cabin in search of the man she'd traveled so many miles to marry.

Callie stepped forward, intent on guiding Clara to the chair, but Clara stepped back. Half exasperated, half understanding the fearful anticipation, Callie stood still, hands up and palms forward in surrender. She wasn't sure how to say the words, having avoided using them even in thought. To speak them aloud made them manifest, yet Clara didn't deserve a lie. Bold and brazen the woman might be, but she'd abandoned her previous life on the promise of a new existence with a man who no longer existed.

Slumping back into the chair, Callie stared at her boots. "Jasper and I had a run-in with a bear near a month ago. It attacked him, did some serious damage to his innards." She swallowed against the lump of tears in her throat, refusing to allow the sobs to find their way to the surface. "He died a few days later." A suspicious tickle made her sniffle, and she wiped at her nose with the sleeve of her shirt. "I sent you a letter a day or two later, but I reckon it didn't get there in time."

"I suppose not." Clara's voice was faint, wooden. "I'm sorry for your loss."

Callie heard a rustle of clothing and looked up to see Clara stumble to perch on the edge of Jasper's bed. Clara's obvious shock at the news indicated she'd had no ulterior motives for marrying a landed stranger in Alaska. *Unless she's upset she missed the opportunity.* Though the idea that Clara was a brassy malingerer with plans to humbug Jasper for his property had merit, it didn't feel right the longer Callie watched her.

They sat in silence for some time, each visiting with their particular specter of grief. Callie fell into her usual trance as she stared at the table, running her fingers over the familiar designs of the wood grain. From the corner of the room she heard the occasional sniffle and movement from her guest but hesitated to interfere with Clara's heartbreak.

"Oh!" Clara hastily wiped the tears from her face. She tucked her handkerchief into her sleeve as she stood. "The cornbread!" She hastened to the wood stove. Using a rag as a pot holder, she removed a cast-iron pan and placed it on the table on top of a towel to cool.

The smell of fine cornbread filled the air, causing Callie's stomach to rumble. *Damn, that smells good. Much better than mine.* Her hunger reminded her of her dinner plans and the caribou still lashed to the sledge outside. Wild animals seldom strayed into the yard in daylight, but the meaty buffet out there would beckon even the shyest to come in for a free meal. She stood and glanced out a window at the darkening sky. "There ain't no way to get you back to town tonight. And I've still got to unload and butcher today's kill." She placed one hand on her hip and rubbed her face with the other. "You can sleep here tonight."

Clara looked like she wanted to argue, though Callie couldn't suss out what was debatable about her statement. Clara suppressed whatever she had wanted to say and nodded. "Of course. Thank you."

Relieved, Callie felt her shoulders relax. It would be a long night with a stranger in her cabin, but there was no reason to take it out on Clara. It had been Jasper's doing and bad timing that had caused this situation, nothing more. Callie gestured at the door. "It'll take me about an hour, then we can grill up some caribou steaks to go with that fine-smelling cornbread."

Her compliment startled a slight smile from Clara, drawing out her beauty. Unable to help herself, Callie grinned back and left the cabin. It was probably a good thing Jasper wasn't here. She had the distinct impression that both she and her brother would have fallen for Miss Clara Stapleton.

* * *

Clara lay in Jasper's bed, in the bed that would have been her marriage bed, the one she'd have called her own after they'd wed. A smaller cot in the other corner of the room held the woman who would have been her sister-in-law. None of that would happen now. Jasper had gone on to his heavenly reward, his soul singing with the angels rather than pining for a young wife. She sincerely hoped he was at peace.

The news of his demise had dashed her dreams. Callie had mentioned twice in the course of the evening that she'd take Clara into town, intent on sending her packing back from whence she came. Clara sighed and faced the rough wood wall. Perhaps she hadn't used those words, but it seemed to Clara that Callie couldn't wait for her to go far away. Clara supposed she couldn't blame her. Callie had obviously loved her brother very much, and Jasper's loss bit deep into her heart. The last thing Callie wanted or needed was a strange woman lingering in her home, reminding her of the man that had been the cause of her presence.

But damn it all! This was Clara's life too. She might not have known Jasper as intimately as she had in her daydreams, but after all the hard work and organization to get here she couldn't pack up and leave after one night! She imagined dragging her tail between her legs back to Boston, the repressed glee from her father, the combination of felicity and sorrow upon Emma's face. She'd see the resumption of the elderly marriage candidates at her door with their bad breath, rotted teeth and prodigious paunches. Either she'd be forced to choose one of them or spend her life as a spinster. It simply would not do! Clara closed the door on that particular path, and considered her immediate future. If she wasn't to marry, there were other avenues to explore.

She'd noted while in Skagway that there were a number of tent establishments that had sprouted off the main street. They offered laundry and sewing repairs and seemed to do brisk business. From all appearances they were crewed or owned by women. Daryl McKenzie had mentioned a number of women had also opened their own restaurants, serving those miners that searched for a bit of home. If worse came to worse, Clara could use the rest of her money to open a similar shop or restaurant. She had a fair hand with needlework and could cook well enough. There wasn't much call in Skagway for embroidery or gourmet meals for which she hadn't the skills anyway.

But she hadn't come here to begin a business. She'd come looking for a home in the magnificent northern wilds, to be a decent helpmate for a husband who would give her several children. Today she'd discovered a small photograph amongst the dusty shelves she'd cleaned, one of a man and woman. The woman was Callie, taken only a year or two ago, which meant the man had been her brother. It was the first time Clara had seen his image. Jasper had been a handsome man, with lively light-colored eyes. Their children would have been beautiful— blue eyes and dark hair—comprising the best of both parents.

Tears sprang into her eyes again as she suffered the loss of her dreams, of the children she and Jasper would never have. Annoyed, she shoved the maudlin imaginings aside and flopped onto her back. Callie snorted and shifted in her bed, her breathing eventually evening back out into slumber.

Clara considered the assertive women who'd clustered together on board the steamer ship she'd arrived upon, smoking their cigarettes and cackling like roosters on the deck. She'd wager that Callie was of the same breed. Callie certainly had the masculinity down, acting the tomboy in her trousers and suspenders. Clara had peeked outside as Callie had unloaded the wheel-less barrow she'd used to haul the carcasses, amazed at the woman's strength. At first glance, Callie appeared fragile, a slender young woman bearing a wounded expression, one who could break with the slightest breeze. But Clara had seen her heft a deer—*caribou*, she reminded herself—that had weighed as much if not more than her. That fragility hid a wiry strength.

Clara stared up into the dark rafters. She shivered at the thought of spiders falling upon her. That hadn't been the only task she'd accomplished, but she was glad she'd at least taken care of the cobwebs. In fact, the entire cabin needed a thorough scrub. Dust still sat thick on many surfaces, the stove was in desperate need of a scour and polish and every piece of clothing and linen needed laundering. Callie had said she'd lost Jasper a month ago, but it had been much longer than that since the interior of the cabin had seen better care. Clara smiled. Callie took after the typical man in more ways than temperament and clothing preference. She seemed ignorant on how to run a household, not comprehending that it took more than chopping wood and bringing home staples from town to live a decent life.

Clara felt the smile wither from her face. How closely did Callie follow a man's perspective? Clara had run roughshod over most men since her age of majority, using her feminine guile to attain her goals. She could almost hear Emma's giggle as she considered her choice of action. It was entirely possible that Clara could ingratiate herself with Callie enough to remain here. At the very least, she could postpone her eviction from the premises for a few days, possibly a week. In that time, she could make herself so indispensable that Callie would have to allow her to stay.

Clara's smile returned full force. Had it been daylight and had Callie witnessed it, Callie would have been dazzled into blindness.

CHAPTER EIGHT

Callie woke to the clatter of pans on the stove and the smell of coffee. She hadn't been alone long enough to become accustomed to the solitude, and it took several minutes along the warm edge of slumber to remember that Jasper was gone and a stranger had invaded her house. Startled at the belated if repetitious revelation, she sat up, and brushed troublesome blond hair from her face as she searched the room.

Clara had fully dressed. She bustled about the wood stove, perfectly at home as she cooked. Either Callie had been seen or heard when she woke because Clara glanced away from the griddle to smile at her. "Good morning, sleepy. I have coffee when you want it. Do you like flapjacks?"

The innocuous question so soon after waking confused Callie. Mind fuzzy, she took a minute too long to ponder her response.

"I'll take that as a yes." Clara returned to her brisk business, and flipped a pancake. "You'd best be up if you want any. I'm hungry enough I might eat them all." She gestured with the spatula at a plate of pancakes on the table.

Hunger fought with dismay as Callie considered grabbing her clothes and leaving the cabin. She received a sharp look from Clara that interrupted her flight reflex and hastily dropped her feet from the bed. "Um, yes ma'am." Her brisk politeness was rewarded with a larger smile, and she helplessly returned it.

"I took the liberty of stripping more meat from the caribou," Clara said conversationally. "I think fried venison and eggs will go well with breakfast. What do you reckon?"

Callie paused and stared. Gone was the lost young woman who'd cried at the news of her future groom's death. Now she efficiently juggled pans of sizzling food. Callie had thought that Clara was from a well-to-do family, one with servants to do the dirty work of butchering and cooking. Clara's handwriting, her use of a perfumed envelope and her wardrobe all pointed to the same. It had never occurred to Callie that Clara could create such wonderful aromas from a little flour and eggs, last night's cornbread notwithstanding.

Clara looked at her again, raising an elegant eyebrow, a reminder to Callie that she hadn't yet responded.

"Oh! Um…" Callie cast about her recent memory. Fried venison. Eggs. "Yes! Yes, I think that'll do fine." She cleared her throat, shying away from Clara's pleasure as she shoved her feet into her pant legs. She used the activity of dressing as an opportunity to regain some equilibrium. She felt as if she swam in unfamiliar waters with a dangerous undertow that she couldn't quite feel. *That's just silly.* What could be more familiar than her bed, her home, her life? *At least what's left of it.*

"Come and get it." Clara placed a plate of eggs and venison at Callie's seat, turning to retrieve the coffee and a dented tin cup.

Jasper's cup.

"Put that down." Callie strode across the room in her bare feet, nightshirt and suspenders dangling below her thighs.

Clara flinched away from Callie's harsh voice, uncertain which item had caused offense.

Callie grabbed Jasper's cup. She whirled about, and hugged it to her chest. There was only one use for Jasper's cup, a use for which she hadn't yet shown the courage. Her throat burned with the pressure of holding her dolorous tears inside. She gulped in air in an effort to gain control of her emotions.

Behind her she heard the coffeepot grate across the stove as Clara set it down. A distant part of her wondered if she'd hurt Clara's feelings, the sorrow of such an action added to the heap of misery she already carried. Coupled with that was the spiteful pleasure that she had. *It doesn't matter.* After breakfast she'd see Clara on her merry way, and life would return to normal. *It'll never be normal*, a voice whispered. Maybe after Clara was gone Callie would have the ability to follow through with Jasper's cup and the bottle of laudanum. Maybe this was the very reason she hadn't done so yet, subconsciously awaiting Clara's arrival if it would come at all.

"It was his, wasn't it?" Clara asked, her voice a whisper.

With great effort, Callie nodded. She felt a gentle hand on her shoulder. It didn't tug at her or force her to turn and reveal the naked grief upon her face. It just rested there, and offered warmth and support, the touch of a woman who comprehended at least a little of the loss she suffered.

"I'm sorry. I didn't know. I promise I won't use it again."

Her calm understanding almost undid Callie's self-restraint. The tableau continued as she wrestled the ball in her throat down by tiny increments until it returned to its home in her heart. She took an unsteady breath and stepped out of Clara's reach, crossing the cabin to carefully set Jasper's cup on the shelf next to her bed. "Thank you."

The sound of movement informed Callie that Clara had returned to the stove. She used Clara's distraction to quickly doff her nightshirt and replace it with a wool one. She shoved the tails into her trousers, buttoning them and pulling the suspenders over her thin shoulders. She turned, slightly awkward.

Clara's eyes held sympathy as she gestured to Callie's chair. "Come, sit down. Have breakfast."

Callie allowed herself to be directed to the table. Despite the punishment her emotions were taking, she was impressed to realize she was still hungry. Since Jasper had left her, she'd been less and less inclined to eat. Her cooking left a lot to be desired anyway, and the grief hadn't added much sauce to her cravings. Now she felt famished, like her stomach met her spine. She fell to her breakfast with controlled ferociousness.

Clara sat across from her with her own plate. She'd procured a bowl to use as a coffee cup, causing Callie a twinge of guilt for her irrational outburst. Clara acted as if everything was hunky dory as she sipped blackjack from her bowl and cut into her venison and eggs as she chatted.

As Callie ate, Clara talked. Most of the conversation was one-sided as she regaled Callie with a narrative about her train trip across country and her week on the steamer ship. It didn't take long for Callie to fall into a sort of trance, listening to the vivid descriptions of places she'd never see, allowing the strange Bostonian accent to wash over her. Before she knew it, Clara had collected her empty dishes and set about washing them.

"Now, Mr. McKenzie should have made arrangements for the rest of the foodstuffs to be delivered today. I expect they should arrive by midday."

Callie blinked, finally focusing on the topic rather than the sound. "Foodstuffs?"

"Of course, silly." Clara transferred hot water from the bucket on the stove to a large pan she'd converted into a wash tub. "I told you, remember? I purchased a thousand pounds of staples in Seattle before boarding the *Queen*. I left it with Mr. Lutkins at Pacific Freight." She rolled up the sleeves of her dress and immersed her hands in water. "Today I'll go through the cabinets and make space for everything. Do you go out on the trapline every day?"

"Um." Callie nodded her head. "Normally, yes. We each had our own lines that we'd check. Now that Jasper's...now that I'm alone, I go out most days, swapping between them."

Clara nodded. She used the bucket to rinse a plate, and set it aside on a fresh apron she'd pulled from her belongings. "Let me make your lunch. You'll need supper on the trail."

Supper? Callie opened her mouth but couldn't think of what to say as Clara dried her hands and proceeded to wrap up a slab of cooling venison.

"I purchased apples in Seattle. When the delivery arrives I'll bake a pie for you." She broke apart the cornbread and buttered it before bundling it with the venison into another napkin. She slid the food across the table. "You have a pack you carry, yes?"

"I do." Callie accepted the bundle. "But there's really no need. I'd planned to bring you in to town today—"

"Oh, don't worry about that." Clara reached out to pat Callie's upper arm before returning to the dishes. "There's simply too much to do around here just yet. And I'd hate to miss Mr. Lutkins's delivery."

Callie gaped at the woman. *What part of "You're going back" doesn't she understand?*

Clara seemed oblivious to Callie's confusion as she finished the dishes. She set another pot of water on the stove and proceeded to pull every plate, cup and bowl from the shelf to wash. Though she didn't say it, her domestic industry created an air of "skedaddle" that Callie couldn't resist. Her mother had been the same way when it came to housework—discretion was always the better part of valor when Mama got started on her chores. Callie thanked Clara for both the breakfast and lunch, grabbed her boots and gear and fled the cabin.

She stood in the yard, and listened to the rattle and splash of a thorough cleaning behind her. Though concerned at what she'd find upon her return, she felt a certain rightness too. It had been so long since Callie had lived in a proper home, she'd forgotten the level of comfort inherent in having a woman about the house. That didn't mean she regretted a single minute of living with Jasper, but it was funny how she'd never recognized the loss of her mama's homemaker skills until just now.

Callie looked toward Jasper's gravesite, the stone barely visible through the scrub. "You'd have liked her," she whispered.

A gust of a breeze caressed her forehead. She smiled and put on her hat. It wouldn't hurt to let Clara stay a little longer. She'd traveled so long and so far; certainly Callie could allow her some time to enjoy the wilderness she'd professed her excitement to see.

And it wouldn't hurt to have someone at home when she returned after a long day on the trapline either.

* * *

Callie walked Jasper's trapline in a daze. For the life of her, she couldn't figure out when she'd gone from the firm opinion of sending Clara Stapleton on her way this morning to this seemingly ineffectual haze of uncertainty. *Is this what men feel when women run roughshod over them?* She had the strange suspicion that it was, and the idea that Clara could bat her beautiful hazel eyes and cause Callie to throw common sense to the winds galled her. As the day passed, she mulled over her options and decided that come Hell or high water Miss Clara Stapleton would be sent away on the morrow.

She spent most the day tramping through the bush, clearing and resetting traps and bolstering her self-confidence. As she sat on the edge of a creek to eat a fine lunch of leftover cornbread and venison, she again vowed to put her foot down upon her return home. Like it or not, Clara was going back to Skagway in the morning. What she did when she got there was up to her. The creek bubbled and chuckled over the rocks, laughing at Callie. Both pleased with and annoyed by her decision—and uncertain why she'd feel irritated over the matter—Callie filled her water skin and continued onward.

Not long after her midday meal, Callie reached the apex of the trapline. Jasper's line headed due north from the cabin and reached the edge of the property closest to Skagway before arcing east and back toward home. Her eyes narrowed when she reached the next trap. It was both sprung and empty.

She crouched over the wire snare, and brushed her fingers over a patch of still-warm blood. Whatever had been caught was gone now, but there was too much blood for it to have disappeared. If it had been killed and eaten by a predator, there'd be bones and fur. She scanned the ground. There were tracks a'plenty but none were animals. A chill washed through her. Men in boots, more than one, and they weren't heading toward town.

She clutched her rifle, thankful that she'd left the sledge a quarter mile back near the main track to the cabin. It would have made an awful racket as it moved, and right this minute she needed stealth. A handful of marmots dangled from her belt, swaying with her movements as she tracked something much more dangerous than a bear or wolf.

It didn't take long to find them. She heard and smelled the men long before they came into sight. The scent of cooking meat over a fire of heavy smoke directed her downwind. She discovered them in a tiny meadow near another of Jasper's traps. It too had been raided.

There were four men, two of whom were known to her. Jamie Perkins sat on a log, laughing at another's jest. Beside him was one of his sycophants, Billy Quinn. Spits of rabbit grilled over the fire they'd gathered around. The rabbits from Jasper's traps. The traps on her property.

Growling, Callie stepped into view, rifle at her shoulder aimed at Perkins. "You're trespassing on my land. Get out."

Perkins hardly batted an eye as he smiled. "As I live and breathe, it's Callie Glass. Your land? Are you sure?" Before she could answer, he turned to the others. "Did anyone know this was her land?"

Quinn smiled, revealing a large gap between his teeth. "I didn't think women could own property. Did you?"

The fellow next to him wasn't as complacent with a loaded rifle pointed in his direction. Rather than answer and possibly get ventilated for his efforts, he shrugged.

"Pack up and shove off." Callie stepped forward, her sights on Perkins's head. "I've got no problem with shooting you, Jamie Perkins. Nor you, Billy." She glanced at the other two men who appeared more inclined to follow orders. They were probably newcomes who'd been swayed by Perkins's reputation and attitude. Neither seemed to be as tightly woven into Perkins's little gang of malcontents quite yet.

Quinn held out his hands as he stood. "Now Callie, it was a simple mistake. We didn't realize this land was taken. Right, fellahs?"

The others nodded and Perkins's chuckled. "That's right. No offense meant, Miss Glass." He tipped an imaginary hat to her, a lewd wink revealing his manners to be a parody. "Though it must get mighty lonely out here by yourself. I'd think you'd find a little masculine company…welcome."

Despite their uncertain danger, the two strangers sniggered with Quinn. Callie felt the heat on her cheeks, and knew that once again her slight stature undermined her initial threat. If she let them keep insulting her, the two strangers would come to the same conclusion as Perkins and Quinn, and she'd be in a world of hurt, outnumbered four to one.

Callie dropped the barrel of the rifle and fired. Dirt and rock kicked up at Perkins's feet. He jumped back with a shout. The others leapt up and backed away, no longer laughing. She reaimed at their ringleader's head. "I ain't repeating myself."

He gave her a look of sheer loathing and spit on the roasting meat. "You will regret your treatment of me, Callie Glass. I guarantee it."

She cocked the rifle, resettled it on her shoulder and rested a finger on the trigger. Her threat clear and no longer doubted, the men grabbed up their gear and stepped back. She kicked out the fire and followed, ignoring Quinn's whining complaints and Perkins's continued innuendo. As soon as they reached the edge of her property, she stopped, and kept the gun up until they disappeared back toward town.

Long minutes passed as she waited—frozen with rifle ready—for them to double back. Eventually the silence after their passage faded to be replaced by birdsong and insects. Still she waited, standing there for a good half hour more before lowering her rifle. Only then did she allow the shakes to take control of her as her knees turned to rubber. She stumbled to a fallen tree and sat down.

It wasn't unusual to find stragglers wandering the woods this close to town, people who didn't know where the property lines began and ended. But Perkins knew better. He'd had it out for her since she'd knocked him on his butt her first year with Jasper. He'd made some sort of snide remark, something he'd never have said to a woman of means or to the relation of a man whose good graces he wanted, and she'd popped him in the nose, knocking him into the mud on Main Street. Apparently he'd decided that with Jasper dead and buried, she was fair game.

Good thing I didn't bring Clara to town today. Who knew what Perkins would have done if he'd made it to the homestead while she was away. She might have come back to find all her earthly possessions going up in a blaze of smoke. Or he could have been lying in wait to ambush her on the main track. If she was dead and the homestead gone, he could go to the assayer and claim it for himself.

When her heart no longer pounded in her ears, she returned to the remains of their impromptu campfire. She confirmed it was completely out, pouring part of her water skin on the coals. The traps in the immediate vicinity would have to be abandoned for some time. No self-respecting critter would brave the recent smell of ash. She looked at the sky to determine the time, a number of rude words in reference to Perkins's paternity and sexual interests crossing her mind. If she hauled ass, she could run the rest of the traps and reach home before nightfall.

As she continued on task, her mind worried away at the encounter. She reimagined it, making different choices in her head to counteract her fear. There were so many things she could have said or done to drive Perkins away. The best one would have been putting a bullet between his eyes. Billy Quinn was a chick'shit; if Callie had shot Perkins, Billy would run like a rabbit, taking his two new friends with him. *And then you'd end up on trial for murder.*

Being hanged would be less pleasant than drinking Jasper's laudanum, sure, but she'd still be with him in the end, wouldn't she? If the Christians were right, then probably not. Being a murderer, she'd go to Hell. *As if I'm not in Hell now.*

She pushed away the thought. There was nothing to be done for it now and she had work to do. She let herself fall into her normal thought patterns out in the bush, ignoring her troubles as she listened to the land and its creatures, allowing nature to spread its balm across her spirit. Most days lately the nearer she came to home the more her equanimity faded, replaced by the dread of returning to a cold and empty cabin, devoid of companionship.

That didn't happen today. The sky grew darker as the sun lowered in the sky, and Callie's pace picked up as she neared the cabin. Despite her worry about Perkins's trespass and obscene threats, she whistled a jaunty tune that lifted her heart.

* * *

Clara fanned herself on one of the stools outside. The sun hovered in the sky, promising her that it was much earlier than it truly was. One thing she hadn't taken into consideration was the amount of daylight available in the northern wilds. Her small watch said it neared six in the evening, yet the sun was nowhere near setting. Longer days certainly meant the ability to get more work done, but she steered clear of that idea. She'd already been quite productive today and she was exhausted.

After Callie had left, Clara had boiled up more water and washed the clothes. She'd brought a bar of soap in her luggage though she'd originally planned to use it for bathing. She had several more bars in the supplies so its use wasn't a sacrifice. Laundry had taken the rest of the morning. She'd draped the blankets and furs from the beds over the windowsills to get a healthy dose of fresh air and sunlight. The mattresses would need a good beating and airing too, but she didn't have the tools or the ability for that chore yet. She'd need a sturdy rack of some sort in the yard to hang the mattresses and some sort of paddle with which to beat them.

McKenzie himself had arrived with her goods. He and a worker from the Pacific Freight Company had unloaded her staples into the cabin while she heated up coffee and fried more venison. She'd served them both supper, handing the worker a five-cent tip as she thanked him. McKenzie had refused money with a tip of his hat and a chuckle at her domestic industry. He'd conveyed his greetings to Callie when she returned.

The rest of Clara's day had been spent reorganizing the few cabinets available and putting away the food and house wares. As promised, an apple pie cooled on the table and a savory stew bubbled on the stove in the Dutch oven her mother had insisted Clara bring along.

Clara examined her surroundings, taking in the yard and outbuildings. The trees whispered to her as she fanned herself, and the sun caressed her skin with its warmth. She closed her eyes and listened to the laundry flap on the clothesline she'd strung up between the two sheds. Perhaps she could convince Callie to put up a more permanent drying rack in the yard. One of the sheds smelled of blood and meat from the carcasses collected on the traplines. Clara didn't want their clothing to smell of rot. And a root cellar! A root cellar would come in mighty handy over the long term.

Provided there is a long term. She pushed the discouraging thought away. She'd spent the day making herself indispensable by cleaning the cabin, cooking a fine meal and adding to their joint supplies. Her hope was that Callie would see the benefits of Clara's presence and that Clara would be allowed to stay. The two of them could live quite well on what Callie procured on the trapline, and if they needed more income Clara could offer baked goods or mending in town. *I could help with the trapping too if she'll teach me.*

Her heart fluttered in her chest. Callie didn't seem the gregarious type, aloof and intent on brooding over every little thing. Clara thought Callie's remoteness was due to Jasper's death. There was a fair chance that Callie saw Clara's presence as an intrusion. If Clara couldn't break through Callie's grief and despair, and show by example that she could be an asset, chances were good she'd be sent packing regardless of her contributions to the household. What would she do then?

She didn't want to return home. She'd observed the countryside as the steamer ship had brought her here, reveling in the mountains, the greenery of the forests, the clean cool air. The Alaska District was breathtaking, full of so much more beauty than Boston and its environs. This land now resonated in Clara's heart. She'd become enamored with it before she'd set foot on the beach at Skagway. Even if she couldn't convince Callie to take her in on a permanent basis, she couldn't leave. If there was a way to fall in love with a place, Clara had discovered it.

But what could she do? Clara had never been interested in mining or setting up a claim. After her first full day in the wilderness, she doubted she'd be interested in the hubbub of Skagway or Dawson City farther north. There'd been enough of that on the east coast. She wanted adventure, but also a home. She desired to live outdoors rather than cooped up in a city, but tramping through the wilderness without someplace to settle didn't seem right. If Callie didn't want her around, she'd have to stake her own claim somewhere, homestead in the wilderness like Callie had. Women were allowed to have claims; it was simply a matter of finding land that hadn't been earmarked for someone else. With everyone heading north there should be plenty of acreage around here.

Maybe she could ask Callie to teach her to trap. Certainly with the number of people traipsing through the neighborhood toward Dawson City and the rich goldfields beyond there'd be plenty of call for more fur and meat. As she pondered her future, the thoughts of husband, hearth and children faded. Her heart swelled with a sense of freedom, her mind with adventure. In Boston she was a spinster. Here in the Alaska District, she'd be one of many strong women making a life independent of the menfolk, standing on her own two feet, a true New Woman like the ones she'd read about in books. If she got lonely, she could send Emma an invitation. The idea of her and her best friend together in this majestic beauty made her smile. *If Callie can make a life out here without a man, why can't I?*

Despite the pleasure of a life with Emma at her side, the thought of staying at the Glass cabin with Callie overshadowed the reverie. Though they'd only just met, Clara found Callie intriguing, just as she had the masculine women on the ship or the occasional one she'd seen in Boston. While Clara had been vaguely terrified of those strong women on the *Queen*, she found that Callie's vulnerability, her grief for her brother's death made her more approachable. In a word, Callie was fascinating.

Warmed by the sun, content with the day's activities and her future plans, Clara indulged in a new daydream—she and Callie Glass with a life together as they ran traplines, made trips to town and puttered about the homestead. They'd build a bigger cabin, put in a root cellar and maybe a yearly garden and grow old with each other, never needing vindication from anyone on how they lived their lives. *Wouldn't that be wonderful?*

* * *

Callie returned home to discover that the hard ground in front of the porch had been swept clean of debris. From this angle the porch looked to have been neatened too, but she couldn't put her finger on what had changed. She continued past toward the storage shed, frowning in thought as she tried to figure out the difference. Clara bustled around inside the cabin, but Callie didn't announce her presence. She studied the crudely hung rope stretched between the two sheds currently festooned with what appeared to be her drawers and socks. A mishmash of hot embarrassment and self-conscious gratitude forced her to look away and focus on the job at hand. *I can imagine what Jamie Perkins would have said if he'd arrived here to see my union suits dangling in the wind.* The knowledge that Clara had touched her underthings forced the warm blush across her cheeks. She mindfully ignored the sight of her unmentionables airing in the sun. It was too late to do anything about them now. Instead she unloaded her catch into the shed, skinning the carcasses as she went. Marmots, beavers and hares went past her knife in a flurry of disregard, the job slower than usual as her attention wavered toward the sounds from the cabin. Clara remained oblivious to Callie's return and didn't make an appearance. It was a disappointment. Uncertain why she even cared, Callie turned her back on the cabin to focus on her task.

From the corner of her eye she saw that another clothesline had been tied between two trees at the edge of the clearing. This one held the bedsheets. She'd already seen her bedding draped outside a cabin window upon her arrival. *Good Lord, has she been cleaning all day?* That behavior didn't strike her as something done by a woman who planned to leave. She scowled as she worked, slicing fur from meat, hanging carcasses from the ceiling of the shed and laying the furs out on the floor. Last night Clara had said that she wouldn't stay so why had she invested all this time and energy into straightening things up? Gratitude for a night or two out of the cold only went so far in Callie's books.

Despite the vague discontent, Callie finished her work. She secured the shed against predators and muscled the sledge onto its side. Since the clothesline took up the sledge's usual spot on the side of the shed, she set the thing up against the shed door, doubly securing it against incursion. She pulled the cover from the rain barrel there and used a ladle to sluice her head, dipping out more water to wash the blood from her hands.

With nothing else to distract her from the inevitable, she crossed the yard toward the cabin. Clara's humming grew louder as she neared. The sound of music both soothed and irritated Callie. Though it was nice to hear another person at the homestead after a long day on the trapline, the knowledge that it was a stranger—one who Callie hadn't wanted around to begin with—triggered her annoyance. She had enough disruption with Jamie Perkins and his malcontents from town trespassing on her property; she didn't need or want another complication in her life. Caring for herself was hard enough. That Clara Stapleton was a complication was not in question no matter how Callie looked at the situation.

A closer inspection of the porch showed that the stools had been dusted off and the cobwebs brushed away. Though the traps that hung from the cabin wall had been left alone, a number of smaller tools had been neatly stacked on a folding table that had once resided inside the cabin. Fresh kindling had been placed on the woodpile, probably from the debris swept up in the yard. The kindling distracted her from her initial disgruntlement of the table being brought outside. It reminded her of a dead tree she'd noted on today's run. She made a mental note to cut it up and haul it home. Wood was chopped every day in Alaska or there wouldn't be enough to get through the coming harsh winter. She told herself to warn Clara that roaming around outside the cabin without a gun close at hand wasn't safe. Did she know how to shoot?

Callie shook her head. Clara was going back to Skagway tomorrow. She didn't need to know the dangers of the wilderness. By this time next week she'd be back in Boston, sipping tea and eating sweets, flirting with the menfolk in her ongoing effort to gain a husband.

A delicious aroma threw off her dissatisfied thoughts, the scent strengthening as she stepped inside. The smell of apple pie, rich venison stew and coffee struck her stomach hard, making her sway on her feet. *How come my stew never smells like this? And is that bread baking?*

"Welcome home." Clara approached and took Callie's pack from her shoulder. "How was your day?"

Callie blinked as Clara hung her pack from a nearby hook. When inquiring hazel eyes turned to stare at her, she cleared her throat with a start. "Oh! Um…it went all right." The smile she received in return caused the memory of Jamie Perkins to fly out the open door behind her.

"Excellent." Clara returned and took Callie's hat, hanging it as well. "I hope you're hungry. The biscuits should be finished any minute now."

"Biscuits?" Callie's mouth watered.

"Biscuits." Clara went to the stove to stir the stew. "Wash up."

Callie hooked a thumb over her shoulder. "I already did in the rain barrel."

Clara raised an eyebrow. "With soap?"

Mouth open, Callie froze. Soap? Was there any left from Jasper's last trip to town? Before she could enunciate a response, Clara chuckled.

"Here." Clara retrieved a used bar and a linen and handed both to Callie. "Wash up with this. Go on." She shooed Callie back outside.

Standing again in the yard, Callie stared at the soap and linen, then over her shoulder at the cabin door. Clara had gone back to the wood stove. From the sounds of it she was dishing up dinner—venison stew, fresh hot biscuits and apple pie to finish. Callie's stomach reminded her to get a move on, its hunger inciting her to follow instruction.

Callie stepped back inside, now smelling strongly of lilac soap. Clara waved in the general direction of a shelf. While she turned back to the stove and began dishing up dinner, Callie returned the soap and linen to the counter. For the first time she got a good look at the interior of the cabin.

There didn't appear to be a lick of dust or a cobweb in the entire cabin. The shelves holding household goods and tools had been neatened, and now appeared overcrowded with new items. Callie peered at the shelf in front of her, noting a new box of candles, matches and tins of condensed milk and corned beef. She scanned the rest of the corner that served as a kitchen. The shelves overflowed with goods and linen curtains had been hung in front of the storage space under the counter. She twitched one aside, stupefied to see fifty-pound canvas sacks of staples. "What the hell?"

"I told you that Mr. McKenzie had made arrangements for the delivery of my shipment." Clara turned toward Callie, a hot plate of stew in her hands. "He arrived while you were out."

Meaning Daryl McKenzie had probably seen Callie's underthings. She sagged, and leaned against the counter. "Why didn't you go with him when he left?" When Clara didn't answer immediately, Callie sighed and turned to fully face her. "I told you yesterday. There's no place here for you."

Clara's gaze dropped down to the table before she straightened, chin up. "Sit down and eat." She set the plate of stew and biscuits at Callie's chair, and whirled about to pour a cup of coffee. "Hurry now. Before it gets cold."

Left without an argument to defend, Callie paused. Clara ignored her, setting down the cup and returning to the stove to dish up her serving. Callie sat, the meaty aroma from her plate doing much to distract her from a strong sense of awkwardness. She realized it was rude of her to speak her mind like that, especially after the woman had gone to such lengths to clean up around the place and fix such a wonderful meal. The apple pie at the other end of the table mocked her resolve to send Clara packing come morning.

Dinner was a repeat of the previous evening's meal as Callie stuffed herself with good home cooking and Clara regaled her with her day's activities. It was only when Clara discussed curtains and putting in a garden that Callie became alarmed. Before she could vocalize her concerns, Clara dished up a slice of the best apple pie Callie had ever had, effectively shutting her up as she adored every morsel.

When dinner was finished, Clara chased Callie out of the house to collect the sheets and make the beds while she cleaned up the remains of their meal. Callie struggled with the unfamiliar chore, stuffing wooden clothespins into her pants pocket as she hefted the material over her shoulder. She remembered how her mother had hollered when she'd let the clean laundry trail in the dirt. The last thing she wanted was to test Clara's domestic authority despite an irrational urge to do just that.

Once back inside, the motions of making the beds distracted her from her thoughts, perhaps even soothed her nerves. So what if Clara stayed another night? Tomorrow Callie would send her to Skagway as planned. There was plenty enough light to escort her into town tonight, but she reckoned it would be rude to tell the woman to shove off so soon after that delightful meal. *Besides which I'm tired. A good night's sleep after that dinner will fix me right up.*

Resolved to take care of business tomorrow, Callie finished the beds, and pulled the furs and blankets in from the windows. She ignored a twinge of consternation as she noted two new quilts and a stack of new books on the shelf over the bed. As she shot a glance at Clara, who had begun drying dishes and setting out a sourdough mix, Callie wondered again if Clara truly understood that she wasn't welcome.

Clara noted her observance, looking back with a cheerful smile. "Would you like some tea?"

Startled at being caught, Callie jerked her head around. "No." She exerted extra effort into her chore, sneaking another peek at Clara, relieved as she began to wipe the table clean. Callie blew out a breath of relief and then wondered why she felt that way. *Women are so confusing.*

CHAPTER NINE

When Clara woke it was already daylight. For the second day in a row, she sat up with a start, half panicked that it was much later in the day than it was. A glance at her watch reminded her that the sun rose and set at vastly different times than she'd experienced in Boston. Breathing a sigh of relief that she hadn't overslept, she looked over at the smaller bed, pleased to note that Callie hadn't been awakened by her panic.

She wished she could roll back into the blankets and furs to sleep a while longer. Instead she eased out of the bed, setting bare feet onto the cool floor. The one thing her mother had drilled into her during her last few weeks at home was the need to be up before her husband in order to make a good impression. Callie wasn't her husband, but the last thing Clara needed was for Callie to catch her napping, not if she wanted to stay. Clara had other ideas about her future, most of which had nothing to do with her being chased off to Skagway so soon after her arrival regardless of her lack of wedded bliss.

Keeping her movements slow and silent, she dressed for the day, pulling her arms into her nightgown and shimmying into her underthings on the off chance that Callie would wake. She left her shoes tucked under her bed, not wanting to make a sound. After twitching her bedding into some semblance of order, she went to the front door and opened it a crack to allow more light into the cabin. At the stove, she retrieved a match and opened the firebox, cringing as it squealed on its hinges. She cast a quick peek at Callie's bed, pleased that there was no movement from that quarter, and lit the fire she'd prepared the evening before.

The fire door safely closed with a minimum of noise, she busied herself by stepping out into the yard to drain the pot of beans she'd left to soak through the night. The cool morning air caressed her skin, so much more refreshing than the swelter of Boston in June. She quickly took care of her business in the outhouse and returned to the cabin, mincing as the soles of her bare feet traversed the rough yard.

She cleaned and prepared the beans for simmering on the stove all day. Breakfast would be a challenge. Callie kept no chickens—all her eggs had to come from town and there weren't enough to both make a loaf of bread and have eggs for breakfast. Preferring to bake bread today, Clara idly considered the efficacy of keeping a flock of chickens here as she prepared another batch of biscuits. Did Callie have the knowledge and ability to build a chicken coop? What were some of the issues of raising chickens through the long winters here? Clara wondered if they'd need a small stove in the henhouse, or would it be easier to build a coop against the cabin and add a grate between them to allow warmth in from the cabin? The bounty of baked goods and boiled eggs might make it worth living all winter with the smell of hen. She popped the biscuits into the oven box to bake.

The caribou venison didn't have much fat, so she fried up a bit of her bacon with some lard. Biscuits and gravy would have to do for breakfast. *Tomorrow I'll fix oatmeal. I can use some of the dried fruit to zest it up.* The cabin began to smell of bacon grease and coffee. Clara put the leftover apple pie on the stove warmer. That would taste mighty good later today. She added flour and water to the fry pan, stirring it into a thick gravy as she considered today's tasks.

Keeping the cabin clean was her top priority. She eyed the shuttered and oil-skinned windows. When she'd filled her shopping lists in Seattle, she'd included bolts of material for clothing and curtains, yarns and string for various craft projects and the appropriate tools to utilize them. Interior curtains for the windows would be a nice touch and wouldn't take too long to create. At home people used rods to hold the curtains in place. She doubted she'd find a curtain rod anywhere in a five-hundred-mile radius here. Surely she could locate nails on the homestead to hang curtains, at least until she had opportunity to create or purchase a reasonable rod.

Sounds of movement from Callie's corner of the cabin disrupted Clara's domestic schemes. She saw the movement of a tousled blond head and congratulated herself on getting the jump on Callie again. The more she made herself an asset, the more leverage she had to counteract Callie's desire to send her away. "Good morning. Coffee's on. Breakfast will be ready in a few more minutes."

Callie mumbled a response, rubbing her face and brushing fingers through her hair.

Clara focused on stirring the gravy. She found Callie adorable in the morning with her sleepy face and mussed hair. Callie's hair was spun gold in the sunlight. Clara wondered if Callie would ever feel comfortable enough for Clara to brush her hair. Back home Clara had always found fixing Emma's hair soothing. A glance at Callie's morning scowl made Clara grin. Perhaps not, at least not until they became much more familiar with one another.

The gravy had thickened. She pulled the pan off the stove and checked the biscuits. Nearly done. Callie staggered past to use the privy outside, unlaced boots clomping on the floor. While she was out, Clara rolled up the oilskins and threw open the shutters to allow fresh air and sunlight into the cabin.

Upon Callie's return, Clara had the biscuits out of the oven. She dished up a plate of them, ladling a liberal serving of bacon-venison gravy over them and placed the plate at Callie's chair. "Breakfast is ready."

Clara had correctly tagged Callie as a Grumpy Gus in the mornings. Despite Callie's natural inclinations toward crotchetiness, it didn't take her long to warm up with good food in her stomach. Pleased, Clara dished her own breakfast and sat across from her benefactor. "Do you have gardening tools in one of the sheds outside?"

Callie paused, midbite. "Got shovels, maybe a hoe. Ain't never been much one to garden around here." She sighed, lowering her fork. "And I don't see reason to start seeing as I'm taking you to town today."

Clara braced herself and gathered her arguments. "I'd rather stay here if it's all the same to you."

"Why?" Callie's question was blunt, any good humor from a fine breakfast fading as she glared across the table. "You came here for a husband. There ain't one here." She waved about the cabin. "Don't get me wrong. I appreciate the work you've done since you got here, but there's no reason for you to stay."

Clara drummed her fingers on the table, her exasperation rising to meet Callie's. "I left everything I've ever known to come to the Alaska District. Yes, it was with the initial understanding that I'd marry your brother, but that option isn't available now. That doesn't mean I'm going to run back to my father's home with my tail between my legs."

Callie stared, mouth open in response to Clara's forceful tone. She snapped her jaw shut, and grasped the sides of the table. "That's not what I'm saying."

"Oh?" Clara cocked her head. "And what are you saying?" She watched a flush darken Callie's freckles. The sight intrigued her. With a mental shake of her head for her odd woolgathering, she focused on the task at hand.

"I'm saying this ain't the place for you," Callie said.

"Fine." Clara ignored her stab of disappointment. Apparently she hadn't made herself as indispensable to Callie as she'd hoped. It was too bad she hadn't had more time to convince her. "If you insist on evicting me from the premises, we should get packing. I'll need at least half of these supplies to live on while I consider my other options."

Callie gaped at her again. "What other options? Even if you don't go back to Boston, you can go anywhere in the world. Why stay here?"

"Because this is where I want to be." Clara rapped one knuckle on the table to punctuate her statement. "This is where Jasper wanted me to be. Even if you don't want me residing here, I'm not leaving Skagway."

Callie groped for an appropriate response, mouth working as her gaze darted around the cabin.

Clara pressed her advantage. "I'd much rather stay here if you'll have me." She put her hands in her lap in an attempt to appear contrite though she wasn't sure of her success. She didn't have a lot of practice with the posture. "I've already unpacked my things and we seem to get along well enough. We both could use the company. I could go into Skagway and open a restaurant or some such to make a living, but..." She looked out the open door. "I'd so miss Mother Nature's bounty. I know I've only been here two days, but I find the fresh air and solitude most refreshing."

The reverence in Clara's tone caused Callie to fidget.

"I promise you that I won't get in the way of your work. I'm more than capable of keeping home and hearth if that's all you need of me." Clara leaned forward, placing her elbows on the table as she caught and stared earnestly into Callie's eyes. "And if you want more, I can do that too. As I told Jasper in my letter, I'd love to learn how to run traplines or hunt and fish. I'm not a shrinking violet!"

"Didn't say you were," Callie grumbled at her plate.

"I know." Clara held up her hands, palms out in concession. "I didn't mean that. I just..." She sighed, eyes once more drawn to the wilderness outside the cabin. "I've dreamed about this ever since I saw Jasper's advertisement. I've never wanted anything so badly. I don't want to lose it before I can hold it in my hand."

They sat in silence for some time. Clara eventually returned to her meal, woodenly feeding herself. She heard Callie's fork scrape and rattle against her plate. If Callie insisted on sending her away, Clara had to figure out what to do next. Perhaps she could check in with the assayer's office. Callie owned land through inheritance. Clara was sure it was legal to put in her own claim, else why would those masculine women have come here? If claiming land truly was available for a woman, she only had a few short months to put in a garden, build a shelter, dig a well. The long list of things to do for a homestead seemed daunting. Chances were good Clara would have to wait until next spring before her home would be habitable. Obdurate, she refused to consider failure as she straightened in her chair. *So be it. Even if it takes me ten years or more I'll have a homestead here.*

"You can stay."

Clara gasped aloud.

"You're right. Jasper wanted you here." Callie shrugged, a sheepish expression upon her face. "I can't say the same, but I agreed to it before he wrote you. It's as much my fault you made the trip. It's only right you have a place here."

"Really?" Clara's voice barely broke a whisper.

Callie sighed and reached across the table. When she had Clara's hand in her own, she squeezed it. "Yes, really. I know I haven't done much welcoming, but I've spent the last day or two enjoying the fruits of your labors. I haven't had a home-cooked meal in forever." She released Clara's hand to gesture at the cabin interior. "And this place ain't been this clean in the seven years I've lived here." She smiled. "Let's take it a little at a time, all right?"

"Yes. Yes!" Clara felt tears spring to her eyes and she clapped her hands over her mouth, heart bursting. "Thank you! Thank you so much! You won't regret this, I promise."

Callie's grin was bashful. "Well, you might."

"Never!" Unable to help herself, Clara jumped up and rushed to the other side of the table, startling Callie with an embrace. She felt Callie's slender strength as she hugged her. After several breathless moments, Callie returned the gesture, uneasily patting Clara's back.

Clara broke away, ecstatic and slightly abashed at her overly enthusiastic response. She dashed happy tears from her eyes and wiped her hands on her apron. "Do you want more coffee? Another helping of breakfast? There's plenty to be had."

Callie made a point to frown seriously at her plate. "No, I think I've had my fill. I'm going to..." She paused as she considered her day. "Uh...I'm going to go fishing."

"Shall I fix you a lunch?" Clara fairly floated to the stove and prepared biscuits and a slice of pie before Callie could answer.

"Sure." Callie's chair scraped the floor as she stood. "I'll just get dressed." She fled to her corner of the cabin. Within minutes she'd donned clothes, accepted Clara's lunch and fled the cabin.

Clara watched her retrieve her pole from the shed and disappear into the wilds. As soon as Callie was gone, Clara spun in the center of the cabin. *I can stay! Oh, Emma! I wish you were here to celebrate with me!*

* * *

Callie trudged through the brush, heading west from the cabin toward Taiyasanka Harbor. The prime fishing time had already passed, but that didn't stop her. She needed to clear out of the cabin and avoid Clara's obvious delight at being allowed to stay. Why Clara's joy made her uncomfortable confused her. Somehow seeing the emotion and feeling Clara in her arms had been too cozy, too...intimate. Callie had watched women from afar, had longed for the touches and embraces they seemed to share with abandon, had yearned for that and more—though the more was a bit of a mystery to her. Having Clara excited and vibrant in her arms... Well, the idea of fishing was the first thing that had popped into Callie's head, and she'd latched onto it for all she was worth.

Why the hell had she agreed to allow Clara to stay? Her obligation to the woman had ended once she'd delivered the news about Jasper. There was no groom for a bride, therefore the bride needed to return home. Besides, Callie hadn't wanted a mail-order bride on the homestead in the first place, least of all a rich one from the big city who couldn't navigate to the outhouse and back without a map, a compass and a guide.

But she'd felt sorry for Clara. Something about the way Clara mourned Jasper, though they'd never met, had struck a chord with Callie. She idly rubbed her full belly. Clara's ability to cook didn't hurt either. *Where does a rich girl learn to bake pies like that? I thought she'd grown up with servants and the like.*

Callie pointedly shoved away the non sequitur in favor of her current conundrum. The moment she'd capitulated to Clara's request the previous morning was when Callie had lost control of the situation. She should have sent Clara back that very first day, dragging her kicking and screaming into Skagway and making arrangements with Daryl McKenzie to come back and pick up her luggage and foodstuffs.

If you had, you might have come home to find Jamie Perkins and Billy Quinn raiding the cabin.

Callie tripped past a tumble of brush and trees. That was a round-about argument, nothing more. Perkins might not have intended to reach the cabin. She'd just as likely have come home to an empty homestead with nothing out of place. "Like that would happen." She swatted at a cloud of insects in her face. Perkins was a townie through and through, too prissy to get his hands and clothes dirty. It was a wonder he survived spring melt what with all the mud begging to ruin his expensive boots. No, his foray onto her property had to have been for the sole purpose of tormenting her. Jasper was gone and he thought her too weak to hold her place.

That was another thing. Callie wasn't doing Clara any favors by letting her stay. What would have happened if Callie had followed the other trapline and Perkins had made it to the cabin to find Clara? If Perkins had nefarious plans for Callie, Clara would be in just as much danger, maybe more. Even if Perkins didn't have schemes beyond picking on Callie, his crowd of lackeys would delight in teasing Clara mercilessly when they discovered that they lived together.

The thought of all those disgusting words being said to Clara sparked a fury in Callie's chest well beyond what she had felt when they were directed at her. Maybe she deserved their aversion, not being a proper lady and all, but Clara certainly didn't merit their foul opinions or invective. *I should turn around and tell her she's not staying. Just pack her up, pouting or no, and get rid of her.*

All Callie could see was Clara's brokenhearted expression when she'd heard about Jasper. The tears she'd cried that night had been as real as her earnest appeal this morning. Callie had noticed that Clara's hazel eyes changed color with the light and her mood, seeming to darken when she was sad or worried; as her humor brightened so did their hue. Callie found that Clara was lovely enough with her dark hair and alabaster skin. With the addition of her brilliant smile and blue-green eyes, Clara was all the more beautiful. Even on this short of an acquaintance, Callie would miss her if Clara were to go.

She silently cursed her moment of weakness and kept walking toward the harbor and the nonexistent fish.

CHAPTER TEN

Clara crouched in the garden, pulling weeds as she hummed. The dirt beneath her fingers wasn't as rich as she'd have liked, but it did the job well enough. Within minutes of Callie's affirmation that she could stay, Clara had found shovels in the shed and started the garden plot. Now, a week later, it was with great pleasure that Clara noted the first sprouts of beans, corn and cucumbers. According to her copy of the *Farmer's Almanac*, it was late in the season to plant these crops in this area, but she hoped to get in at least one decent harvest before the first frost. It might not be much but the more food she grew, the less they'd need to purchase from town. Next year she could get a proper start on seedlings to increase her yield. For today's project, Clara planned to erect a fence to keep out the rodents and deer. There was already some evidence of nocturnal pilfering.

She completed the weeding and stood. She stretched as she ruefully massaged the ache in her lower back. Homesteading was harder work than living in an established house with a maid and a cook. It had been a pleasure to discover that the personal satisfaction of her accomplishments went a long way toward easing the pedestrian pain of sore muscles and the occasional scrape or bruise. Some might say, "Pride goeth before a fall," but she couldn't help but swell with it as she observed her new home. Sometimes she wished she was able to voice her joy like a songbird, trilling her pleasure to anyone who would listen. There were days she felt near to bursting with the delight of it all! She dusted off her dress, and gathered the weeds into her apron.

"Ho, the cabin!"

Clara spun, heart in her throat. The homestead was fifteen miles south of Skagway; who would possibly travel hours through privately owned land? Callie had warned her to keep the rifle handy, and here Clara stood on the far side of the yard, the weapon leaning against the porch woodpile. Her gaze scanned the forested edges of the yard, and she wondered if she'd have time to reach the weapon before the uninvited stranger made his appearance.

Daryl McKenzie came into sight, a packhorse behind him. His grin was wide in his white beard as he cradled his rifle and waved.

Warm relief caused Clara to shiver as she patted her chest. She returned his smile and wave as she disposed of the weeds, promising herself to not let the rifle be out of reach again. She crossed the yard. "Mr. McKenzie! What a nice surprise. What brings you out this way?"

He tipped his hat to her. "I thought I'd come round to check on you and Callie, Miss Stapleton. Haven't heard a whisper from these parts since I dropped off your goods last week. Thought it would be neighborly to see how you've settled in."

She gifted him with a rueful eyebrow. "And whether or not I needed a ride back to town?"

The elderly man flushed, but his smile widened. "I know Callie can be a terror when her dander is up. You being unfamiliar with these parts, I thought I'd offer my services as guide if you needed to return to Skagway."

She patted his forearm with a laugh. "While I appreciate the offer, sir, there's no need." She gestured toward the cabin. "Come sit on the porch and share some tea with me."

"I'm never one to pass on food or drink." He walked beside her across the yard, and hitched his pack animal to the porch post. "I also took the liberty of bringing along a little something to share if you've a mind." He dug in one of the sacks hanging from his horse, and revealed a tin of fruit. "Canned peaches. Fresh from California."

"Oh, my!" Clara waved for him to take one of the stools. "I'll be right back with the tea." Soon she sat with him in the morning light, the taste of lukewarm tea and the syrupy sweetness of canned peaches on her tongue. "These are delicious."

"Yes, they are. And the tea hits the spot."

"Thank you."

McKenzie scanned the yard, noting the new additions to the homestead—the fresh garden with fencing material nearby, the compost pile set almost in the forest and a series of more permanent clotheslines Callie had strung up at Clara's insistence. "The homestead is looking mighty fine," McKenzie said.

Clara laughed. "It's a little cleaner, yes."

"I bet that took a spell of time," McKenzie allowed.

"It did." Clara sipped her tea, wishing she had ice handy. Though Alaska didn't enjoy the same temperatures as a Boston summer, she'd toiled hard enough today to sweat. "Callie's not much for the feminine arts. She said the place hadn't been this clean since she initially moved here."

McKenzie shrugged. "I wouldn't be surprised. Jasper was a bachelor through and through when he came here. And Callie…" He shook his head with a fond grin. "Callie's Callie."

Clara silently agreed with him. Callie was indescribable some days. Clara had spent many hours attempting to portray her in a letter to Emma, but with little success. What could she say that would make sense to her best friend, that would explain the almost supernal attraction she felt for Callie? The woman had so many amazing peculiarities, but Clara seemed unable to properly explain them or the fact that she didn't find those oddments offensive. The whole package that contained Callie Glass was a conundrum.

"When I delivered your goods and discovered Jasper had passed, I was surprised that she didn't turn you out the first day," McKenzie said. "I expect she's been inconsolable. Jasper was her whole life."

"I imagine so." Clara frowned. "It's only been a few weeks. I don't know what she was like before. I only know her as withdrawn, somber, uncertain but still self-assured." It was the latter that intrigued Clara. Callie's poise and confidence in the face of such a personal tragedy served to make her all the more appealing.

"She's got an impish side to her, never fear." McKenzie's countenance was one of fond remembrance. "She and Jasper had a war of ongoing pranks, always trying to do one better than the other."

Clara wished she could see that side of Callie now. "Perhaps one day she'll move past her grief and reveal such to me."

"I expect she will. Why one time…"

She listened to him reminisce, imagining Callie putting on a joke with her brother, laughing and smiling. McKenzie's rendition portrayed a Callie whose humor was rich and earthy, just like good farmland, a place where planted seeds yielded the best fruit. His Callie was one who wouldn't remain sublimated for long, not without serious consequences to her mind and soul. Clara could only hope that some kernel of his Callie still existed beneath the stoic exterior she'd come to know, and that Clara could coax it from the darkness.

"Well I'm sure I've bored you enough." McKenzie stood, and dusted off his pants. "Thank you kindly for the tea, Miss Stapleton."

"Hardly boring, Mr. McKenzie! You've reminded me that I miss the occasional visit." Clara rose. "I wouldn't trade this for the world, but it's nice to sit and converse with a friend. Thank you for the peaches. They were delightful." She followed him to his horse.

"I might have a cure for those blues." He rummaged in a saddlebag. "Perhaps you two would like to come to town two days hence. There's a social in the works—a new piano player and some dancers arrived last week. The plan is to block off Main Street for an evening of dancing. There may even be a talent show." He handed her a folded paper. "It'd probably do Callie good to come to town. I hear she ain't been in but once since Jasper got hurt."

The idea seized Clara as she opened the paper. It was a hand-drawn flyer providing details for the upcoming dance. "Thank you. I'll see if I can convince her to go."

"Good luck on that score." McKenzie mounted his horse. "Though it was my express purpose to do the same, I didn't think I had much of a shot so soon after Jasper."

Clara smiled. "I was able to convince her to allow me to stay."

He laughed. "Then you should do fine. Convey my greetings to Callie, and perhaps I'll see you in town day after tomorrow."

"If not, would you be so kind as to deliver my correspondence to the post in town?" At Daryl's assent, she gave him the letters she'd written to Emma and her parents. She said goodbye and watched him leave, amazed to note an urgent need to follow, to bring him back and sit a spell longer. She turned slowly back toward her garden fencing. It had been a long time since she'd had a proper visit with anyone; she was loath to be alone again so soon. Contrarily, she didn't feel the urge to return to Skagway or even Boston, preferring the solitude she'd discovered here. It didn't help that Callie wasn't much of a talker, though whether that was normal behavior or a result of her grief remained in question. The fact was she probably needed more contact with people too, just like Clara did. *Perhaps we can visit every two weeks or so. That should be enough to assuage the need for distraction and conversation.*

She nodded to herself, hands on her hips as she studied the fencing material. "No more dillydallying." As she got to work on her next project, she resolved to drag Callie into town the day after tomorrow. Getting her to go would be a struggle, but Clara was up for the battle. As she worked she began a mental shopping list of things they could use from town.

* * *

"You can't be serious."

Clara cocked her head, a frown twitching her lower lip. "Of course I am." Her hazel eyes began to darken, a sure sign that her spirits drooped.

Callie turned in a huff, arms akimbo as she resisted the urge to run out the cabin door. She'd noticed a decided difficulty when naysaying Clara's ideas and much preferred it when Clara's eyes were bright with happiness. Perhaps it would go easier if Callie couldn't see Clara's disappointment. "It's a cockamamie plan."

She heard the swish of clothing as Clara moved closer, though for a wonder she didn't actually touch Callie this time. That had been something to get used to, Clara's need for tactile affirmations when they talked. "It's just for a night. I have enough money for a room at the hotel. It'll do us both good to get out for a bit."

Callie doubted that. The thought of spending a full day in Skagway made her shoulders and gut tense as she imagined all the hostile stares and whispers. "I don't need to get out. I'm right where I want to be."

Clara sighed. "Maybe so, but even you need a change of scenery once in a while. Mr. McKenzie said there's going to be a talent show and everything!"

The talent show did have its appeal; the idea of it teased the edges of Callie's denial. She'd never seen a talent show before. Still she couldn't shake the fact that Jasper wouldn't be there. She'd spent the last seven years toughening herself up but secretly doubted she could protect herself from Jamie Perkins and his ilk. It was sissifying to recognize that she was as weak as she looked. The realization galled her. And if she couldn't protect herself, how was she supposed to protect Clara too?

"We still have to go to town every so often for staples. You've got to trade your skins and meat, otherwise what's the point of trapping?"

Callie sighed. Clara had a valid point, one that Callie had struggled with for near a month. If she didn't get her goods to town soon, she'd lose money. As it was, she'd smoked and brain-tanned everything she could to avoid the meat and skins going bad, but it wasn't enough to stave off the natural order of decomposition forever.

Against her better judgment, she turned toward Clara's hopeful face. "It ain't safe in town. I'll go alone." The stern expression she received forced Callie back a step, her resolve wavering in light of Clara's disfavor.

"You most certainly will not! If it's that dangerous in Skagway, I'll not cower here at home and leave you to the perils of travel. For wont of any other word, we are partners in this endeavor!"

Callie stared at Clara, astonished at her ferocity. What had happened to the well-to-do debutante who had invaded her homestead? That pleasant young woman had become this veritable Valkyrie, bristling with righteous fury as she prepared for battle. Callie brought her hands up to waist height, palms forward as she patted the air to calm Clara. "Fine. We won't need to go into town. I'll arrange to have the goods picked up." Even as the words spilled out she knew they wouldn't happen. No butcher or furrier would bother with a trip when every other trapper delivered to his or her doors. If she couldn't bring herself to make Skagway trips, she'd lose business.

"That's silly." Clara's face mellowed from its battle-readiness to the simple sternness of a mother talking sense into her recalcitrant offspring. "Even with the staples I brought with me, we still need more things from town—axe handles, crockery, butter and eggs. We can combine all our purchases and sales in this one trip and still have time to watch the entertainment."

Callie rubbed the back of her neck as she searched for other arguments. She'd never admitted her fears to anyone, not even Jasper. She certainly couldn't do so with Clara Stapleton, a complete stranger. "I don't like staying away overnight."

"It'll only be the one, Callie. We'll make certain everything is closed up tight, nice and secure. Most nights nothing happens anyway."

But what if Perkins sees me in town? Callie couldn't use that logical argument since she hadn't told Clara about Perkins's foray and their confrontation the week before. She searched for another reason. "What about the distance?" she asked. "Have you ever walked fifteen miles before? We only have the pony to draw the goods to town. He's not for riding."

Timidity softened Clara's adamancy. "Not exactly." She rolled her eyes, the Valkyrie returning on swift wings. "But I'm not a weakling, Callie Glass, and don't you forget it!"

Startled, Callie again held her hands up to ward off attack. "I won't! I didn't mean—"

"See that you don't." Clara crossed her arms over her chest, obstinacy in every line.

Callie sighed, whether in relief or consternation she couldn't tell. The one thing she'd learned from Clara over the course of her stay was that Callie knew absolutely nothing about women in general. "All right, I'll concede that I need to go into town every so often. And I'll concede that you can take care of yourself well enough to come along."

Clara smiled, chin raised.

She's so pretty when she smiles. Mentally shaking her head, Callie forced herself to focus on the conversation. "But I ain't going to some soiree, and that's final! If it's going to be a big party and all, I can guarantee you that the town leaders will be attending. Look at me." She held her arms wide, inviting a thorough examination as she looked down her body. She wore rough spun pants with patches in the knees and crotch, scuffed dusty boots and a threadbare shirt. "Nobody wants to see me like this."

"I could make you a dress," Clara offered in a cautious tone.

"A dress? Hell, no!" Callie sneered. "I ain't been in a dress in forever, and that's not going to change. I like my trousers just fine, thank you." Clara bowed her head, and Callie felt sheepish and sorrowful over her outburst. She felt her shoulders sag, fighting the urge to leap forward and apologize.

Clara spoke to the table. "You still have Jasper's clothes, and I can sew. I could adapt some of his better clothing to suit you." She glanced quickly up to measure Callie's reaction before dropping her gaze again. "I know he has one suit that's in good condition. And I've material enough at least for a new shirt."

Callie scowled, unable to devise a valid counterargument. She needed to go to town to trade. Clara seemed to feel the need as well, especially with a talent show in the offing. Callie felt more than heard the grumble in her throat. *Damn Daryl McKenzie!*

With an explosive sigh, she threw hands into the air, and dropped them to her sides. "Fine! We'll spend tomorrow preparing and leave day after tomorrow after breakfast."

Clara's eyes sparkled, their color almost a turquoise blue, as she finally looked at Callie, with a brilliant smile. "Truly?"

Despite her personal consternation, Callie felt her lips twitch in an answering grin, wondering why she even cared. "Truly." She pointed a finger at her. "But if there isn't a room available in town, we turn right around and come back."

"Of course!" Clara nodded emphatically, unable to stifle her happiness with an expression of earnest accord. "Of course." She fairly trembled with excitement for a brief moment before closing the distance between them. "Oh, thank you, Callie! We'll have so much fun, I promise!"

Callie returned the embrace without the hesitation she'd shown at first. Clara was a demonstrative woman, and Callie was becoming used to the constant touches and hugs. At first the affectionate displays had made her feel uncomfortable—she and Jasper had never had such a relationship. It was different with Clara though; Callie couldn't figure out how that was so.

She relaxed into Clara's arms, and soaked in the physical touch, a part of her warming to the expression of friendship she'd never experienced before.

CHAPTER ELEVEN

The morning of their outing came much faster than Callie had hoped despite her private merriment over Clara's anticipation. The previous day had gone by in a flurry of activity as Clara flitted about the cabin and yard—sewing, packing, washing, packing, making dinner and packing. Callie couldn't recall ever needing so much preparation for a trip into Skagway, but any attempt to dissuade Clara had been met with resounding disapproval.

Callie stomped alongside the packhorse, uncomfortable in her stiff new shirt and what had once been Jasper's trousers. Clara walked beside her, discussing the scenery and wildlife that they passed along the main trail to Skagway, her musical voice an excited burble in counterpoint to birdsong and creaking trees.

Rather than focus on personal insecurities that seemed to grow into epic proportions as they neared their destination, Callie distracted herself with admiration for Clara's skills as a seamstress. There was no way Callie could have altered Jasper's clothes to suit her smaller frame, not with any decent results.

Yet Clara had done so in less than a day. While Callie had spent yesterday sorting through the hides and meat in the smokehouse, Clara had kept busy on the porch with a flashing needle and thread. It had been the only time Callie had seen her seated except at meals. Clara had done a fine job with her straight and even stitches. The cut of the pants and the design of the shirt somehow made Callie look less like a woman swimming in men's clothes and more like the outfit had been designed for her.

Callie had spent years hiding inside men's clothes. She felt a little out of place at the way these fit, tight in places they shouldn't be and loose in areas she'd grown used to chafing. She was nervous about how people would perceive her now. Did she look more like a weak woman than she had before or did the new clothes portray her as stronger and more confident? Jasper had never invested in a full-length mirror for the cabin; neither Glass had been vain enough to need more than the little shaving mirror he'd owned. Regardless, Callie didn't look forward to the reaction from the Skagway townsfolk. She hadn't been completely vilified in Skagway since she'd arrived, but most folks found her odd. She'd seen it in their eyes, in the way they'd whisper to one another after she'd passed. Only the lowlifes and roustabouts spoke aloud their negative opinions of her, but the rest were just as judgmental, maybe more so. She was sure of that.

"Oh! We're almost there!" Clara laughed, distracting Callie from her intellectual malaise by squeezing her arm.

A bolt of terror caused Callie's heart to leap into her throat. They'd reached a rise in the trail. Below and to the east across the inlet was Skagway. It nestled between two juts of land, an aggregation of buildings, outbuildings and tents covered by a layer of hazy smoke from a multitude of cook fires. Though she and Clara were still more than two miles away as the crow flew, sound spilled from the small harbor town, discernible even at this distance—the low rumble of hundreds of voices in conversation, the industrious sounds of chopping wood and hammering and barking dogs; the ringing of blacksmith's anvils, the creaking of ropes from the ships in the harbor and the continuous splash of ocean water against the mud flats. The sights and sounds were accompanied by smells. Callie's sharp inhalation stung her nose with the odor of wood smoke, wet fur and an aroma that only occurred when hundreds of unwashed humans gathered.

Clara's grip was the only thing that kept Callie along the trail. The sound of her blood pounding in her veins eventually faded, to be replaced by Clara's excited and entirely one-sided conversation in regards to the hotel room they would rent, the purchases she had in mind and speculation over what talents would be on stage that evening. Callie let her ramble, glad for the inattention as she gathered her courage for the ordeal to come.

An hour later Callie's nerves were no better, but at least she wasn't a complete wreck as they entered Skagway.

"Why haven't you purchased a boat?"

"What?" Callie blinked at Clara. "A boat? Why would I buy a boat?"

Clara gestured back the way they'd come. "We've gone, what…five miles out of our way as we skirted the water to reach Skagway? If you had a boat, you could row your goods right down the inlet to town. A boat would lessen your transit time. We'd have been here long ago."

Callie's mouth stood open as she searched for something to say. Why hadn't they ever thought of that? Jasper had complained at least once a month about the inconvenience of passing Skagway on the west bank of the Taiya Inlet to circle through Dyea and back in order to reach town. She wondered how much a boat would cost and how she could get it and the horse and sledge home.

Clara tapped Callie on the nose, ignoring her startled flinch. "Something to think about." She promptly continued down the street.

Rubbing her nose, Callie followed with a thoughtful frown.

The noise of human habitation was frightful as it enveloped them. Now they made out distinct voices—drunken arguments, barroom poker games and hawkers selling everything from gold mining equipment to the latest scientifically improved medical elixir. Women's laughter drew Callie's focus as they passed a whorehouse. She stared in speculative fascination at the three women in nothing more than their bloomers as they lounged on a second floor balcony. One of them smiled knowingly at her and blew her a kiss. Her face burned and she quickly turned away. She heard the women laugh and felt their eyes upon her back.

"To whom do you deliver your hides?" Clara studied Callie. "Are you all right?"

"I'm fine!" Cursing her light skin, Callie scowled and rubbed her face before she answered Clara's first question. "We go to Hansen's. It's up another two blocks and left."

Clara cocked her head, eyes narrowed as she studied Callie. The close examination didn't appease Callie's blush, and she felt the heat of it grow along her chest and throat and neck. Clara glanced behind them, as if searching for the cause of Callie's abashment. Panic flashed through Callie's chest. She and Jasper had never discussed her unnatural attraction to women with the exception of her informing her brother that she would never marry and why. She'd yet to mention her deviant ways to Clara however, perversely not wanting to drive her away despite not wanting her at the homestead in the first place. What would she do when she discovered Callie's aberration?

Before Clara could make the connection between Callie's shameful secret and the teasing whores, Callie urged the packhorse forward. "Come on! Time's a 'wasting." Clara hustled to catch up a few steps later. Callie breathed a sigh of relief at a disaster narrowly averted.

* * *

Clara happily strode along beside Callie, the bustle of activity a balm to her soul. The solitude of life at the Glass cabin was equally as satisfying, but she'd definitely missed people with their bounty of characteristics and foibles. She held no illusions that she wanted to reside in town—she preferred the isolation of the cabin to this uproar—but the occasional visit was a nice reminder that humanity marched forward.

Besides, there's so much to see and explore! As they pushed through the crowd of people, she noted multiple transactions as men bought and sold goods. Though it had only been two weeks since her first visit, the town seemed so different from what she remembered. The smell of fresh-cut wood permeated Main Street, and she noted at least three new buildings that had been erected since her first visit. Another hotel had opened, along with a new saloon and what appeared to be a telegraph office. *Skagway boasts a telegraph?* It seemed civilization had indeed arrived in this wilderness.

A faint stink, acrid and metallic, grew stronger as Callie led Clara to a building that was part wooden structure and part tent. A sign nailed to a post indicated that this was Hansen's Butchery. Rough-hewn trestle tables held mounds of meat as a heavyset man wielded several knives, slicing and dressing his goods for his customers. Doors had been thrown wide, and Clara saw several piles of furs inside with a number of unrefined men picking through them.

Callie pulled her sledge alongside of the establishment, tying the packhorse to a post. "Stay here. I'll be right back."

Clara nodded, clasping her hands before her as Callie disappeared into the tented section of the business. She watched the activity around her with avid interest, her imagination wild with stories for every person who caught her eye. Her nose wrinkled at the heavy copper smell of blood and the scent of tannin, but she didn't complain. There was too much to see and hear, distracting her from her fleeting discomfort.

A burly older man escorted Callie back outside. He wore a heavily stained leather apron over his shirtless torso, and his voice was the sound of gravel. "I was beginning to wonder when you didn't show last week."

Callie shrugged, her cheeks red. "I was busy at the homestead."

The man nodded, preparing to continue the conversation until he caught sight of Clara beside the sledge. "And who's this then?"

"This is Miss Clara Stapleton." Callie scratched the back of her neck. "She's been staying at my place."

"I can see why you've been busy." The man pushed past Callie and held out his hand. "Malcolm Hansen at your service."

Callie's blush reached imposing colors as Clara smiled and accepted Hansen's hand. She wondered why Callie seemed out of sorts, but Hansen's presence prevented her from asking questions. "It's a pleasure to meet you, sir."

"Darling, the pleasure is most certainly all mine." His grin was snaggle-toothed. He kissed her knuckles, scratching her skin with his bushy brown beard. "And what brought you to the Glass homestead?"

Clara's smile faded. "My intention was to marry Jasper Glass, sir."

Hansen's face also fell. A brief but awkward moment drew out over the trio. His glance flickered to Callie who had turned away to stare over at a crowd of men near a saloon. "Then you have my most sincere condolences, Miss Stapleton."

"Thank you, sir. They are most welcome and appreciated." Clara rewarded him with a small smile as she retrieved her hand.

After a respectful moment, Hansen turned to Callie. "Well, Cal, what do you have for me today?"

With an almost relieved air, Callie unlashed the ropes holding the canvas tarp over her goods.

Clara watched and listened as the two dickered back and forth over the meats and furs, noting the range of prices they discussed. She glanced toward the front of the building where the worker sold the meat to customers. The boards with posted prices were within easy view. She frowned as she did the math in her head.

"Three hundred," Callie said as Clara returned to the negotiation. "And six fifty for the furs."

Hansen made a show of sniffing the hides. "I don't know, Callie. Do you smell mold here? Maybe if you'd arrived last week, but I just got a delivery in from Weller yesterday. I don't know that I'll be able to sell half this before it goes bad."

Clara stepped forward and cleared her throat. "If that's the case, why are you charging so much for beaver and fox pelts?"

Boggled by her interruption, they both stared at her before Hansen spoke. "I beg your pardon?"

"Beaver and fox pelts." Clara waved at the clearly visible board with its prices. "You're asking top dollar for them, but you don't think our furs are worth six hundred fifty dollars? You wouldn't ask for or receive so much if you had overstock." She made a show of sniffing the hides on the sledge. "And I don't smell a bit of mold here. Smoke maybe; we keep them in the smokehouse back home."

Hansen opened his mouth and then closed it. He and Callie shared a baffled look before he smiled. "It appears you've brought a ringer, Callie."

"I reckon so," Callie mumbled back, staring at Clara.

Clara preened under Hansen's rueful regard. "I'm quite good at arithmetic."

"I'll say." Hansen grinned despite himself. "All right, you've got me as far as beaver and fox pelts. I'll give you that." He smoothed out the length of his beard as he considered. "Five fifty for the pelts and two fifty for the meat."

Callie blinked with unexpected satisfaction. "That'd be fine."

Hansen nodded. "I'll send Ervin out to unload your sledge."

As he went back inside, Callie stared. Clara closed the distance. "Did we do well?"

"Are you kidding?" Callie gaped at her. "I didn't expect to get half that! Jasper always did the better bargaining. I can't talk terms for anything."

Pleased, Clara hugged Callie, releasing her when two men, one of whom was presumably Ervin, exited the tent to begin unloading the goods.

Hansen called them inside. He carefully counted out the money and handed it to Callie. "There you go, eight hundred dollars."

Clara almost laughed as Callie thanked him and pocketed the cash, chest puffed out and pleasure.

"You're welcome." He hooked a thumb at Clara. "And I suggest you bring her to town more often. Cain't find many folks who understand money and bargaining like that."

Callie grinned. "I will."

Her resolve warmed Clara's heart. Finally she'd found something worthy to offer Callie, something the younger Glass couldn't do for herself. It was more and more likely that Clara had found her new home.

They made their goodbyes and left the business. Hansen's men had made short work of their task, and Callie unhitched the packhorse from the post. "Where to now?"

"How about finding a hotel and stable?" Clara scanned the immediate vicinity. "And a restaurant. Bargaining has made me peckish."

"I'm a mite hungry as well."

"Excellent! I think we passed a new hotel on our way here. No doubt they'll have a room." Clara basked in Callie's good humor, noting how her pleasure seemed to brighten everything about her. Callie was a pretty woman, with an upturned nose dusted in freckles, and her smile accentuated her fine features. Her golden hair was tied back, but Clara had realized she liked seeing it about her shoulders. She hadn't been able to convince Callie to allow her to brush it yet, but she held out hope that she'd eventually wear Callie down. Enchanted, she walked beside Callie as they searched for a likely establishment to eat and rest before tonight's show.

* * *

The evening was more magical than any Clara could recall ever having experienced before. She had attended both the ballet and opera in Boston, had seen any number of plays with Emma at her side, but nothing quite compared to the earthy humor she'd been exposed to tonight. The perfect capper was sharing a bag of peanuts with Callie as they enjoyed the show, shoulders rubbing as they listened to the commentary of their fellow spectators or laughed at the antics onstage. Callie had laughed more often than Clara had seen from her in the two weeks of their acquaintance.

Skagway had yet to build a concert hall so the talent show took place in an alleyway between two buildings. Sheets had been strung up and painted as a backdrop and a rudimentary stage had been built for the occasion. Benches and chairs had been procured from nearby establishments, and Clara shared a bench with Callie in the second row. The acts that crossed the stage varied from the newly arrived and celebrated piano player with his rendition of Chopin to a trio of saloon girls wearing sequins and net stockings as they pranced about the impromptu platform. Aghast and awed at this latter act, Clara spent most of it with her hands covering her mouth as she blushed. *At least I'm not the only one*, she thought, taking into account the deep red of Callie's cheeks.

The crowd was equally as rowdy as those plying their stagecraft. Wolf whistles and thunderous applause met even the most lubberly of acts. Clara had been impressed to discover not only miners and their ilk in the audience but the upper crust as well. The town fathers were in full attendance as were their wives. Until now, Clara hadn't realized the number of well-to-do women that resided in Skagway. There were far more than she'd thought, convinced that they would want nothing to do with the wild frontiers of a mining boom town. Being an unwed woman—a mail-order bride promised to a deceased trapper— didn't do her any favors as far as the good opinions of those in high society, but she felt a little more comfortable knowing there were others of her social standing in town.

Intermission arrived and the audience stood and stretched. Lanterns were lit on the stage to counteract nightfall. Clara looked up at the sky with the sudden realization that the sun was setting. "My! It's past our bedtime."

Callie nodded. "Yep." She muffled a yawn. "Do you want to stay longer...?"

Clara hooked her arm through Callie's as she pulled them both to their feet as she stood. "No, unless you do?" At Callie's negative shake of her head, Clara hugged her arm. "Let's get some sleep. We'll need an early start tomorrow."

"Why?" Callie walked them away from the audience and out into the street, their abandoned bench seats immediately taken by a fat man dressed in sweaty furs. Callie steered them sideways to avoid a horse and cart that trundled past, dust kicking up from the animal's hooves.

"I want to stop at the general store on the way out of town. And you wanted to check the hardware store, remember?" Clara strolled along beside Callie, intent on tomorrow's list of tasks. "Axe handles."

"And eggs."

Clara shared a smile with Callie. "And eggs. Lots of eggs. And rose water, a bolt of that exquisite material they had on display, two new pie tins and a rifle for me."

Callie patted Clara's hand on her arm. "Whoa, whoa, whoa! All that? Why not just buy out the store?"

"Because I don't need the store, silly." Clara stuck her tongue out at Callie, enjoying the startled chuckle. It had taken a bit of work to jolly Callie out of her worries, but the results had been wonderful. It was nice to see the fun-loving side of Callie, the tip of the prankster iceberg that Daryl McKenzie had mentioned two days previous. Callie's grief over Jasper would be a pall over her spirit for months and years yet, but at least the healing had finally begun.

"Well, lookee lookee here! It's Callie Glass, boys!"

Clara gasped at the three men in their way. The central man, the one who had spoken, seemed a prissy fellow with a forked beard and delicate features. He looked vaguely familiar to Clara but she couldn't place him. Flanking him were two pugnacious blokes bristling with agitation. A cloud of alcohol fumes enveloped the lot of them, making her nose wrinkle.

"I'm surprised to see you in town, Callie," the effeminate man said. He made a show of looking her all over. "I don't see a rifle. Guess you're not planning on shooting at me again."

Shoot at him? Again? Clara glanced back and forth between the oily little man and Callie, amazed to see sheer hatred in her friend's face. "You shot at him?"

"He'd be dead if I had. He was trespassing on my property," Callie growled. "I'll do it again if he tries it a second time, only this time I won't aim at the ground."

"And look at you with a woman on your arm." The man wiggled his eyebrows, his tone suggestive. "I hear your husband-to-be met his end. Guess you didn't want a real man even after my generous offer."

Ice washed over Clara as her memory cleared. This was the man who'd been rude to her on the day of her arrival, accusing her of being a tom—whatever that was.

"Shut your hole!" Callie slid out of Clara's grasp, and stepped forward. "You don't talk to her, Perkins, you got it?"

Perkins masterfully held back a flinch, though Clara saw a faint twitch around his eyes. He matched Callie's hostile stare. "Or what?"

"Or I'll wipe the ground with you again. I've done it before; I can do it at will. I don't need a rifle."

Clara gaped, mouth open. In the past couple of weeks, she'd seen Callie gruff, depressed, confused and exasperated. These past few hours had added satisfaction, pleasure and even a bit of happiness to the list. But Clara had never seen this hot fury before.

She studied the men, the animosity between Callie and Perkins flaring. The two roustabouts seemed to swell as they leaned forward, much like rabid dogs on leashes, ready to attack on their master's order. In that instance, Clara knew things would not go well, that even if Callie had the ability to defend herself against Perkins, he was not a man to allow a woman to win in a fight. He'd fight dirty or not at all, especially against someone of whom he was secretly afraid. In the course of the last few months Clara had been nervous and excited about her adventure, worried over packing lists and whether or not her future husband would be acceptable to her and she to him. This was the first time that she felt outright fear.

She tugged on Callie's arm. "Let it go. We don't need this." Brief relief caused her knees to shake as Callie glanced aside at her. *If I can just get her away from them.*

"Back off, woman. This isn't about you." Perkins brushed Clara's hands away from Callie.

Callie's growl was full of fury as she forcefully shoved Perkins backward. "Don't. Touch. Her."

He bounced against his two burly companions, quickly rebounding to shove her back. The brunt of it pushed Callie back a couple of steps. Before Clara could intervene, Callie launched herself at Perkins and they both went down into the dusty street.

The abrupt violence stunned Clara. She stood for untold moments as they scuffled. Perkins grunted as he hit Callie; she howled with anger as she returned his punches. Blood spattered the dry ground, not enough to dampen the rising cloud of dust, but enough to frighten Clara with its crimson contrast against Callie's pale skin.

When Clara finally found her voice, she turned to the growing audience. "Help! Stop them! He'll kill her!" Her pleas were met not by assistance but by the boisterous cheers of unpolished miners as they wagered on the outcome, swapping money and gold between hands. Clara searched for anyone to assist, flitting around the circle of spectators as she tugged and begged ineffectually. No one was inclined to stop the fight. There was only one thing left for her to do. She interceded herself, knowing she'd suffer the same violent fate as Callie, but she couldn't leave her friend to these rabid dogs.

Callie was on the ground, her face a mass of bruises and blood. Perkins straddled her, gleefully hitting her again and again.

"Stop it!" Clara tackled him, knocking him over into the dirt. "Leave her be, you big bully!" One of his companions intercepted her before she could get in a swing, pulling her up and away from Perkins's prone form.

Perkins laughed through split lips. "Aren't you the little tomcat?" He struggled to his feet, then leaned over with his hands on his knees as he spit blood onto the ground. Around them the crowd shouted congratulations or demanded more. Perkins raised his hand to acknowledge the crowd, straightening with an almost audible creak. "Once I kill your little bed warmer, I think you should come with me and my friends. A long night with us and you'll forget about this little bitch." He squeezed his crotch.

Horrified at his crude language and behavior, Clara sagged in his companion's arms, unable to comprehend the level of depravity to which Perkins alluded. Icy terror filled her veins as she searched for help, no longer seeing a crowd of rough men. Instead she saw slavering animals, yelling for her blood.

"Let her go," a man said.

Perkins whirled. The crowd parted and allowed three men into the impromptu arena. One of them was Daryl McKenzie, and all three were armed.

Clara had never been so happy to see anyone in her life. She thought for sure she'd drop to her knees when her captor released her.

McKenzie brought the rifle to his shoulder. "You heard the man. Let her go."

The crowd had quieted, though they were by no means silent. They whispered as they drifted back, no one wanting to stand behind the man holding Clara. New bets were made on the likelihood of someone else dying this evening.

Perkins winced as he grinned. With a wave, he ordered Clara's release.

She indeed dropped to the ground, her knees unable to hold her weight. Crawling forward, she reached Callie's side, more concerned with her injured friend than the tableau around her. The relief at seeing Callie's chest rise and fall almost caused her to swoon, and darkness teased the edges of her vision.

"All right! Fun's over," one of McKenzie's companions called. "Get moving."

Disgruntled by the interruption of their entertainment, the crowd began to dissipate.

"And you stay away from these women if you know what's good for you." McKenzie lowered his rifle though it remained pointed at Perkins.

"Sure, old man. You keep telling yourself that." Perkins grunted as he bent over for his hat. He slapped dust off it before planting it on his narrow head. He grinned down at Clara, a hand on the brim in politeness. "I'll see you later, sweetheart." He sidled off with a chuckle, his cohorts with him.

"Are you all right?" McKenzie knelt on the other side of Callie's unconscious form.

"Fine," Clara ground out. Now wasn't the time to faint or dissolve into tears. Callie was safe from more reprisals, but needed medical attention and recuperation. Clara could break down later. "He pushed me away from Callie and she attacked him." She leaned over Callie, and stroked the bruised and bloodied face, her brow tightening with worry. "She needs a doctor."

McKenzie looked up at his companions with a nod. One said he'd fetch the town physician, and the other ran off for a stretcher. By now the rowdy men had disappeared, replaced by concerned citizens who helped block pedestrians and horses from trampling Callie and the people around her. The sound of piano and fiddle music started up at a nearby saloon, along with the raucous cheer of its patrons.

"You said you were going to get a hotel, yeah?"

Clara gently stroked Callie's hand, unable to look away from her wounded face. "We have a suite at the Golden North."

"We'll get you to your room." McKenzie stood at the arrival of a hastily lashed together stretcher. "The doctor will see her there."

In no time Callie was bundled onto it. McKenzie and another man hauled her toward the hotel, and Clara hovered beside her the entire way.

CHAPTER TWELVE

The darkness was swept with aches and pains—nothing solid, just the amorphous sensation of discomfort, making escape into deep slumber an impossibility. The scent of a woman's perfume, the familiar smell of lilacs soothed her. She heard the sound of trickling water and felt coolness across her brow. The pleasant touch accentuated the aches, the pain more pronounced, yet she yearned for more.

Someone, two men, murmured in the near distance. A door opened and closed, the sound muffled by Morpheus's cotton in her head and ears. She heard the scrape of boots on a wooden floor drawing near.

"Thank you." A woman's voice, the woman of the lilacs.

"You're welcome." A man, a familiar one, not...*him*.

"Do you mind telling me what is going on? I know today wasn't the first day these two have met up. He said she'd shot at him."

Shot at him. The words echoed in the darkness, seemingly unable to latch onto anything of import. *Shot at him*. Shot at whom? *Him?*

"Well, I don't know nothing about that, but there's been bad blood between her and Perkins from the beginning."

Perkins. An image flickered in the darkness. Narrow face, brown eyes, a scraggly chin beard that dripped down into two forks. A sense of loathing chased away the darkness, pursuing the soothing comfort of lilacs and coolness.

The man spoke. "He's been in town almost as long as Callie has. Worked at a saloon for a bit. Not sure what he's doing these days." Rustling clothes, the creak of wood. "Anyway, he said something to her years ago and she whipped his a—pardon—his butt all over tarnation. He's had it out for her ever since."

Satisfaction swelled as she recollected beating Perkins into the ground all those years ago. *Wasn't there something today?* A frown twitched her lips accompanied by a sharp twinge of pain around her mouth, an unnatural stiffness in one cheek. *Ow.*

The woman spoke again in a tone that hinted at frustration. "I'll concede there's bad blood there, but why now? Why tonight?"

Clara. Hazel eyes, smooth milky skin, lilacs, full lips just made for kissing. She swallowed and sighed, feeling a curious restriction around her ribs. Something was wrapped there, tight as could be. The darkness faded as she listened to the conversation. Flickering lights hovered on the edge of her perception.

"Jasper's gone."

Her world crashed as the weight of loss suffocated her. The sound of it was the roar of an angry grizzly bear. *Jasper's gone. How could I forget?*

"Perkins hated Callie, but he feared Jasper. She didn't know it, but Jasper confronted Perkins a few days after their fight. Told him he'd kill him if he laid a finger on his sister again."

I had no idea. Such an action would have been just like her brother though. He'd have done what he could to protect her without letting her in on the secret, allowing her to believe she'd taken care of herself without his help. How many others had heard about Jasper's threat and been warned off? *Have I ever been able to protect myself? Has it always been the fear of Jasper's reprisals that kept me safe?*

Cool fingers removed the cloth from her forehead. The bed shifted beneath her and she heard the trickle of water before it was replaced. Longing filled her soul, desire for something that could never be. Life would be so much easier if God had created her as a boy. She'd have been a fine man, able to protect and provide for a wife and children. But this? This half-life was all that was left for her now that Jasper was dead.

"Whatever the past, they've had a confrontation recently. You said Callie hasn't been in town but once since Jasper's death. She said she shot at Perkins because he was trespassing."

The man—*Daryl*—sighed. His chair creaked again as he shifted in it. "Damned if I know, pardon-my-language. I haven't heard a thing about it." He paused. "Maybe he's interested in the property now that Jasper's gone. He's always been a no-account townie, but his hatred for the Glasses would be fuel enough for him to do whatever he could to destroy her. Driving her off her land would be a start."

"That ain't gonna happen." Callie peered out of one eye, unable to open both of them. Her voice seemed rusty and she cleared her throat. It felt rough like she'd swallowed a mouthful of arid sand, and she coughed, clutching her abdomen as shards of agony shot through her.

Her words brought on a flurry of activity from Clara who sat on the bed beside her. "Callie, you're awake! Thank goodness!" She removed the wet hand towel from Callie's forehead, hazel eyes dark with concern, one hand caressing Callie's temple. "I was so worried."

As much as she enjoyed the solicitousness, Callie batted Clara's hands away. She attempted to sit up and groaned at another stab of fire through her chest.

"Careful! You have two cracked ribs." Clara helped Callie sit up, undeterred by Callie's surliness. She offered her a glass of water from the side table.

Thankful and trying not to show it, Callie took the water and sated the dryness in her throat. As she drank she took note of her injuries. Cracked ribs, one eye swollen near to closing, the sting of cuts on her face. She used her tongue to explore her mouth and found the taste of copper where her teeth had cut the inside of her lips and cheeks. It seemed Jamie Perkins had indeed gotten the best of her. She looked at McKenzie sitting on the edge of a chair. "How'd he look?"

"Like he'd tangled with a wildcat." McKenzie grinned but his eyes reflected concern. "You got in a few good licks before he knocked you out."

Callie winced at the complaint from her ribs. "I reckon so." She tentatively rubbed her face, fingers finding neat stitches along one of the cuts. Her knuckles were split and bruised. "I'm guessing the doctor has been by?" She flexed her hands, gauging the damage. At least she hadn't broken a knuckle.

"He just left." Clara retrieved the glass from Callie and stood, crossing the room to pour another from the pitcher on the armoire. "He gave me some medicine to help with the pain. I'll make you some."

"You'll be fine." McKenzie leaned forward, elbows on his knees. "Though dancing is out for the next month or so."

Callie snorted her derisive opinion of his sense of humor. With the care of an old woman, she turned to place her feet on the floor. Clara hastily returned to her side, and Callie waved her away. She'd be damned if she'd show any more weakness than she already had. "What happened?"

McKenzie and Clara shared a look, one that sparked irritation in Callie's heart. Was that pity? She didn't want pity, not from anybody and especially not from Clara Stapleton.

"What do you remember?" Clara asked, voice cautious. She cupped her elbows as if she were cold.

Callie thought back to the tumult of crimson anger. "I went after him. Punched him a few times. He weighs more than he used to though. Got the jump on me. Last thing I recollect is him whaling on me while I was on my back in the dirt."

Clara sighed. She crossed to the room's sole window and stared into the night.

Callie blinked. She hadn't realized it was full dark already. How late was it?

"I tried to get others to help, but no one would." Clara faced the window. "Finally, I...I knocked him off you."

Callie stared. She wasn't the strongest looking woman around, but Clara was even less physically imposing than her. Callie never would have thought Clara had the necessary fortitude to attack a man, especially one that had two others ready and able to defend him.

"That may have been when I came in."

Callie's head swiveled to McKenzie.

He nodded a chin toward Clara. "One of them had hold of her. Perkins was dusting himself off when we got there. The fight was all but over when we drove them off."

"We?"

McKenzie shrugged. "I enlisted a couple of boys from the saloon when word came 'round."

So the entire town knew that Perkins had bested her in a fight. Callie scowled. Perkins had been drinking and he was a townie. He didn't have the requisite woodsman skills to reach her homestead tonight. It was possible that he'd make a try tomorrow though. She had to get there before him.

Looking up, she nodded at McKenzie. "Thanks for helping out. Much appreciated."

"Any time, Callie. You're like family to me." McKenzie pushed to his feet. "It's late and you need rest. The doc said he'd be by in the morning to check on you. Until then, get some sleep."

"Will do."

Clara spun around, and wiped at her eyes. With a false smile, she approached McKenzie and took his arm. "I'll escort you out, sir."

Callie watched them cross the room together and disappear into the entry alcove of the suite. They held a murmured conversation that did nothing for Callie's peace of mind. Either they conspired against her, treating her as the weakling invalid she was, or there was something more between them than she'd first thought. *Jealous of an old man and a friend? I'm ineffectual enough as it is. At least Daryl can give her the protection she needs to survive here. I certainly can't.*

The door opened and closed, and Clara paused to lean against the wall of the entry. "Can I get you anything?"

She seemed so unsettled, so closed off, unlike the gregarious Clara of Callie's recent experience. Callie's heart sank as she recognized the barrier being erected between them. Clara now understood the true dangers of Skagway, of being an unmarried woman in this town. She'd come to realize that Callie had little to offer her in the way of security, that perhaps she'd gotten more than she bargained for considering the feud between Callie and Perkins. The townsfolk had always looked down upon Callie for her mannish clothes and ways, though few actually denigrated her as thoroughly as Perkins and his ilk. She'd been secretly afraid that once Clara had opportunity to see things from the townies' point of view, she'd feel the same.

Just as well. I knew it wasn't a permanent arrangement anyway. Callie stamped the tears into her gut where they could fester with the rest of her sorrow and anger and self-contempt. The emotions kept her warm when nothing else did. She realized that somehow over the past two weeks she'd begun to consider a long life with Clara. She knew now that the whole scheme was a silly thought. Callie wasn't proper material for any woman; she wasn't the settling type.

With effort she pushed to her feet. "Where are my boots?"

"What?" Clara crossed the room, hands out to urge Callie back into bed. "You don't need your boots. You need rest."

Callie spied her boots at the foot of the bed. She brushed past Clara and grunted as she bent to retrieve them, forced to hold the bedpost to keep from toppling over. When she straightened, dark spots flashed in her vision as she stumbled to the chair that McKenzie had vacated.

"Callie! Get back into bed this instant!"

"No."

Clara glared at her, hands at her hips. "Callie Glass, you get back into bed right now! The doctor said you should rest until tomorrow."

Callie stomped her foot into one boot, panting as she struggled to tie the laces. "I'm not waiting around here for the doc to decide to visit. Perkins wants me off my land. If I don't beat him to the cabin, he'll raze it to the ground."

"He'd do that?" Clara's voice became hesitant, the stern schoolmarm fading as her hands dropped to her sides.

"He'll beat a woman on the streets. Why wouldn't he do that too?" Callie refused to look at Clara, knowing that to do so would crumble her resolve. She finished with one boot and began the other. "He might not know the exact location of the cabin, but he's been searching for it. It won't be long before he finds my home. I'll be damned if I'll let him destroy it without a fight."

Clara made some sort of decision. "Fine. I'm going with you." She marched to the armoire, intent on packing her things.

"No!" Callie shot up, clutching at her broken ribs. "No, you're not. You don't belong there."

"What?" Clara turned, hands full of clothes. "Of course I belong there. The cabin is my home too."

Callie steeled herself against the darkening hazel eyes, the flash of fear and anger that sparked from them. "No, you don't. You're not a trapper, not a fisher or hunter. You're a mail-order bride without a husband, and I don't need a wife."

Clara blinked and swallowed, her expressive eyes glassy. "I don't…I don't understand," she whispered. "I started the garden, put up the fence. Up until Mr. Perkins accosted us we've had a wonderful visit here in town. I helped with Mr. Hansen and the bargaining. I made you those clothes…"

Callie felt wretched. Clara had only just begun to see Callie for the abomination she was, she hadn't had time to absorb the full import of a life with someone like Callie. Eventually she'd fully comprehend the situation and close the door between them. Knowing the heartbreak would come, knowing that Clara didn't deserve this treatment, Callie sneered at her. *Push her away now before it's too late.* "It takes more than deals and sewing to survive out here. You can't defend yourself any better than I can in a fight. What good are you?" She stood, swaying briefly as the room spun, holding out a warning finger to keep Clara from rushing to her aid. Callie's hat and coat were on the coat rack by the door. "You stay here. I'll pack your things and bring them to town tomorrow or the day after."

"Callie…"

"No!" She closed her eyes as Clara flinched away from her roar. With difficulty Callie forced herself to calm down. "Whether you go home to Boston or not is up to you, but you ain't welcome in my home anymore. Goodbye."

She collected her hat and coat and fled the suite, leaving the door standing open as she clattered down the stairs, clutching the railing to keep her unsteady feet. By the time she arrived at the base of the steps, she heard the door close above her. The finality of the sound echoed in her heart as she closed off the hope she'd allowed to grow there.

Pausing, she put on her hat and slowly eased into her jacket. She wished she could see through the wooden planks above her and catch one last sight of Clara. The only thing Callie could offer her was sorrow and death. Silently, she wished Clara the best life, whatever it might be—a full life with a husband and children, property of her own.

A man cleared his throat, and she looked over at the lobby counter where a gaunt man with long blond hair eyed her. She gathered herself, tipped her hat at the clerk and exited the hotel. She had to get home before Perkins decided to make the trip. With heavy heart she marched into the darkness, intent on the stable.

CHAPTER THIRTEEN

Clara sat on the edge of the rumpled bed, hands primly in her lap as she waited. A clock ticked the seconds past, the only sound in the room save her breathing. The sun had come up some time ago, but dawn in Alaska was a good two hours before people rousted themselves from bed and businesses opened their doors. She waited, fully dressed and bags packed, waited for Daryl McKenzie or the town doctor to check on Callie's welfare.

Callie should have arrived at the cabin by now, providing she'd ridden the packhorse. If she'd limped along with her current injuries—and Clara could easily see the recalcitrant woman doing just that—it might be another hour or more before Callie reached the homestead to collapse in exhaustion and pain. How she could possibly expect to defend her cabin from Perkins's anticipated invasion in her current weakened state was a wonder. She'd probably pass out on the cabin floor before she made it to her bed.

A surge of worry pushed at the edge of the knot in Clara's throat, and she refused to allow her imagination free rein.

She reached for her anger to combat the sorrow, a trick she'd recently learned during the long night past. It galled Clara that Callie could abandon her so easily. Clara had prided herself on her ability to acclimate to the rural homestead after life in a veritable metropolis. Now she realized that those tasks she'd completed—putting in the garden, protecting it from predators, cleaning the cabin and providing home-cooked meals—were the tip of the iceberg when it came to self-sufficiency here. In a world full of wild predators and unruly men, it took more than keeping a good house to survive.

The worst thing was that though daylight burned, Clara couldn't follow Callie home. She didn't know how to get there, having paid more mind to the birds and trees on both her trips to and from the cabin rather than the trail itself. She could find her way out of town easily enough and circle the end of the inlet, but there her memory failed her. Was it this trail or that one? There were a number of homesteads to the west of Skagway, and any one of the tracks she'd come across could lead her to them instead. *I swear to God I'm going to purchase a boat.* Had she the experience and knowledge of bushcraft, she'd have been right behind Callie last night, even in the dark. Instead she'd been forced to sit in this hotel room for hours, sleepless with worry for both her future and Callie's well-being.

That's going to change. As soon as McKenzie arrived, she'd march to the nearest general store and pick up a gun or two as well as ammunition. He could teach her to shoot if Callie wouldn't. And if Perkins came anywhere within a mile of either of them, Clara would kill him herself.

Once she had purchased a weapon, Clara would ask McKenzie to take her home. Callie might have the misguided idea that she could throw her weight around and chase her off, but Clara had other plans. Callie was a pigheaded woman with deep insecurities. The fight with Perkins had brought all of those anxieties to the fore. Though shocked at the time of Callie's departure, Clara'd had hours to consider the underlying content of Callie's words. It wasn't Clara she didn't trust; it was herself. Callie didn't believe she was capable of defending both herself and Clara. Her abandonment of Clara had little to do with rejection and everything to do with protecting her because of Callie's own failings. Though Clara still felt rich fury at being cast aside in such a cavalier fashion, she at least understood more of Callie's inner cognitions than Callie herself did. This mess wasn't about Clara or her capabilities. Callie was running scared.

Clara took a deep breath, and slowly let it melt away from her. Outside she heard the sounds of increased activity as the townsfolk began to wake. She even smelled coffee and bacon from the hotel restaurant, and her stomach grumbled. As much as she didn't want to waste the time, she knew she'd need to eat before she left. She couldn't handle fifteen miles of travel without sustenance. *Perhaps I can have them pack me travel food.*

A soft tap at the door interrupted her thoughts. She leapt up, crossing the room to open it, and almost sagged against it as she saw McKenzie. "Oh, thank goodness, you're here."

The old man's bushy white eyebrows wrinkled. "Why? What happened? Is she—?" His gaze flickered over Clara's shoulder, but he couldn't see the bed from the door.

"She's gone." Clara stood aside to allow him entry. She left the door open as was proper for a lone unmarried woman with a male visitor. "She left for home not long after you said goodnight."

"What? In the dark?" He shook his head, confusion evident. "Why would she go and do a stupid thing like that?"

Clara glanced at the open door and lowered her voice. "She thinks Perkins will raze the cabin if he finds it. She didn't want him to get there before her."

McKenzie shook his head. "Well, she ain't thinking right. He ain't an idiot. If he showed up to do something like that so soon after their fight last night, everyone would know it was him what did it. That kind of thing has to be done on the sly, even if it is against a woman."

The idea that being a woman meant being a second-class citizen riled Clara on the best of days; it didn't help today. "Will you take me home, please? I'm unfortunately unable to find my way there without a guide."

"Of course!"

"We'll need to make some stops along the way. We didn't pick up many supplies yesterday. Will that be a problem?"

"No. No problem. Would you like me to rent a cart like last time?" McKenzie asked.

Clara nodded. "I believe so. Not so big a one, and I'll cover the cost of its rental."

McKenzie took a step back. "I'll take care of it, Miss Clara. You've enough to worry about."

With a reluctant dip of her head, Clara consented. "Thank you. You're a good friend."

He gave her a reassuring pat on the shoulder. "Like I told Callie last night, she's family. That means you're family too." He gave a tiny bow and backed away. "I'll go get that cart. The sooner we get started, the sooner we can check on Callie."

Clara returned his smile. "And I'll go downstairs to purchase breakfast for our trip." She closed and locked her door as they left her room, relieved to finally be doing something. The hours of inactivity had taken a larger toll on her nerves than last night's altercation had. Soon she'd be home where she could convince Callie of her folly.

* * *

Callie woke with a gasp. She attempted to roll over, and her ribs bitterly complained when she twisted. With a grunt, she struggled to sit up. The cabin was dark, shafts of light penetrating past the closed shutters to illuminate brilliant dust motes. Puddles of sunlight had gathered in strange spots along the wall; it was far later in the day than she was used to seeing upon rising.

She grumbled, and scrubbed weary eyes with the palms of her hands. Leaving town in the middle of the night had been foolhardy. It had taken her far longer than normal to return home and made her veritably worthless upon her arrival. By the time she'd gotten to the cabin, she'd reeled with exhaustion, barely able to make it to her bed. *Did I even put up the horse and sledge?*

Fear shot enough adrenaline through her to get her up. She'd been so tired…had she left the horse outside? Her booted feet hit the floor, a brief shock that she quickly set aside. If she'd been too tired to take care of her obligations toward the packhorse, why would leaving her boots on in bed surprise her?

She stumbled across the cabin, and threw the front door open. Brutal late morning sunlight blinded her one good eye, and did nothing for the ache in her head as she squinted to see through the agony. She expected to see her horse's half-eaten carcass on the ground in a sea of blood, a bear or a pack of wolves snarling at her. Instead she noted the sledge parked in front of the cabin and no horse in sight. As her eyes adjusted, she saw that the shed had been secured. *Maybe I put him up when I got home?*

Of course, she'd closed up the shed before she'd left the homestead yesterday. Maybe Perkins was already here and he'd taken her horse. He could be out there, waiting for her to show herself.

She slammed the door closed, light-blind as she searched the inner shadows for her Winchester. It lay across the dining room table where she'd apparently dropped it last night. She picked it up, checked its load and returned to the door to reinvestigate the yard. Cracking open the door, she peered outside. Nothing seemed untoward—there'd been no damage done to the outbuildings or Clara's garden and fence. The sledge sat in silent reproach for having been left out. Movement flickered in the trees as birds and rodents flitted about their business, oblivious to the dramas of humanity.

Callie hissed as one of her cuts on her face tugged at its stitches when she frowned. *Maybe he ain't here yet.* Cautious, she eased the door open and stepped outside, rifle clutched in both hands. Still nothing. She would have chewed her lip in uncertainty if it hadn't been split in two places. Instead her nerves jangled as she scanned the homestead. "I can't stand here forever." Resolved, blood pounding in her ears, she ventured away from the porch and across the yard.

Nothing happened.

She reached the shed and leaned her back against it, eyeing the yard from a different angle. Still nothing out of place and no indication of unwanted visitors. The horse snorted from inside the shed, having caught her scent.

Callie felt all manner of foolish. She sagged against the shed. In her fatigued state she'd put the horse up for the night before stumbling into the cabin to collapse on her bed. Perkins wasn't here. No one was here. Not even Clara.

Her heart sank at the last thought, but she set aside the sorrow. It was too dangerous for Clara to be here, plain and simple. Even if Perkins didn't have the tenacity to follow through with his threats against Callie out here in the bush, he had no compunction to leave her alone during her trips to town. He'd be looking for her to return. If Clara was no longer attached to Callie, he'd have no reason to target her.

That's when she heard the rumble and clop of a horse and cart. Rapid-fire emotions of fear, sorrow and the return of terror caused her stomach to heave with nausea. She clutched the rifle in her hands and stepped away from the shed. The new arrival traveled on the main track from Skagway. Either it was a legitimate visitor or it was a ruse by Perkins to distract her from his mates moving into position all around the cabin. Callie ducked around the back of the shed, and studied the brush and tree line for ambushers.

"Ho, the cabin!"

Her head swung around, causing her vision to swim. Slightly unbalanced, she put a hand out on the shed to steady herself. Was that Daryl McKenzie's voice?

"There's the sledge. She at least made it home."

Callie's heart soared at the sound of Clara's voice even as anger swept over her. *Damn it! I told her I'd bring her things to town! And damn Daryl too for bringing her back!* Wrapping herself in her choler, Callie circled back around the shed.

Clara had reached the open cabin door and peeked inside, a rifle in her hand. McKenzie stood on a cart with his rifle, scanning the yard. He saw Callie first and lowered the weapon. "I see you made it back in one piece."

Clara drew back into the yard, grim worry in her expression. Callie didn't know whether Clara meant to confront her or bring her gun to bear. To avoid the looming altercation, she focused on McKenzie, the lesser of two evils. "I did. Thanks for your concern. Now head back the way you came and take her with you."

"He most certainly will not!" Clara settled the butt of a brand new rifle on the ground, her other hand planted on her hip. Callie wasn't sure if she should be more afraid of Clara's fury or the fact that she'd followed through on her threat to buy a gun. "You have no right to drive me away from my home."

Her home? Where did this highfalutin woman get off saying this was her home? She'd been here less than a month and had no legal claim. Callie gathered her vexation to bypass the sudden shameful desire to roll over and bare her belly. She pointed a finger at the daunting woman in her yard, mindful not to get too close lest Clara bite it off. "Then you need to talk to the assayer's office because I don't recollect your name being on the paperwork." Pleased with the logic of her argument, she breezed past Clara and into the cabin, firmly latching the door behind her.

Once inside, her confident manner fled. Clara had followed her back. Somehow Callie doubted Clara would accept Callie's final judgment on the matter. A manic snort of laughter escaped her; Clara hadn't let Callie have the final word on anything since she'd arrived. Why would she start now?

In counterpoint to that thought, Callie heard fumbling at the door. She held her breath, and grasped the latch mechanism, forcing it to remain closed as Clara struggled on the other side. Her ribs ached with the effort.

"Callie Glass, you open this door right now!"

Even her split lip couldn't interfere with the inexplicable grin teasing Callie's mouth. She recalled a similar and more juvenile incident with Jasper, mad as a hornet, stymied by this very same tactic. Callie huffed laughter at the exasperation in Clara's voice. *I'm going crazy, that's it.*

Clara scrabbled at the door. "I mean it! Right now!"

McKenzie called from the cart, "I'll just unload these things here on the porch."

Callie held onto the latch for dear life, not certain whether she wanted to laugh hysterically or cry. Jasper was dead, Perkins wanted to drive her away—maybe kill her—and the woman she was trying to protect was having none of it.

Clara stopped trying to get inside. The abrupt cessation dashed the humor from Callie's face. She put her ear against the door. What would Clara's next move be? Would she try at one of the windows? The sight of prim and proper Clara climbing through a window might almost be worth the bother. Callie heard movement and the sound of heavy items being placed on the ground as McKenzie unloaded Clara's purchases. "If you don't open this door," warned Clara in voice barely audible through the wooden door, "I'll use your full given name in front of Mr. McKenzie."

Callie blinked, mouth agape. She hated her full given name with a passion, and the only person who'd known it besides her parents was buried on the edge of the yard. She turned, back against the door to scan the cabin. Did Clara really know? "You're bluffing."

"Try me, *Calpurnia*."

Aghast, Callie threw open the door to stare at Clara. A hasty glance showed McKenzie out of hearing range at the cart. "Where did you hear that?" she demanded in a whisper, the situation no longer humorous.

Clara strode past, nose in the air. "I have my sources."

Her domain thoroughly invaded, Callie crossed her arms over her chest, partially in defiance but the stance helped to hold her chest still. The less movement the better at this point. Her pain had moved past discomfort and into the realm of serious distraction.

Clara walked a circuit of the cabin, nose wrinkling at Callie's rumpled bed. She leaned the new rifle against a chair and opened the shutters to allow fresh air inside. "You'll be happy to know that Jamie Perkins is currently lounging in a saloon with a spittoon as a pillow. Though he should probably be awake by now." She removed the light coat she wore, and hung it from its hook by the door. "The odds against him attempting anything more today are rather steep."

The news loosened a knot in Callie's chest. She didn't allow her relief to melt her resolve as far as Clara was concerned. "Regardless, you're not staying here. I don't need you and I never wanted you!" She shouted the last, internally wincing at the crestfallen expression on Clara's face. *Buck up! You're saving her stubborn life.* "You don't belong here, Clara, not by a jug full. This is my land, my place and my mess."

"Has your head always been full of wool, or is this a new development?"

Callie blinked at the ferocious woman in her cabin. Her self-deprecating anger disappeared, overshadowed by the tempestuous glare in Clara's dark hazel eyes.

"Well, let me remind you of a thing or two," Clara continued. She marched forward, poking Callie in the sternum. "You. Don't. Own. Me." She dropped her hand, and mirrored Callie's stance, arms across her chest. "Your brother invited me here, and I've stayed long enough that I doubt the law would be on your side. You can go back to the assayer's office and begin eviction procedures if you wish, but I doubt you'll get anywhere with them."

"Eviction procedures…?" Callie started to shake her head. She stopped when her brains rattled and the dull ache behind her eyes grew stronger.

"Possession is nine tenths of the law, I've heard. If you want me out, you'll need to secure a lawyer." Clara's smile was smug.

"A lawyer?" Callie gaped at Clara's self-satisfaction, her anger rapidly making a comeback. "Leave it to a brassy woman like you to threaten a lawsuit where you're not wanted. What I need is to bend you over my knee and spank the living daylights out of you!"

Clara gasped. "You wouldn't!"

"Wouldn't I?" Callie rolled up a sleeve, taking a step forward, immensely pleased that Clara no longer acted so superior.

Instead she backed away, hands out and palms forward in a supplicating gesture.

"I've put everything on the porch." McKenzie stood a healthy distance outside the doorway. "I'll be heading back to town now."

"The hell you will! Not without her!" Callie whirled to confront him. Her vision blurred. The edges of it darkened and she squinted at McKenzie. Why was the door listing to one side?

When her vision cleared again, she was seated at the dining room table. Clara knelt beside her and caressed her face. Callie shivered at the touch, feeling her heart vibrate in her chest.

"She all right?" McKenzie asked.

Callie turned her head, hearing her neck creak. He'd entered the cabin and stood on the other side of her, hand on her shoulder.

"She seems to be." Clara's caress drifted down to Callie's other shoulder.

A spark of annoyance reasserted itself. "Hello. I'm right here. Quit talking like I ain't."

McKenzie chuckled. "Yep. She's all right." He released Callie and headed toward the door. "I'll be going now."

Clara stood, but remained at Callie's side, still touching her. "Of course. Thank you so much for doing this. I never would have gotten here without getting lost once or twice."

McKenzie doffed his hat to Clara. "Remember, stick to the left trails…"

"Except where I need to stick to the right. Of course."

He reseated his hat on his head and winked at Callie. "And you get better, sprite. You've got a trapline to run."

Still out of sorts from her near faint, Callie nodded. "Yes, sir." She sat in mute silence as he listened to his horse clop away. *So much for driving Clara off.*

Clara let out a breath. "So. That's that." She squeezed Callie's shoulder. "Let's get you comfortable and back into bed. Once that's done, I'll cook up some breakfast. I bet you're starved."

Callie internally measured the breadth and width of her body. "I reckon I could put something on my stomach. I'm not hungry though."

"That's the injuries talking." Clara stroked her hand down Callie's arm, taking her elbow and urging her to stand. "Once you've had some food and rest you'll feel better."

Allowing herself to be led away, Callie wondered why she'd let Clara domineer her yet again. What was it about the woman that counteracted every attempt Callie made to drive her off?

Not long later, Clara had administered the pain medication the doctor and Callie had left at the hotel, and Callie no longer felt the depth of her aches. She drowsed in bed as she watched Clara put on water for tea and prepare broth. What was it about Clara? At first glance she seemed weak, ineffectual, a prissy high society girl who'd complain about the smallest obstacle. But that slight exterior hid a tenacious formidability, one that Callie was beginning to learn wasn't easy to overcome. Was that why she couldn't stand up to Clara? Was Clara the stronger of the two of them?

Despite the dissident thoughts, Callie listened to Clara hum as she worked, filled with a sense of peace that had nothing to do with the medicine she'd taken. Though Callie had never been much one for women's work, as a child she'd always enjoyed watching her mother cook or sew. A woman in the house, one who truly enjoyed being there, was what made it a home, gave it a soul. Callie hadn't realized how much she'd missed that until Clara had arrived to show her different.

It was more than that though. Clara wasn't just any woman. Callie liked Clara, enjoyed her chatter about her day at meals or her plans for bettering the homestead. Clara had a sharp wit that matched Callie's and was quick to catch a play on words. Even the trip into town had become fun with Clara at her side, overshadowing the best of times with Jasper. Without expecting it, Clara had become Callie's friend.

She drifted to sleep on that thought, dreaming of a friendship that she'd never had but had always envied in others.

CHAPTER FOURTEEN

Dearest Emma,

My, but it seems like forever since I last saw you! I miss you dearly each and every day, and so wish that you could be here at my side to experience the majesty and wonder of the wilderness here! You must plan a visit as soon as may be!

In my last letter, I regaled you with descriptions of my new home. I have produced a number of changes about the homestead since then.

For one, I have put in my very first garden! The beans and cucumbers are doing quite well. Alas! My corn does not appear to appreciate its current location. I expect I will need to move that crop to an area that receives more sunlight. There is a perfect spot near the smokehouse, but I am concerned that the smoke will interfere with plant growth. I suppose it is an experiment best left for next spring.

I also have tried my hand at building a fence for the garden. While not an extreme success, it has done well enough to keep the plentiful deer from nibbling through the vegetation. The next time we go to town, I will see if I can locate some chicken wire. Perhaps if I attach it to the bottom of the fence, it will repel the plentiful rabbits that have discovered a liking for my carrots.

Additionally, I cajoled poor Callie into building a more permanent solution for my rudimentary clothesline. Now after laundering clothes, I am not concerned about the amount of space I have to hang the wash. She still blushes when she sees her underclothes on the line however. She can be so prudish over the silliest of things!

Callie, how can I describe her to you? I find the English language exceedingly lacking in this regard. I cannot seem to find the words. (I can hear you laughing now. Me? Speechless? It must be a sign of Armageddon. Quick! Call Reverend Marsters!)

She has golden hair that falls halfway down her back. It is an absolutely beautiful hue, and reminds me of early morning sunrise upon a meadow. And her eyes! They are a striking blue with dark rims around the iris. She is as tall as I, which is a wonder. You recall how I always towered over the other girls. Her skin has a golden glow from living outdoors. My mother would have a conniption over it. And freckles! Callie has the cutest smattering of freckles across her nose and cheeks.

You would think there would be a line of suitors tramping the fifteen miles between Skagway and the cabin to call upon her, but nary a man has shown interest. It is such a shame that her beauty languishes so, though I cannot help but be relieved. Would she have allowed me to remain if she had a husband on hand? I very much doubt it. Besides, I am not quite certain she would appreciate having a husband. She is not inspired by the feminine arts.

Do you recollect the women we saw near the theater on Federal Street that one time? Harsh looking women, they were, their walks and gestures more masculine than expected. Callie reminds me very much of them. She has the same air about her, the same manly ways of moving. Though some might be put off by such a deviance in behavior, I find it quite striking in a woman of her stature and beauty. The women on Federal Street seem more brutish in nature than Callie could ever be.

I wonder at times if she takes after her brother in temperament. If so, I can only mourn his passing more for he would have made a fine husband had he been half the man. It has been a mere two months since his demise, and Callie still feels the bite of his loss. As much as I wish to comfort her, she shuns my touch. Perhaps she is concerned with losing control of her emotions if she were to allow her vulnerabilities to show. If there is one thing she cannot stand, it is appearing weak and ineffectual, an odd affliction from a woman who is the strongest, emotionally and mentally I have ever known.

She says she does not want me here, and I have been firm in my resolve to stay. On our first trip into town, one week past, there was an altercation between her and a man who I can only charitably name a layabout. Callie jumped into a brawl, defending my honor! It was both exhilarating and horrifying! I feared for both our lives! The end result was her being knocked unconscious with a multitude of injuries.

A friend arrived in the nick of time, but Callie has been recuperating from broken ribs among other things. She attempted to utilize her defeat in the fight as reason enough for me to go—she being unable to protect me from the world and its ills. We engaged in a healthy "discussion" over the matter and she eventually capitulated. Whether she yielded due to my logic or her constraining injuries is debatable, but I was more than happy to accept her surrender.

The doctor was by yesterday afternoon. She is healing well. He has stated she can return to the trapline in two days' time. She has spent many hours in concern that she is unable to work it. Certainly the moneys I received from my father will keep us well until Callie can return to trapping. Such sentiments do not ease her heart. She spends much of her time attempting to be as solid as a rock, not realizing that rock can be brittle and break.

If I knew where to go and what to do, I could ease her worries. Until presently, however, she and I have been satisfied with my taking on the standard household chores. My next task is to convince her that I am capable enough to learn the trapline. While I do not expect medical emergencies such as this to happen often, it is best to be prepared for any eventuality, think you not?

Me running a trapline! Did you ever dare think it? Not I, not even in my wildest imagination!

I have just read over this letter and I must say that I am positively blushing. Waxing poetic over Callie to my best of friends? You must think me a loon. Or a fickle friend, prepared to toss your sweetest of companionship aside for the first person that comes along. I swear to you that such is not the case! You will always be my deepest and dearest of friends, Emma. But I cannot argue that Callie Glass has most certainly come to reside in my heart with the fondest of affections. At times I wonder at the rapidity and profoundness of my emotions, and would they have fixated on Callie so firmly had Jasper still been alive? And what if they had? Could I have remained married to a man when my heart belonged to his sister?

My goodness! I cannot believe I just wrote that. Oh!

Clara carefully set her pen down, studying the words she'd written. Slowly, to avoid notice, she turned her head to check on Callie.

Callie slumbered in her bed, a hand tucked beneath her cheek. Her face was relaxed in the late evening sunlight, the brush of freckles plainly evident on her face. She'd lost some of the golden tan with a week indoors, and her thin frame had become frailer from bed rest, though Clara doubted it would take much time for Callie to be back to her irascible self. She'd been a force to be reckoned with as she struggled back to full wellness, and it wouldn't take long to finish her healing.

Unbidden, a smile crossed Clara's face as she watched the gentle rise and fall of Callie's chest, the vulnerable expression on her face. Callie had become much less annoyed with Clara's touches since their return home and subsequent squabble, and Clara had exploited that acceptance every chance she could. Though she still hadn't been able to brush Callie's golden hair, her brief touches and caresses had become more abundant, some even instigated by Callie herself. Clara wondered if the trend would continue, or would Callie put up the walls once more when she attained her full health?

I think I love her. The thought brought a hot rush of both pleasure and confusion to Clara. She'd spent her life accepting the societal precepts of her status—daughter of a well-to-do businessman with certain obligations and expectations. As a child she had played house with her brother Bradford and Emma, always knowing she'd grow up to marry, have children and raise a family.

That prospect had become somewhat stymied in adolescence when she'd discovered several novels on the topic of New Women. The books evinced a feminist ideal of women who controlled their own social and economic lives without sovereign men dominating supreme. The novels, which she had wickedly shared with Emma, took the concept past propriety, and delved into hints of lesbianism between the primary characters, each book filling Clara with the secret hungriness for an intimate relationship beyond what she shared with Emma. *Is this what I am? Is that what I desire?*

She frowned, uncertain. She'd had a tendency to overexcitement, an affliction from which most teenaged girls suffered. Giggling with Emma over the illicit material had been both effusive and oddly inadequate. Emma's cheeks had flushed just as brightly, her eyes sparkled with the same impish delight, but she hadn't been as intrigued by those mannish women as Clara. They would playact through parts of some scenes, but Emma always balked when it had come to the kissing.

The idea of kissing Callie in the manner of those books sprung fully formed into Clara's head. Her heart thumped and she felt a sensation in her abdomen that made her dizzy. "Oh, my!" She stared at Callie.

I'm in love with her!

* * *

"She's driving me to distraction. I don't know what else to do anymore. The more I push, the more she digs in her heels. I tell her it's for her safety, and she either ignores me or gives me a stern look and accuses me of treating her like a child." Callie sat at Jasper's grave, frowning at the pile of twigs in her hands. She'd spent the better part of a quarter hour peeling bark from the wood as she vented her exasperation with Clara to the only person who would listen without recrimination. She gave his headstone a significant glare. "This is all your fault, you know. You wanted a wife and now I'm stuck with her."

Movement from the cabin drew her attention. Clara, large bowl in hand, crossed the yard to her garden and let herself into the patch. She spied Callie and waved with a smile.

Callie waved back, bits of bark and wood fiber flying from her hand and into her hair. Grumbling, she brushed them away as Clara knelt to weed her garden. "You should be here, not me. Some days I wish you were back so I could kick your behind for leaving me with this mess." She stewed a moment. "Oh, and I heard what you did with Jamie Perkins that one time. I'd kick your butt for that too. What did you think was going to happen if something ever happened to you? Everybody in town knows that you had to protect me, and now you ain't here to do the job. He's had it out for me for years because of you. He's expecting payback."

She tossed the twigs aside, hands automatically searching for more to do in the undergrowth. Sullen anger faded into sorrow. "I'm sorry. I know you were just trying to help. Hell, I'd have done the same thing if our positions were reversed." In silence, she pulled grass stems from the ground. She heard the whistle of yet another steamer in the distance as it made its way up the Taiya Inlet to Skagway, filled with more newcomes looking for the red. A gentle wind played along the trees, and she heard the forest groan and whisper in counterpoint to birdsong and the buzz of insects. She even heard Clara humming as she weeded the garden. Clara sounded like an angel.

"I think you'd have liked her," she told Jasper. "She's stubborn as all get out, but other than that she's almost above reproach. When she got here, she took the cabin over by storm. I can hardly find anything now." Despite herself, Callie grinned. "And her cooking! She's a marvel at baking bread and pies. I've yet to taste anything of hers that I didn't care for. She's got a gentle touch with the spices that sits well with me. You know how much I hated it when you poured salt on my eggs. I swear, you must have gotten your taste buds from Pa; he was just the same."

Callie's gaze found Clara, and she watched as the woman worked. "She wants to build a chicken coop out here. I'm still not convinced it's the thing to do what with all the predators. Chickens would just be waving a red flag at them, don't you think? 'Want a free meal? Head over to the Glass cabin!' Still… she has a good idea about butting a henhouse up against the cabin, using our heat to keep them warm in winter. That close, it'd be easier to know if they were in danger, too." Her eyes drifted to the side of the cabin, imagining a chicken coop there to provide plenty of eggs for breakfast and desserts as well as the occasional drumstick at dinner. A body could get mighty tired of venison when that was all that was available. "I don't know. We'll see. If this thing with Perkins doesn't settle, it won't matter anyway. I expect one of us to be dead first."

She looked at Jasper's headstone. "Sometimes I imagine you ain't dead, that you're here and you've married Clara. For a wonder, I'm glad she wrote you. I don't think another woman would have been near as compatible with either of us. She's got a wonderful sense of humor, kind of brassy if you know what I mean, very much in line with yours. For being a high society gal, she sure knows how to play a joke. I think it's because she has those large, guileless eyes—you think she's being true when in reality she's cutting a shine." Callie chuckled. Again she watched Clara work.

"She's a hell of a beauty too. Striking. Creamy skin and hazel eyes that reflect her moods. I love the color of them when she's in a good mood." She snorted and stared at her hands. "Not the bad moods though. That color is a warm cinnamon then. Gorgeous. But she's…volatile when she gets her dander up. She's the bossiest thing I ever met at those times." Callie placed one of the grass stems in her mouth and leaned back on her hands to stare at the trees. "No, when she's happy her eyes are almost a silvery blue, not gray-blue like yours. I'd wager you two would have had a whole passel of beautiful children, each with curly dark hair and hazel eyes."

She pulled her lower lip into her mouth as she thought. "Even though she's bossy, she's got the gentlest of touches too. She changes my bandages, and I hardly feel the pain. I don't know why. When the doc came by a couple of days ago he did the same damned thing and it hurt like a son of a bitch." She straightened her legs, and rested on her elbows, feeling the muscles in her chest stretch and her ribs twinge. The discomfort didn't stop her as she forced herself to remain in that position a while longer.

"Doc says I can go out on the trapline again starting tomorrow. It's probably a hell of a mess and it's going to take a lot of work. As much as I can't wait to be doing something instead of sitting around all day, the thought of leaving Clara here all alone isn't sitting well with me. Not that she can't take care of herself! I've been teaching her to shoot her new rifle, and she's a natural marksman! I just…" Her voice trailed off as she searched for the words. She verified Clara wasn't within hearing. "I just think I'll miss her." Sitting up, she shook a warning finger at Jasper's headstone. "Don't you dare tell her that either!"

Callie dropped her finger as she stared at his headstone. Jasper would keep her secret, not because he was a loyal brother but because he wasn't even there. He'd gone on to his great reward, his soul oblivious to the scrabbling of his mortal sister on this plane. Her chin sagged to her chest.

Though she would never be happy for Jasper's loss, she had to admit deep in her heart that the more she came to know Clara, the happier she was that Jasper wasn't around. Her brother had been a gregarious, confident and outgoing man— the perfect husband in Callie's books. Had she ever met a man like him, she might have considered changing her stance on men and marriage. Jasper would have swept young Clara off her feet in a whirlwind romance that would have left all three of them breathless. It would have also left Callie on the outside, falling for a woman she could never have.

Her spine straightened with a jolt as she corralled her wandering thoughts. She shot a look at Clara as though expecting her to have witnessed her epiphany. *I'm falling in love with her?*

Clara chose that moment to look over at Callie for a brief instant. Their eyes met, and Callie swore she saw a flash in Clara's even at this distance, a white-hot connection that disappeared as soon as it came. She gasped aloud.

Unmindful of how the shared look had affected Callie, Clara simply smiled and returned to business.

Callie physically turned her back on Clara. Her blood pounded in her ears as she attempted to grasp the seriousness of the situation. She was falling for her brother's promised bride! How could she do that? Now she was more thankful that Jasper wasn't here to witness her nefarious thoughts. He'd known of Callie's predilection for women and had never denigrated her for it. Once she'd heard him say that God had made man in His image—Callie was just another manifestation of God's will. It wasn't a popular opinion among the religious folk. *Would he have changed his tune knowing that I coveted his wife?* Wife-to-be in any case.

She frowned. Had Jasper and Clara married, it was possible Callie wouldn't be thinking this way. Clara would be her sister-in-law, a pleasant enough woman but hardly a potential love interest. She sneaked a glance over her shoulder, immediately enamored of the sun reflecting from Clara's dark hair. Callie tore her gaze away. She may have developed a crush, but who didn't once they came to know Clara? Even old Daryl McKenzie was wrapped about her little finger.

The frown faded into a faint smile. She imagined spending the rest of her life with Clara—building that henhouse, expanding the garden and strengthening the fence, enjoying the companionship of someone who intrinsically understood the vagaries of being a woman in such a rustic existence. They'd enjoy a freedom with one another in a manner they couldn't attain with menfolk, a gentle camaraderie and intimacy that Callie had never seen between a man and his wife.

She'd seen Clara in her nightgown, ankles brazenly revealed when she slipped into bed at night. Sometimes Callie laid awake, listening to Clara breathe, wondering what it would be like to hold her as she slept, to be held. She imagined slipping into Clara's bed in the middle of the night, Clara waking just enough to snuggle together, Clara's welcome smile…

Clara wasn't a deviant like Callie.

The thought dashed cold water on Callie's aspiration.

Clara had come here to marry a man, not a woman. She didn't find herself attracted to women at all. Which meant that Callie's idealistic vision was fiction. Clara had insisted on staying but for how long? How long would it be before she'd feel the biological imperative to have children? When that happened, she'd be gone like a shot to Skagway. And it didn't matter how close she and Callie became, Callie would never allow another man to live on her property. None would ever compare to Jasper, and she couldn't stand the thought of anyone lesser residing in his stead.

With a deep sigh, she set aside her woolgathering. She'd already accepted a friendship with Clara—an annoying and exhilarating friendship, but a friendship all the same. And Clara had shown a remarkable obstinacy when it came to threats against Callie. Despite Jamie Perkins and his feud, Clara refused to budge from her position. *Perhaps she feels that we're friends too.* Callie nodded, proud to have figured out that much at least. She'd never had a close female friend before and had no similar relationship with which to compare. She could only accept Clara's words and actions at face value.

"That's that then," she murmured to Jasper. "We'll be friends and support one another for as long as it takes before she figures out what she wants in life. After that…" Her voice trailed off, smothered beneath the weight of past and potential sorrow. After that, perhaps she'd see if Jasper's laudanum was still viable.

CHAPTER FIFTEEN

Clara smiled as she and Callie returned to the homestead. The packhorse pulled a laden sledge, its breath puffing mist into the winter air. Clara felt the cold of the season upon her cheeks and nose but little else, bundled as she was in heavy clothes and long underwear.

Callie scooped up snow and threw it at her.

She ducked and laughed before she returned the favor. In no time there was a monstrous snowball fight in the yard. The packhorse flinched out of the way, moving his load to the shed that doubled as his stable while the two women continued their play.

After a face full of snow met its mark, Callie left off the snowballs to tackle Clara. Hysterical laughter caused Clara to fall into a snow drift, and Callie straddled her.

"Got you now," Callie said.

"Yes, you do." Clara pulled Callie down and gave her a thorough kiss, triggering a liquid heat.

With a gasp, Clara sat up in bed. She panted, and patted her chest as she surveyed the room. In the other bed, Callie snorted and rolled over. *A dream! It was just a dream.*

The urge to both laugh and cry assailed her. She pushed both responses away as she calmed her ardor. She was overwarm and tossed back the covers. Again she glanced at Callie, the dream-kiss emblazoned across her senses. Clara swallowed against a rush of heat and longing. Her blood pulsed through her veins and pooled uncomfortably in her nether regions. She shifted, and the sensation was both pleasant and embarrassing. She'd been taught that masturbation was a sin against God but had never accepted that He would allow her to feel this ache without allowing some sort of relief. Unfortunately with Callie a mere few feet away, Clara couldn't chance being discovered should she attempt to ease her desire.

Her respiration calmed, though her desire did not. She slowly lay back in bed, the blankets pooled at her thighs, and allowed the cooler night temperatures to leech the fire from her body.

Her dream wasn't a surprise, not after her recent self-revelation regarding Callie. Clara had experienced similar dreams throughout her adolescence, dreams of yearning for one or another young man who had captured her fancy. There had even been a few with Emma in the role of Clara's True Love, so it was no oddity to see a woman now. Besides, the New Women Clara had read about believed in equality of the sexes in all things, including whom one should love and bed. Why, some of them had been known to bed one man after another, and then slept with a woman right after! Though Clara didn't care for the idea of nonmonogamous relationships, a shared life with another woman wasn't far-fetched.

Perhaps that is why I've always been fascinated by women of a masculine stature. She turned toward Callie's bed. The issue was whether or not Callie felt the same. Just because a woman didn't have an effeminate nature didn't necessarily mean she was interested in intimate feminine companionship. There had been one girl at Clara's secondary school who'd been as mannish as they came, yet she had pined for the boys worse than Emma ever had, swooning over the cutest lads in town. That girl had unfortunately suffered multiple horrid experiences among her peers. Men were fickle and overly confident; they required women to meet a certain level of physical attractiveness to win them. By the time Clara had graduated from school, the masculine schoolgirl had grown into a bitter young woman who shunned her former friends, having been the butt of far too many cruel japes.

Callie tended to shun people too. She'd shown an irrational reluctance to make the trip to Skagway to sell her goods or pick up supplies. To hear her tell it, she'd only been in Skagway once since Jasper had died, and he'd been gone for two months or more. If Clara hadn't arrived when she did with a thousand pounds of supplies, Callie would probably be starving to death or living off squirrels and wild onions, loaded down with moldy hides and meat that no one wanted.

Clara's heart ached for Callie's secret vulnerability. She wished there was something she could do to protect her from the slings and arrows of disdain from men like Perkins. Even if Callie wasn't interested in her as a—what would she be? Partner? Wife? Was there even a term for what she considered? —Clara couldn't abandon her now.

She lied on her back and stared at the dark ceiling as she drew the blankets up to her chest. The physical desire lounged in her body, relaxed and easy as it awaited an opportunity to surge forward again. In the meantime, Clara focused upon the earlier part of her dream.

Callie had said she would teach Clara how to trap, but their argument and Callie's injuries had brought that plan to a halt. Now that Callie was well enough to go back out onto the trapline, perhaps it was time for Clara to become insistent. She considered what needed to be accomplished to counteract Callie's immediate resistance. If there was one thing Callie knew, it was the word "no." Clara needed resourcefulness and imagination to put herself in a position that made "no" impossible.

Once Clara negated every argument Callie could come up with, she'd be able to convince Callie of the efficacy of her plan. She felt a smile cross her face as she dipped deeper into contented slumber.

* * *

Callie panted as she walked beside the horse. She'd argued against the packhorse, knowing the trapline would be a disaster after her absence, but Clara's insistence and Callie's private worries that she'd weakened too much in her convalescence had forced her to say yes. Now she was glad she had. The doctor had said her ribs wouldn't be fully healed for another month. The walk alongside the horse was exhausting enough; hauling her pack on her own would have been agony.

Wood smoke and fresh-baked bread heralded her proximity to home, and she picked up her step despite the exhaustion in her bones. A hot meal with fresh bread would hit the spot, especially when served by Clara Stapleton. Callie smiled, grabbed the horse's bridle and urged it to greater speed. She wondered what Clara had done all day. Clara would be sure to regale Callie with her exploits as soon as they sat down to dinner. *Garden and baking, o' course.* The day-to-day chores rarely changed. What intrigued Callie was Clara's voice as she spoke about her day, her thoughts and her new discoveries as she roamed the homestead.

Callie had no reason to announce her arrival. Clara would have heard the horse and known she was home. Instead, Callie led the packhorse across the yard, past the veritable greenery of Clara's garden, and opened the smokehouse door. The trapline had been a mess of sprung traps and rotting carcasses. She'd hunted a couple of marmots and a willow ptarmigan but hadn't brought home much else. The rendering of her kills wouldn't take long.

"Need some help with that?"

"Naw, it ain't…" Callie turned. Her words trailed off as she stared.

Clara stood proud in a pair of trousers, a shirt, and her jacket. She held her arms out from her sides, a wild grin on her face as she spun around. "How do I look?"

Callie gaped. Her brain refused to function. She worked her mouth in an attempt to answer but couldn't find her voice.

The satisfaction faded from Clara's face as she pursed her lips. "You look like a fish."

Callie snapped her mouth shut. Her mind finally gave the correct commands, and she said, "Why are you dressed like that?"

"Well, I certainly can't join you on the trapline in a dress, silly." The smile returned. Clara twirled in place once more. "I altered some of Jasper's clothes while you were away. What do you think?"

Callie forced herself to examine Clara from head to toe. It almost seemed indecent to see her dressed so. *Is that how people see me? Indecent?* She didn't know how to feel about that, but it would explain how people had treated her all her life. Obstinate ire brewed as she considered all the slights and outright venom she'd received from people since she'd started dressing in men's clothes. Oblivious to the thought processes of her detractors, she'd only ever felt hurt that no one had deemed her worthy of friendship. Now she experienced the immediate knee-jerk judgment that the general public bestowed upon those who didn't follow societal rules, Callie's sadness transformed into anger. *Who gives a damn how a woman dresses so long as she's comfortable with herself? Why do we have to wear all that frippery? To appeal to folk who aren't even in our skins and don't know our private thoughts and feelings? That's bullshit.*

"Callie?"

Startled out of her fury, Callie blinked. Clara's initial joy had begun to fade, probably due to Callie's angry look. Clara's eyes darkened, and by the tilt of Clara's eyebrows Callie knew it wasn't anger but unhappiness painting itself across that beautiful face. She stepped forward and touched Clara's upper arm. "You look fine."

Clara peered at her to ascertain whether she was being truthful. A slow smile broke through the clouds and her eyes began to show more blue. "Really?"

"Yes, ma'am." Callie rubbed Clara's arm and released her. She stepped back and made a circle around Clara to tug lightly on the jacket and straighten the shirt collar. "It looks like they were made for you."

Shoulders sagging, Clara laughed. "Do you think so?" She held out her arms and studied her alterations. "I'll be honest—I used some of your clothes as a measure." Abruptly, as if the thought had just occurred to her, Clara stared at Callie. "Do you think Jasper would mind?"

Her concern for the feelings of a man she'd never met—a man who had meant everything to Callie—caused a wave of affection to flood Callie's soul. She took Clara's hands in her own and held her fingers between them. "He wouldn't mind none at all. I think he'd support you just as he supported me all these years."

Clara's smile was tremulous.

Callie's concentration narrowed down to those full lips. The touches between them had increased daily since the brawl in Skagway, but this was the first time she'd fully instigated the intimacy and the first time it didn't involve Clara caring for Callie's injuries. *What does she taste like?* Clara's tongue darted out to wet those wonderful lips.

The horse interrupted Callie's thoughts with a snort, a reminder that she stood in the yard with her kills and a horse to put up, holding the hands of her brother's promised. She dropped Clara's hands as if they were hot brands. She unconsciously wiped her fingers on her trousers and backed away.

Clara seemed taken aback by the abrupt change in atmosphere, swayed in place. A slight indentation between her eyes indicated a frown that didn't quite make it to the rest of her face.

"I've got to take care of this." Callie gestured vaguely at the packhorse. "Put the horse up."

"I'll take care of the horse." Clara's expression cleared and she smiled.

Pleased that she hadn't offended her friend, Callie returned it. "Thanks."

"That's what partners do for each other." With Callie's help, Clara pulled the bags off the horse and led it across the yard to the shed.

Callie looked after her. *Partners? Is that what we're becoming?* She shook her head to dislodge the idea. *Work first, think later.* Faintly euphoric despite her tumultuous emotions and physical exhaustion, she prepared to skin her catch.

CHAPTER SIXTEEN

"Oh, this is impossible!"

Callie looked up from the snare she was setting.

Clara knelt a few feet away, attempting to set up a secondary snare of her own. She'd sat back on her heels, the wire looped in her fingers. "For the life of me I cannot set this trigger properly."

"It's all right. It took me months to get it down." Callie abandoned her work to help Clara. She studied the layout of the trap. "There's your problem." She took up the trigger, a small stick with a notch cut into it. "A deeper angle here won't be amiss." She pulled out her knife, and swiftly cut a more pronounced slant into the wood. "Now it'll sit together better but still be touchy enough to catch your prey." She handed the stick back to Clara who examined the adjustment.

"Should all triggers be that angle?"

Callie shook her head. "Trapping's an art form. You gotta figure out where to place a snare and use the natural environment you're given to set it. Sometimes you have to build it from the ground up with stakes. Other times you don't need anything but the foliage already there."

The answer didn't appease Clara. She held the snare for a moment before returning to the task of setting it.

Callie turned to her trap with a sympathetic smile. She remembered the same frustrations when Jasper had taught her how to work a trapline. It might take a few months, but she had faith that Clara's strong love of the outdoors and delicate control of her hands would go far in making Clara an adept trapper. Anyone who stitched the way she could had the ability to finesse a wire snare. Once she learned everything about the wildlife—identifying their prints and runs, understanding which traps and snares to utilize according to prey and environment—she'd be a force of nature. Callie could then help her set up her own trapline, one she'd run on her own just like Jasper had done.

The thought of Clara out in the wilderness alone worried her but she set it aside. Unable to do anything else all week, Callie had been teaching Clara how to shoot her new rifle. She'd discovered that Clara was a crack shot with a marksman's eye. Clara could hit damned near anything to which she'd set her mind. Callie carried both a rifle and a pistol when she was on the line; she'd have to look into a pistol for Clara. Jasper's was much too heavy for the smaller woman to use with any comfort, and it was a necessary tool in the bush. In some cases, the pistol at the hip could mean the difference between life and death. A charging grizzly didn't leave much time to unsling a rifle and take aim.

In her mind, she heard the roar of the bear as it bore down on Jasper. She shivered with the memory.

"Got it!" Clara exclaimed.

Glad for the distraction, Callie examined Clara's work. "Very good. Keep that up and you'll be running your own trapline in no time." She patted Clara's shoulder.

Clara glowed with the praise. She carefully scooted away and stood, shouldering her pack. "Where to next?"

"South and west." Callie picked up her pack as well. "I've got some leg traps laid out over there, mostly fox and hare trails. We'll see if any have been sprung, and I'll teach you how to set one." She led the way through the underbrush, in constant search for evidence of predators and potential snare-worthy trails.

"This is actually rather entertaining." Clara kept up with ease. "Much better than being stuck in a stuffy old cabin all day."

Callie laughed. "You won't think that come winter. That stuffy cabin will be nice and warm while you freeze your hind end off out here."

"A point in your favor." They continued in silence for several minutes. "You and Jasper weren't both gone at the same time, were you? I seem to recollect you saying something about alternating days…"

"Yes, though that depended more on the weather than anything. Most days we'd go out at the same time, but that didn't mean one of us wouldn't arrive home earlier than the other." Callie pushed through a stand of saplings, holding their branches aside for Clara. "Leaving a critter trapped for more than a day ain't humane. Some days we'd be out for most the day and others only a couple of hours."

"So who took care of the homestead if you were both away?"

Callie cast an impish grin back at her companion. "To hear you tell it, we didn't."

Clara leveled Callie a stern look.

Chuckling, Callie turned back to the trail. "It depended on who got home first. Most days we left a pot of something bubbling on the stove. Perpetual Stew, we called it." She recalled the many evenings that she and Jasper recounted tales of the trail as they shoveled stew and hardtack biscuits into their mouths. "We'd add whatever meat we'd caught, toss in wild or dried vegetables, add more water and let it go on and on."

"Was it edible?"

"Edible enough. Not as good as your cooking, though." The compliment caused Clara's skin to redden, a sight that Callie found most provocative. She stumbled over a root and cursed as she caught herself. Heat infused her cheeks as she forced her mind back to where she planted her feet.

"Though I don't doubt such a lifestyle worked for you and your brother, I can't do the same." Clara grunted as she climbed over a deadfall. "How did you split the chores?"

Callie shrugged. "Whoever thought of it did it, I reckon."

"Hence the reason there was dust three inches thick upon my arrival." Clara's said wryly.

"Exactly." Callie said. "Neither of us was much for household tasks." She pointed. "There's our next stop, and I can see we already have something." As they neared the sprung trap, she indicated others in the area. "Watch your step." She approached the fox and dispatched it with her rifle. "From the look of it, he just got here yesterday. Had he been here longer, he'd probably have chewed his paw off. See where he's already started?" She showed Clara the telltale teeth marks of a desperate animal. "That's why we'd go out most days. The noise and blood smell is one of the reasons why some days you don't find much on the line. It scares other critters away."

She looked at Clara to ascertain her level of queasiness. When Callie had begun trapping, she'd felt squeamish about the butchery, having never killed anything beyond the occasional chicken in Oregon. Clara had done a wonderful job to overcome Callie's unfavorable preconceptions about her past; butchering wasn't a task with which many city people had experience. Clara's complexion was pale, but the set of her shoulders and jaw indicated she wanted to continue the lesson.

"Now we'll release and field dress him. Field dressing is important when it comes to preserving the meat and hide. We've got to open him up and remove his innards, else the meat will go bad faster and poison the skin." Callie proceeded to put words to action as she deftly sliced the fox open from sternum to sex and divested it of its inner organs. "If we're hunting predators, we can use some of this to bait the trap once we've reset it. If not, we want to discard it away from the trail so as not to spook other animals."

She continued through the process, showing Clara how to reset a foot trap. After she sprang it, she oversaw Clara's attempt, instructing her in the safe use of traps. "These smaller ones, now…they'll break a finger easy, so you've got to be careful."

"Don't you have bigger ones back at the cabin?" Clara frowned. "Hanging outside on the porch, right?"

"Yeah. Those are for larger animals. Bear and wolf, for instance. We don't pull those out unless we see scat or tracks. Don't want a bear loose on your trapline. And those traps will break your leg if you step in 'em. They can kill you, sure as shooting, if you're not careful." Callie tied the fox carcass to her pack and pointed out the animal's prints and scat. Soon the area had been cleaned up and the traps reset and camouflaged. They continued on their way to the next traps along the line.

Clara picked up the threads of their earlier conversation. "While I do enjoy most housework, I'll need your assistance with it should I run my own trapline. You know that, yes?"

Callie had enjoyed the cessation of household chores. "Yeah, I understand."

"And my level of cleanliness is…um…much higher than yours."

A smile teased the edges of Callie's lips at Clara's tentative tone. "I reckon," she allowed, drawing it out.

"If we're to be partners at home as well as on the trapline, then we'll have to work together toward a common goal." Clara took a deep audible breath. "Would you be willing to consider taking over the occasional cooking or cleaning duty?"

Callie considered a more realistic life with Clara, one where they worked side by side, not only to survive but also to flourish. Her cautious thoughts were met with pleasure rather than dissonance. Jasper had requested a wife, and Callie had gotten one instead. *No, not a wife. Like Clara said, a partner.* So she'd have to cook and clean more than she liked, but they'd both reap the benefits of working together.

"I'll warn you now. My cooking ain't much. You'll be lucky to get anything better than Perpetual Stew."

Clara's laugh was musical. "No worries. When I allow you near the stove I'll happily suffer the consequences."

Callie felt a sharp twinge in her ribs as she twisted to bypass a mountain ash shrub. The reminder of her injuries dissipated her whimsical thoughts. There was still the issue of Jamie Perkins and his threats of violence. Would it be right to accede to this domestic contract between them when he was out there, waiting for any sign of weakness? Clara's arguments to remain had hit Callie with all the strength of a freight train when she was at her weakest physically. If Callie agreed to this now, Clara would share in the danger of Perkins's threat.

Do I have a choice? As she'd noted many times since Clara's arrival, the woman was a law unto herself when she set her mind. Arguing hadn't change it, nor had abandoning her in Skagway. Callie stopped and turned to face Clara. "What about Perkins?"

Clara cocked her head. "We can't let him scare us away. This is your land, your home."

"And yours," Callie blurted. She received a quick smile as reward.

"And we're partners." Clara grasped one of Callie's hands. "We'll deal with him together. We're stronger together than we are apart."

Still troubled, Callie nevertheless allowed Clara's words to soothe her. "It won't be easy. He's an opinionated ass with a lot of dangerous friends."

"We've got friends too." She shook Callie's hand when Callie evinced disbelief. "We do! And let's be honest, we're far smarter and prettier than Jamie Perkins and his fellows will ever be."

A snort of reluctant laughter disrupted Callie's worries. "If only it were that easy."

"It is." Clara released her. "You're concerned he'll have his men surround the cabin. What if we put out those bear traps? That would be both unexpected and an excellent defense."

Callie was amazed at how cutthroat this young high society woman was. Her dismay held a begrudging note of awe rather than disgust, and her thoughts furiously chased each other as she considered more strategic defensive moves they could make to protect themselves.

Oblivious to Callie's shock, Clara continued. "Perkins doesn't have a thimbleful of our intelligence. With a little forethought, we'll drive him clear back to Skagway if he tries anything." Clara laughed aloud. "We may even send him packing all the way to San Francisco."

The thought of Jamie Perkins running with his tail between his legs all the way to California was a fine one. Callie shared

Clara's laughter although privately, she doubted the reality of the idea.

"Now, where to next, teacher?"

Callie accepted the change of topic and led Clara down the trail to the next set of traps. She pushed Perkins from her mind. She only had one other concern, and it left a sickly feeling in the pit of her stomach. *What happens when Clara finds a husband in Skagway?*

* * *

Clara put the finishing touches on the fox carcass. She'd done her best to follow Callie's instructions and examples, but Clara still thought her fox skin seemed too thin in some places. At least she hadn't gouged any holes into it this time.

"Not bad."

Clara scoffed and pointed her knife at the marmot hide in Callie's hands. "Not anywhere near as good as yours, nor as quickly done."

Callie bumped her shoulder. "I've had a few more years' experience. For a first effort, it's mighty neat." She reached over to take the fox hide, holding it up to the sunlight. "See? There ain't as many light spots as you'd expect." She turned it over and laid it, inner side up, on the sledge. "Though there doesn't seem to be as much artistry on this side."

Clara returned the shoulder bump, both blushing in embarrassment at the evidence of hacking on her hide and secretly pleased with the praise. "Like you said, I'll get better with experience."

"That you will." Callie scooped up the hides to place inside the woodshed.

Clara carefully wiped her new hunting knife on a cloth and sheathed it at her hip. It felt strange and exciting to wear trousers and a hunting knife. *If only Emma could see me now!* The thought caused a brief flurry of confusion—would her best friend applaud Clara's daring challenge of societal mores or would she disapprove of Clara's strange ways? Depending on the day and her mercurial moods, Emma could jump to either side of the argument, a character idiosyncrasy that had inspired many a lively debate between them over the years.

Does it matter? Clara admired the masculine cut of Callie's feminine form. Emma had never understood Clara's draw toward women like Callie, nor was she here to experience the wonder of the wilderness. Why should Emma's opinion matter? The fact was, Emma Whitman's views had little to do with Clara's current life. Though she loved Emma, Clara was glad there was no constant reminder of her Boston debutante lifestyle. Here on the frontier, on Callie Glass's land, Clara had the freedom to be herself without the constant reminder. The sensation liberated her and brought giddiness to her heart.

She helped Callie put the sledge up, tilting it onto its side against the smokehouse to allow any blood or bile to run off and dry from its surface. Then she hooked her arm in Callie's as they crossed the yard. "This is your second day on the line. How are you feeling?"

Callie arched her back. She massaged the muscles of her lower spine. "A mite sore." She patted her side. "And I think the bandages have slipped a little."

"I'll rewrap them for you before dinner." Clara hugged Callie's arm. A week ago, Callie would have backpedaled, hands waving as she hastily explained that she didn't need any help. It was satisfactory to know that she'd become much more comfortable with Clara's touch and proximity.

Inside the cabin they doffed their coats. Clara shooed Callie toward her bed. "Off with the shirt. Let's have a look."

Dutifully, Callie followed orders and sat down on her bed, She unbuttoned her shirt, face red with embarrassment as she revealed her union suit underneath. Clara lit the stove and started a pail of water to heat. She didn't need the water for anything, but the activity gave Callie a moment of privacy. By the time Clara turned toward her patient, Callie's blush had faded. Her shirt lay on the bed beside her and she'd shed the top half of her long underwear. It was a summer set with no sleeves and short leggings, made from linen rather than heavy cotton.

Bandages swathed her torso from waist to armpit, twisted and rumpled at the top where the day's exertions had been too much for the bindings.

"It looks like we'll have to unwrap them a bit to return them to their place. Do you want to turn around?" Clara fully expected Callie to do exactly that and stepped back to allow her room to stand.

Fiery color returned to Callie's face. Her eyes remained on the floor and her butt on the mattress as she shook her head. "No need. You've seen most the rest of me already."

Clara froze for an instant that seemed like forever. She'd only seen Callie's breasts when the doctor had wrapped her ribs that first night at the hotel. Since then, Callie had protected her privacy by presenting her back to Clara when her bandages needed to be changed or adjusted.

"Is that all right?" Callie's flush deepened.

"That's…that's fine!" Clara croaked. She cleared her throat, and dusted her hands off on her hips. "That's fine. I just…" She trailed off, with a sharp shake of her head. "I'll just need to… get closer." She closed the distance between them and began to unravel the bandages. As she did so, she chattered to distract herself. "You haven't complained much about the pain…not that you complain much anyway. And the cuts and bruises have healed up nicely."

"Complaining won't make it better." Callie wouldn't look at her, and her jaw was set at its grumpiest level.

"No. But sometimes it feels good to vent your frustrations." Clara's concentration drifted away as the procedure slowly revealed Callie's breasts. The long strip of linen had left angry indentations against the perfect milky skin. Callie's breasts weren't large. To Clara, they were the perfect size for her shape, with rosy nipples that peaked when she uncovered them. Clara didn't know how long she paused, her initial discomfort superseded by desire. She wanted to touch the tender skin, ease its irritation, feel its softness. Did Callie's nipples feel as hard as they looked? Were they as sensitive as her own? Did they ache for attention? It would be so easy to…

"Clara?"

She smiled into Callie's pensive face. "Sorry. Woolgathering." With brisk efficiency, she rewrapped the bandage that hid Callie's beauty. She didn't want to give Callie a reason to distrust her, especially after their recent discussion on the trapline, and reminded herself that Callie did not necessarily share her predilection for women. "I have some salve in my things. Perhaps you could rub it into your skin. It may help with the chafing caused by the bandage." As she tied off the linen, her knuckles brushed against Callie's warm inner arm, strengthening the urge to caress her.

Callie twisted at the waist to test her bindings with a satisfied grimace. "That would be nice. My back itches something fierce; I'd appreciate an application of salve on my back."

I'd much rather apply it to your front. Clara blushed at the ribald thought. Her heart raced as she spun and walked away. "You get dressed while I get dinner ready." Her hands shook as she slapped a dollop of bacon grease into a frying pan. As it warmed, she prepared a simple dough of flour, water, baking powder and salt, tossing in a handful of rosemary to add flavor. A little fry bread to supplement the pot of beans from the day before would make a fast and filling dinner, one that wouldn't require Clara to pay close attention to her work. The last thing she needed to do right now was chop vegetables. She'd lose a finger for certain. As she diligently focused on the cooking, she heard Callie's approach.

"Are you all right?"

Clara focused hard on the pot of beans, giving them a vigorous stir. She couldn't look up. Would Callie be angry, denigrating Clara for her evil thoughts? Clara couldn't stand that. She forced a brittle brightness into her tone and plastered a smile onto her face. "I'm fine."

"No you're not." Callie leaned over the stove in a failed attempt to catch Clara's eye. "Was it something I said?"

"Of course not." Clara tapped the wooden spoon against the pot before setting it on a spoon rest. Callie's nearness was too much. Clara had only recently discovered her deviant feelings for the woman and had almost made a fool out of herself not two minutes ago. She whirled away from Callie to put distance between them. The tactic seemed to work. She wet a rag and scrubbed the dining table. Clara could see her out of the corner of her eye, no doubt frowning as she crossed her arms over her chest. *Goodness! What is wrong with me? I must control myself or she'll send me away!*

"I'm sorry."

Clara froze, mid-swipe.

Callie did indeed have her arms crossed over her chest, but the frown on her face wasn't obstinate or confused. Her expression was worried as she stared at the floor.

Clara straightened and swallowed, rag on the table. "What are you sorry for?"

"I shouldn't have…" Callie flushed. She shrugged her shoulders. "You don't need to rub anything into my back. And I shouldn't have let you…" she waved vaguely at her bed, "you know, do the bandaging like that." Her hand returned to cup her elbow as she hugged herself.

She thinks she did something wrong. A rush of dismay neutralized Clara's embarrassment. "Oh, no!" She laid a hand on Callie's shoulder. "That was fine. That has nothing to do with—anything!"

The smooth skin between Callie's eyebrows furrowed. "Are you sure? You were fine before, happy even. Then you couldn't get away from me fast enough."

"It has nothing to do with you, I swear." Clara rubbed Callie's arm. *And it has everything to do with you.* She was unable to hold the intense gaze. Her heart pounded in her chest. She felt the heat of a flush throughout her body. How could she explain herself and avoid banishment?

Callie pulled away from Clara, circling the table to sit at her usual place. Clara couldn't help but notice that she'd put the table between them. Was it a conscious effort to build a barrier between them?

"Sit down."

Clara placed the fry pan on the warming shelf and settled into the chair across from Callie. Her friend examined the tabletop studiously, hands clasped before her. Clara's worry suddenly blossomed into dread. Was it just moments ago that they had discussed domestic chores and planned a life? *This is all my fault. She's disgusted with me!*

Callie sighed. "There's something I haven't told you."

Clara frowned at the apparent misery on Callie's face. "What do you mean?"

"Something about me, about what I am." Callie's countenance became more wretched. One of her fingers traced an aged gouge in the wood surface of the table.

Relieved that this tableau hadn't occurred because of her reactions to Callie's nakedness, Clara reviewed her recent memories. She unearthed nothing that could account for Callie's somberness. Grasping for anything that would cause her friend such distress, she thought, *Did she kill Jasper?* The idea was horrible and ludicrous, not to mention completely irrelevant to the situation, and she chastised herself accordingly. Something had happened in the last few minutes to have caused this abrupt mood shift; this wasn't a reaction to or confession of Jasper's demise.

Callie opened her mouth, closed it, and shook her head. A furious scowl crossed her face. She straightened in her seat. "I'm a tom. A deviant."

A tom. Perkins had used the same word to refer to Clara at their first encounter. She hadn't known what it meant then and certainly didn't now. Thorough mystification quelled her anxiety. "I don't understand. A deviant? In what manner?"

Familiar exasperation twisted Callie's expression. "You come from Boston! I thought you knew of these things."

Choler piqued after the emotional morass she'd recently slogged through, Clara lowered her chin. "Apparently I'm not as experienced as you assume. Please explain the term to me."

Callie's ire faded with a flinch. She gathered courage to speak. "A tom. Someone who likes women." She paused. "A woman who likes women. Like men do." She deflated as soon as the words left her mouth, sullenly slumping in her chair as she picked at the rough tabletop.

A tom. Is that what I am? Clara's peevishness faded into wonderment as she discovered a new word that described her. She knew only a handful of terms, words that had become more significant as she'd come to know Callie—lesbianism, tribadism and Sapphism. She'd never heard this slang term before. "How interesting."

Her intrigued tone garnered Callie's rapt concentration. "Interesting?"

The implications of Callie's confession became clearer to Clara. "Indeed. I've heard a handful of words to describe what I feel, but never that one." *She's a tom. I'm a tom. We're both toms!*

Multiple emotions flickered across Callie's face before it settled into lines of faint annoyance. "Wait, what you feel?"

A burble of hysteria broke past Clara's throat. "Yes! What I feel!" Excitement and relief made it impossible to remain seated. She jumped to her feet and danced about the table, cajoling Callie to stand so she could take those work-worn hands in hers and reel her around.

Callie lurched backward and away from Clara's grasp. Clara continued past without her, circling the table with gaiety. "You've gone crazy! Stop that!" Callie intercepted Clara, her hands grabbing Clara's hips to hold her still.

Clara chuckled, and brushed a strand of hair away from her face. "I'm not crazy. I'm happy! Ecstatic! Joyous! Elated!" With each word her voice grew louder until she shouted at the low ceiling.

Callie shook her head. "Because I'm a tom?"

"No! Because I think I'm a tom!"

"What?" Callie dropped her hands and took a step backward so fast that she stumbled. She fortunately caught herself on a chair rather than the hot stove.

Clara filled her lungs with the bracing breath of freedom, releasing it as she settled down. She clasped her hands before her, and focused on her skittish friend. "I've become quite fond of you during my sojourn here, Callie. I find you attractive, intriguing and quite the distraction."

"Me?" Callie squeaked.

Clara bowed her head. "You." The news was an obvious shock to Callie who put the dining table once more between them. Clara didn't pursue. She hardly expected Callie to feel the same joy. Callie's life had been fraught with intolerance, forcing her to be ever on the defensive in every situation.

"You think you're a tom?"

"I've suspected for some time." Clara hugged herself against the need to dance again. Such action would spook Callie. "Women such as yourself have always intrigued and frightened me."

Callie's freckles scrunched with her nose. "I frighten you? That wasn't my intention—"

"It most certainly was!" Clara smiled. "You tried to drive me away from the moment I arrived. Of course you intended to frighten me."

Callie reddened and gave a sideways nod of acceptance. She sank into her chair as Clara followed suit across from her. "How long have you thought you…liked women? Instead of men, I mean."

"I read some books two or three years ago with my friend, Emma Whitman. They were about the New Women." At Callie's blank expression, Clara grinned. "Women who believe that all women should be allowed to vote, to own property in their own right, to run for public office or attend university beyond the accepted societal courses."

Amazement fought through Callie's dismay. "Public office? University?"

"Yes! These women have gathered together to demand the vote—it's called the Women's Suffrage movement."

Callie considered. "I recollect hearing something about that once. Jasper brought home a newspaper and we read it aloud to one another. One of the articles had those words." She focused again on Clara. "And those women, the Suffrages, they're all toms too?"

Clara snorted laughter. "No, not all of them. But some of the books I read were a bit more risqué than what you'd expect to find in a newspaper."

It took a moment for Callie to comprehend. Her mouth dropped open. "Really?"

"Yes, really." Curiosity ate at Clara. "How long have you known?"

The change in conversation momentarily confused Callie. "I don't know. All my life, I reckon. I was a laddie boy as a child, running wild and helping Pa around the farm. Jasper left when I was a toddler, so it seemed right to pitch in." She shrugged, fingers once again finding the wood grain of the table. "Mama tried to teach me my proper place, but it didn't take."

"And women? When did you know you liked women instead of men?" Clara pressed.

"About the time I was twelve. There was a girl at school—Adelaide Martin—who meant the world to me. I kissed her once, but after that she'd have nothing to do with me. You?"

"I believe I've suspected for the last couple of years…" Clara paused, suddenly losing the ability to speak.

"And…?"

You've traveled across half the nation alone. You've spent weeks in the wilderness. You can trap and shoot and have the necessary funds to build your own homestead if necessary. Don't back down now. "It was you." She saw Callie's startled expression. "I've been intrigued by you from the beginning. Everything about you has caught my eye and my imagination." She swallowed as she dry-washed her hands in her lap, her previous burst of ecstasy and excitement diminished into uneasiness. "I believe it would have been an absolute misery for me to have married Jasper because I can only think of you."

They sat in long silence, broken only by birdsong and the sound of a steamer whistle down in the inlet.

Frightened that her confession had ensured her immediate expulsion from the homestead, Clara stared into her lap. She'd never spoken ill of Jasper before and didn't know how well Callie would accept her words. Eventually Callie's chair scraped upon the wooden floor, a harsh punctuation to the inevitable final confrontation. Her boots thumped closer until she stopped beside Clara's chair and knelt beside her.

Callie covered Clara's fidgety hands with strong, warm ones, causing Clara to gasp aloud. Clara felt such a pressure in her chest, making her head pound with the sound of her heartbeat.

"It would have been a misery for me too."

"Truly?" Clara said, unable to do more than whisper.

"Truly." Callie's smile was sad as she reached up to caress Clara's temple, running the rough pads of her fingers through the dark hair there. The sensation caused a ripple in Clara's already overexerted heart. "I think it was too late from the first moment I saw you. You're a beautiful and strong woman. I would have envied Jasper for having you when I couldn't."

Her words caused Clara's eyes to tear. She laughed as she sobbed, cursing her cathartic heart at the same time as she enjoyed the release of tension. Her laughter grew stronger at the stricken expression on Callie's face, forcing Clara to nearly double over with the guffaws.

"I'm so sorry! I didn't mean to make you cry." Callie patted Clara's back, her touch frantic and awkward. "Can I get you anything? Do you want some laudanum? There's some still about—"

"No! No, I'm fine, I promise." Clara brought her apron up to wipe at her face, still chuckling. "I'm just extremely relieved and happy that we are of the same opinion."

"And are we?"

Clara studied Callie's face. Vulnerability stared back at her, hopeful yet suspicious, preparing to wince away if the situation called for it, to shore up the weak points in the inner wall that she'd erected. Clara cupped Callie's cheek. "Yes, we are." She struggled against a bout of nerves, and leaned close to kiss Callie on the lips.

Though she'd kissed Emma on the lips upon occasion, this was different. Callie's lips remained stiff and still for an instant before she returned the favor. Her lips were rough from windburn and exposure, yet simultaneously soft and yielding. Clara vaguely wondered if this was how a man's lips might feel before the thought was whisked away on the crest of desire.

Of the two of them, Clara had a better intellectual idea of what to do. Callie, for all her confident outward appearance, hadn't a clue. Clara teased Callie's lips with her tongue, surprising Callie to stillness for another brief moment. Clara attempted entry again, and Callie cautiously opened her mouth. Fire burned through Clara as she entered Callie for the first time, echoing her groan as their kiss became much more than a simple connection between them.

Clara explored Callie's mouth with her own, thrilling at the sensation of calloused hands in her hair, thumbs along her throat and ears and neck. She caressed Callie's tresses and throat, luring Callie's tongue toward her. The feel of it when Callie complied was like nothing Clara had ever felt before.

Several minutes passed before they broke apart, breathless, heads bent together. "Oh, my." Clara swallowed and licked her lips.

Callie chuckled, the sound of it rusty. "I take it you weren't expecting that?"

"No. Were you?"

"No. But I certainly enjoyed it."

Clara smiled. "As did I."

"Well, that's good. It would be a shame if you didn't benefit from it too." Callie dipped in for another kiss but didn't prolong the connection. "I think I could do that all day."

"And I think I'd let you."

Callie gave a hearty laugh as she sank back onto her heels. She took Clara's hand in hers. "So what happens now?"

I take you to my bed, supper be damned. Despite her desire, despite the knowledge that Callie shared her attraction, Clara felt a sliver of circumspection. It would be easy to tumble into bed and slake their desire, but could fondness bloom into love? *Would it have with Jasper? I came here knowing I might never actually love my husband.* Why that mattered now, with Callie, when it hadn't with Jasper, confused her. Clara patted Callie's hand. "Now I finish making supper. We're both starved."

Callie became vaguely befuddled at the change of subject. "Of course." She released Clara and stood. "How long will it be?"

Uncertain both about herself and about Callie, Clara wiped her hands on her apron for something to do. "The fry bread shouldn't take but a few minutes, and the beans are already heating."

"How about I draw more water and clean up then?"

Relief eased Clara's tension. "That would be fine."

Callie brought Clara's hands to her lips and kissed the knuckles. "I'll be right back."

Clara felt a sense of loss and confusion as Callie left. *What in blazes is wrong with me?* She woodenly returned to the stove. She pulled the fry bread pan from the warming shelf and set it to the heat. After several days of visualizing this very instant, she'd fled from the possibility of consummation. Her heart was full to bursting with joy and trembling with outright terror.

What would happen now?

* * *

Rather than approach the well in the yard, Callie drifted toward Jasper's gravestone. She dropped to her usual place, seated with her back to the cabin.

What the hell had happened back there? Callie had regretted allowing Clara to rebandage her ribs as soon as Clara began acting funny. Terror had raced through Callie, the same terror she'd felt when the bear had mauled Jasper. But there was no weapon against an attack on her heart, an attack that she'd instigated. *Why didn't I turn my back to her like I usually do?*

Her mind was awhirl with private castigation as well as the touch of soft lips, the near-hysterical laughter, the sight of Clara dancing about the cabin with happiness. *She's a tom, just like me. She feels something for me as I do for her.* Then why did it feel like Callie had been chased out of the cabin?

She sat at the engraved stone, stern. "This is all your fault, you know." She leaned closer to Jasper's grave and lowered her voice, "You're the one who wanted her." Jasper didn't answer.

It didn't matter; Callie knew who wanted Clara now. She could torment herself with guilt over lusting after Jasper's bride, but what would be the point? He wasn't here and never would be. Any right he had to feel betrayal had left with him on his angel wings. For a change, the thought of his absence didn't bring the familiar rush of agonizing bereavement. The hollowness was still there—like a sore tooth that she couldn't help but poke at—that empty place in her heart that would never fully heal—but the sorrow didn't seem as unfathomable as it had before.

Besides, Jasper hadn't had a mean bone in his body. If he looked down upon her to see if she was all right, he'd be happy that his little sister had found someone to care for and to care for her, regardless of how that person had arrived in her life. He wouldn't begrudge either his sister or his former bride some measure of happiness; he'd be pleased that it had come about.

Callie looked at the cabin. *Does she care for me?* The memory of the kiss blindsided her. That had been one hell of a kiss, one that Callie had never experienced before. It left her wanting more kisses and more…something. But she couldn't figure out what that vague desire was for, couldn't suss out what to do next. Had she ever had the courage to hire a woman at one of the brothels in town she'd know for certain, but for now she was at a loss.

An image of Clara dancing around the cabin assailed Callie, Clara's arms wide in joyous celebration as she understood who and what she was. *A tom. She's a tom like me.*

Callie reached down to pull at the scrub beneath her fingers. She'd realized early in her life that she wasn't like other girls—eschewing dresses and preferring to work the farm with her father to keeping the house. Her best friends had been all boys. Like them, she'd found girls incomprehensible. Eventually she'd heard rumors naming her a tom, delicious whispers among her classmates and fellow townies. They had begun not long after she'd kissed Adelaide behind the schoolhouse. It took some time to figure out the word's definition, but she remembered when the truth of it had hit her. The knowledge had engendered both an epiphany and a penal sentence as she discovered a core truth about herself, one that forever released her from ignorance but also condemned her to shame for the rest of her life.

She straightened from her slump. "That must be what Clara's feeling." Again she confirmed she was alone. Clara remained in the cabin, though Callie couldn't hear her. Chances were good she was as confounded as Callie right now, working through this new knowledge about herself.

Clara may have always suspected she was different from other girls. She'd as much as said so a few minutes ago. But there was a world of difference between reckoning and reality. Now that she'd come to realize the truth of her deviant nature, she'd need time to work through it all just as Callie had so many years ago. Callie didn't know if it was the natural order of things but her experience was all she had.

Feeling less befuddled, she brushed scrub from her hands. She'd give Clara time to sort through the morass of feelings. Clara was her friend; she deserved to be treated with respect and care. If and when Clara was ready to explore something more than friendship, Callie would be...amenable. She tamped down a surge of animal arousal with an iron will. Standing, Callie dusted her butt and turned toward the well to fetch water.

CHAPTER SEVENTEEN

Clara entered Skagway, a firm sense of accomplishment raising her spirits. She'd made it through the wilderness without a guide for the first time. *Hooray for me!* She'd discussed the trip with Callie but had waited until her housemate left for the traplines before loading up the packhorse. Callie was of the opinion that Clara shouldn't go alone—she'd lose her way, run into a bear—or worse, a woodsman with a gun and a lecherous attitude. Rather than argue, Clara had utilized the same tried and true method she'd used in Boston with her father—she'd waited until Callie had gone and continued upon her course of action anyway.

Clara observed the sky to gauge the time, boisterous with success. There was more than enough time to reach Hansen's Butchery, stop by the general store for a few essentials, and return to the homestead before Callie even noticed her gone. Clara would greet her friend with evidence of her accomplishments, thereby assuring Callie that she needn't worry so much for Clara's safety.

She mulled over her favorite topic as she pushed through the crowds, idly noting more new establishments that had been erected since her last visit two weeks ago. Callie hadn't kissed her since that first one a week ago, and Clara couldn't figure out why. Callie hadn't given any indication that the intimacy had been anything other than an exquisite experience, one that Clara wanted to repeat despite her personal skittishness. But Callie had done a gentle backtrack, avoiding situations that might trigger a delightful recurrence. While she'd kept her distance in that regard, she hadn't reverted to the nondemonstrative ways she'd exhibited at the start of their friendship. There were still touches and soft expressions, even caresses, but nothing more.

At first Clara had been relieved. The lack of pressure on Callie's part gave Clara time to think her way through her feelings about the situation. Despite having always known about her attraction for women, Clara had never confronted or accepted that draw until she had an avowed lesbian before her, one for whom she'd begun to deeply care. She supposed her hesitation was caused by the idea that such thoughts were no longer an abstraction, but a reality. She'd yet to come to terms with it. Callie had helpfully shared her life experiences so that Clara could better comprehend her own.

But a week had passed. Clara was beyond the initial stage of fearful discovery and well into frustration. No matter how much she schemed, pushed, and outright raged, she'd been unable to cajole Callie into another kiss. That was part of the reason Clara had decided to take this solo trip into town. She couldn't help but think that Callie viewed her as a helpless damsel, a ninny who needed rescuing rather than an equal partner in life. That Clara had developed and maintained her own trapline might have raised Callie's opinion of her somewhat but apparently not enough for her to view Clara as a peer, not a child. That had to be the root of why Callie had been reticent to explore any more intimacies. She needed a life partner, not a child to protect.

So Clara strolled alone along Main Street in Skagway, a packhorse with her personally caught hides and meat at her side. Perhaps when she returned home, Callie would understand that Clara didn't need or want a nanny. What Clara wanted was Callie.

A scruffy man blocked her path. "Well, good morning to you, sweetheart!" He briefly touched the brim of his hat and snatched her hand, pulling it to his mouth.

Appalled, Clara yanked her hand away, aborting his rustic chivalrous attempt. Had he been a handsome rogue, she might not have responded in such a brusque manner, but his abrupt and shabby appearance had startled her manners into flight.

Her insult caused a smile that didn't reach his eyes. A thin mustache swooped down to bracket his mouth, failing to hide a pronounced overbite. He took a single step back, and doffed his hat to reveal slicked-down hair, as dark as his eyes, painfully parted in the middle. When he spoke, he revealed a sizable gap between his front teeth. "My apologies! Allow me to introduce myself—Billy Quinn, at your service." His dead eyes left a greasy sensation as they roamed over her.

Years of propriety prevented her from a strident reaction. Besides, he'd taken a firm grasp of the packhorse's bridle, making immediate escape problematic. She drew herself up into the haughtiest of stances. "Miss Stapleton. If you'll excuse me, I'm on a matter of urgent business."

"Miss Stapleton!" Quinn seemed to taste her name as he returned his hat to his head and closed the distance between them once more. A sour cloud enveloped them, an odor of sweat and stale beer. "And from the sound of your accent, you're from Boston way, yes?" He licked his lips as he examined her.

His unwanted engrossment felt shameful, confusing Clara since she'd done nothing of which to be ashamed. She breathed through her mouth to avoid the rancid scent of him, staring over his shoulder as heat rushed up her chest and throat to warm her cheeks. "Yes. Now excuse me." She attempted to squeeze between him and the horse, but he sidestepped to block her.

"I've been to Boston once or twice. More likely once." He laughed. "Have you ever been involved in a Boston marriage? I bet you have, haven't you? Are you one of those wild New Women?"

Clara hardly comprehended the leer on his ugly face. The term "Boston Marriage" referred to two single women building lives together, something the author Henry James had written ten years earlier, and described exactly what Clara had been attempting to build with Callie. Clara didn't know which was more implausible—this unlettered malcontent having the intelligence to read a work of literature above the third grade level or that he'd approach her without any knowledge of who she was and who she knew with such insinuations.

Does he know Jamie Perkins? She cast around with a jolt of fear to confirm Perkins and his muscle men didn't observe from the sidelines with lubricious grins. Suddenly, the idea of a solitary trip to Skagway didn't seem a good one. If Perkins would beat Callie with little provocation, what did she think he'd do to her? *I can't believe I didn't think of this.* She'd been too busy searching for a way to prove herself to Callie to listen to the warnings Callie had given.

"Oh, don't worry." Quinn lightly caressed Clara's upper arm with the back of one finger. "What Callie Glass don't know won't hurt us."

The use of Callie's name confirmed Clara's suspicions, and a shock of horror took her breath away.

"Whaddya say we have a little fun? I can show you things that Callie sure can't." Quinn wiggled his eyebrows and eased closer until a hair's breadth separated them.

Clara searched for assistance but no one paid them heed. Terror vied with revulsion as she realized that she was on her own. She cringed back from his face, smelling the onions upon which he'd recently dined.

Who is he to do this to me? A man? More like a rodent. Fury bloomed in her heart, a fierce and righteous anger. This was the sort of behavior Callie suffered whenever she came to town— the remarks and innuendos, the suggestions that she didn't matter because no man had claimed her, that she was deviant because she wore men's clothing and refused to succumb to the "proper" society. With Jasper gone, no one could protect Callie from the dregs of society that had abused her. Eventually the

Jamie Perkins's of the world would utilize more than words and the occasional brawl to put Callie in her place.

Clara couldn't have that.

Her knee shot up into Quinn's groin. The action wasn't swift, her legs catching in the folds of her dress, but it was enough to get her point across as he grunted, a gust of foul breath blowing into her face. His hands shot to his crotch and he'd bent slightly at the waist, turning his hips aside to thwart a second attempt. As much as she hated to touch him, Clara grabbed his collar and pulled him closer until she growled into his ear, bits of ear wax and dandruff sickening her farther. "Now you listen to me, you little rat. If you ever talk to a lady like that again, I'll use my shiny new hunting knife to gut you like a deer. Do you understand?" She pulled back just enough to glare at him.

It was Quinn's turn to stare at her, open-mouthed, his eyes now filled with pain and dread.

When he didn't respond, she shook him, marveling at the strength her terror had given her. "Do you understand? Or should I take your ear right now?" She pulled her knife from its sheath at her waist. "Perhaps an eye instead."

"I understand!" Quinn's head swiveled about to see if anyone in the vicinity had noticed his abrupt emasculation.

Clara cast a swift look around as well. The potential witnesses were more concerned with their business than a man and woman in close discussion on the street. She shoved him away, and he stumbled as he minced. Without another word, she sheathed her knife, took the packhorse's bridle in hand and marched past.

The street seemed louder than usual as she strode away with a stiff back and expectant of retaliation. The animal part of her brain urged her to flee, to run as fast as humanly possible to escape danger. She'd be damned if she'd give Quinn the satisfaction of thinking she was scared, however. Instead, she panted and hung onto the bridle to keep from stumbling, ears open for any sound of approaching revenge. None came.

At the corner, she looked back. Quinn was nowhere in sight, and no one appeared to be after her. She continued onward, her emotional buoyancy at having navigated the wilds of the Alaskan bush gone. Would Billy Quinn scuttle away and hide? Would he run to Jamie Perkins and spill his guts? She gave a brisk shake of her head as she mulled over her thoughts. No, he'd not want other men to know a woman such as her had bested him. If he went for reinforcements at all, he'd trump up some sort of lie to gain their help.

Clara forged her way to Hansen's, keenly aware of her surroundings. Men seemed to stare at her wherever she looked, fueling her paranoia. Her nerves were shot by the time she reached the butchery. *Get the deed done, pick up the supplies, and get home. You'll be safe there.*

With a forced smile she greeted Malcolm Hansen and began the dickering.

* * *

Clara felt immeasurable relief as the yard came into sight. The trip home from Skagway had been fraught with worry. Every noise had startled her, no matter how unremarkable. Birdsong or insects hushed as she passed, the crackle of twigs and the rustle of underbrush all served to put her on edge. But she was home now. Everything was where she'd left it. The sledge wasn't at the smokehouse and there was no smoke from the cabin, so she knew she'd arrived home before Callie. *Another boon.*

She didn't know what she would tell Callie, who had become quite adept at sensing Clara's emotions. She'd smell a lie from a hundred paces. Prevarication wasn't an option in any case— Clara didn't believe in beginning a relationship in a way that would foster ill will in the future. Better to be truthful now than deal with hurt feelings later. She could easily imagine Callie's expression when Clara told her about Billy Quinn.

I won't mention him, not by name. I'll simply explain the altercation and how I de-escalated it. That would be the truth. Clara would simply omit a tiny bit of information that didn't matter in the long run. Callie wouldn't have a name to attach to the attacker and she would be unable to retaliate if she was of a mind, which would keep her safe.

Feeling better, Clara tied the reins to the porch. The sooner she unloaded and put up the horse, the sooner she could get on with things. She'd purchased more eggs and wanted to get a cake in the oven before Callie returned. Besides, cooking always soothed her, and she definitely needed the comfort at the moment. She still felt dirty from Billy Quinn's eyes.

"Nice place! Got a good view and everything!"

Heart in her throat, Clara whirled.

Billy Quinn stood a few feet away, hands on his hips as he marveled at the homestead. "Sweet little garden going there too. Is that yours?"

She was unable to form words as he strutted toward her, a sly grin on his unhandsome face.

"I asked is that there garden yours?" He stopped just within arm's reach. "Are you always this impolite to visitors? Didn't your mama teach you civility?"

Clara refused to show her fear. She straightened and put a scowl on her face, hoping to play off her earlier threatening demeanor. "Get off my property before I gut you."

Rather than cower in fear, Quinn laughed. "Oh, you are a feisty one, I'll give you that!" His smile faded, his expression darkening as he grabbed for her. "But I like a good fight."

* * *

Callie hauled the sledge up the slight incline toward the yard, pleased with the day's kills. She'd spent the afternoon entertaining the notion of making another supply run soon. Clara had nattered on about going on her own, but Callie had talked her out of the idea. Skagway was dangerous enough for someone who knew what to look for; Clara was a babe in the woods. As much as Callie hated town and the people in it, she knew that both she and Clara needed to make the occasional trip—Clara for purely social reasons, and Callie to take care of business. Providing Perkins didn't get in their way, a trip to Skagway would be beneficial to both of them.

She paused with a frown, and the noise of the sledge faded as she perked her ears. *What's that?*

Sound carried well out here, and she'd distinctly heard something odd. *Are those voices? Is that a man?* Whoever it was, didn't sound like Daryl McKenzie. And there was something else, something that could only be the violent slap of flesh on flesh followed by a grunt and a squeal of pain.

Horror filled Callie as she dropped the sledge ropes. She raced up the remaining few feet, unslinging her hunting rifle as she burst into her yard. The packhorse stood in front of the cabin, tied to the porch rails. The sight of him confused her. *Why is he wearing his tack?* McKenzie's horse wasn't there, nor were there any others. Beneath the animal and partially hidden by its bulk, she saw movement. Boots kicked up dust on the porch and an unfamiliar hat dropped to the ground. She brought the rifle to bear, kept her distance, and swung around the stomping, snorting packhorse.

Clara was pressed against the cabin door, hands pinned behind her by a dark-haired man. Unaware of Callie, he'd covered Clara's mouth with his own, performing a parody of the kiss she and Callie had shared last week. His free hand was planted against Clara's breast. Dirty fingers dug into the bodice of her dress.

Time slowed to a crawl. It was fortunate for the man that Clara was too close. Any shot Callie considered in that brief instant would potentially hit her, the only thing saving the miserable cur's life. Against her better judgment, Callie raised the rifle and shot into the air over the cabin roof. The horse reared at the thunder.

The man pulled back, releasing Clara as he turned toward Callie.

Billy Quinn?

Clara bent over behind him, panting and spitting onto the ground. Her complexion was green as she scrabbled for the door.

Quinn smiled and picked up his hat. He dusted it off and placed it on his head, walking toward Callie with his hands carefully in view. "Hey, Callie! Nice place you got here."

Callie set the rifle to her shoulder and put Quinn's forehead in her sights. Behind him, Clara slipped into the cabin, slamming the door behind her. Relieved that her friend was out of immediate danger, Callie focused on Quinn. "Stop right there if you want to keep breathing."

He held his hands out at his side, palms forward as he halted. "Now why you gotta be so unwelcoming? You've always been that way. Ain't you supposed to invite a visitor in? Offer him coffee? That's the hospitable way to do things."

"I don't offer coffee to trespassers." Callie backed away, putting some distance between them.

Quinn tsked at her as he stepped sideways. The two of them circled one another as he edged away from the porch. "I ain't no trespasser. Your woman there brought me here. We were gonna have some fun in town, but she had bizness to attend to."

Callie refused to show the alarm she felt. Clara brought him here? That didn't make any sense. *Unless she's decided to stop waiting for you to get your head out of your ass.* She shoved the disquiet aside, and concentrated on the problem at hand. "I don't know how you got here, but you'd better leave, lickety-split, or I'll put a bullet in you."

"Have you ever killed a man before? It ain't a pretty sight, you know. Any woman would feel horrible about taking a life, even one like you. I mean, women are the givers of life, right?"

Callie refused to be drawn into this bizarre turn of discussion. "Get walking."

He backed away toward the main track. "Why don't you ask your pretty little bride about how much fun we had in Skagway this afternoon, huh?"

In Skagway? Now the packhorse in the yard made sense. Clara had gone to town against Callie's wishes, and this bummer had followed her home. She vaguely wondered why she hadn't caught his earlier insinuation.

Her shock must have registered on her face because Quinn laughed aloud. "Oh, ho! You didn't know she'd gone!" He slapped his hands against his thighs, and let out another guffaw. "Now that's rich! You wanting to be a man and all, but you cain't control your bitch worth nothing."

Callie's finger tightened against the trigger. "Take that back."

When Quinn realized he was on the raggedy edge, his laughter subsided. "Which? The part about you wanting to be a man, or the other?"

It would be so easy. Just a little more pressure…

The cabin door flew open, and Clara emerged with her own rifle. "You heard her, Billy Quinn. Get off our property now."

Quinn raised his eyebrows at Callie, his mouth a begrudging moue. "'Our property', is it? Guess I was right about that Boston Wedding." Something about Clara's presence behind Callie galvanized him, because he waved his hands in surrender as he walked backward. "I'm going! I'm going!"

Callie leaned toward him, feeling her lips draw back as her prey made his escape.

He tripped on a rock and smirked, tipping his hat. "Now don't be shooting an unarmed man in the back, girls." He turned and strolled down the main track to Skagway, a jaunty whistle on his lips. As he drifted out of sight, he called, "I'll be back for that dinner you promised, Miss Stapleton. I'd love me a fine bit of dessert after too. Mmmm mmmm."

Callie marched after him, just to make certain he left her property. It wasn't because the desire to see him gutted like one of her kills was strong enough to make her tremble.

"Callie?"

She shot a glance at Clara. "Stay here. I'll be back."

CHAPTER EIGHTEEN

Callie returned an hour later. She stopped at the tree line and observed the homestead.

The horse had been put up and the sledge had been brought in from the trail. Clara sat near the smoke shed, up to her elbows in blood as she worked her way through the carcasses Callie had collected from the line. From where she stood, Callie could see that Clara had made a fine dent in the pile and stacked each hide neatly inside the open shed.

A pang shot through Callie's chest as she watched Clara. She'd told Clara not to go to town alone, yet Clara had done so anyway, bringing one of Perkins's lackeys back with her. The remote danger that had bubbled beneath the surface since Jasper's death had finally boiled over. Quinn would tell Perkins where the Glass cabin was located. In turn, Perkins would amass his malcontents and burn them out, but not before torturing Callie with the loss of everything she held dear.

This mess was Clara's fault. Her headstrong ways and lack of common sense had doomed them both. *And I love her.* The dichotomy of emotion made Callie nauseous. She was angry, absolutely furious at Clara's ignorant disregard about the threat to both of them. Was it her well-to-do upbringing, her educated ways? Had Callie been ineffective in expressing the seriousness of the peril? Had Clara never been subject to strife or the illogical malice of others? How could she have gotten so far along in life without ever once having had to deal with the practical realities of hatred and bigotry? Her inexperience with the vagaries of life frustrated Callie to no end.

At the same time, Callie's fear for Clara's safety was so strong that she wanted to weep and gnash her teeth. While she railed against Clara's pragmatic ignorance, she also adored it. Clara's idealism and intelligence were only two of a number of things that had drawn Callie from the start. Clara, with her book smarts and noble-minded thoughts, had unique perspectives that intrigued Callie. The last thing she wanted was for Clara's mind to be stopped, her voice silenced forever, her beautiful hazel eyes glazed over in pain and death.

Quinn would arrive in town within the hour. Callie doubted it would be long before he located Perkins and spilled his guts. She didn't think Perkins would come out tomorrow. Always one for plans, he'd want to gather his resources and make schemes before attacking Callie's homestead. No. She had two days, maybe three at most, before he showed up to burn her out. *And I'll be damned if Clara will be here.*

Callie remained on the edge of the trees until she obtained control of her riotous emotions. Since her arrival, Clara had always been able to wrest control from Callie; that couldn't happen again. Callie couldn't show any weakness, not the slightest chink in her armor. This time she'd have to do and say anything to drive Clara away. *Come Hell or high water, Clara Stapleton is going to leave this place.*

Stoking the anger in her heart, she marched toward the homestead where Clara, knife out, whirled to confront whoever was there. Callie felt a measure of respectful satisfaction at Clara's speed and apparent deadliness, then quashed it immediately.

Clara examined Callie for injuries or evidence that she'd murdered Quinn. "He's gone?"

"Yeah, but not for long. Get up."

Wincing at Callie's rough tone, Clara stood. Her hand shook as she returned the knife to its scabbard. "I'm sorry. I—"

Callie cut her off as she impatiently sliced her hand to one side. "Doesn't matter. You're leaving."

Clara turned white as she stared. Her mouth worked, attempting to find words, but nothing emitted from her lips.

Rather than allow Clara an opportunity to argue, Callie took her by the upper arm and marched her toward the cabin with brisk efficiency. "Pack up your things. I'll get the horse ready. It'll be dark soon, so we don't have any time to waste."

"But—"

Callie spun Clara around and dug her fingers into both of Clara's upper arms. "You're leaving and that's final." She mentally apologized for her next words. "I never wanted you here in the first place. I knew you'd be trouble, and I was right."

A hint of recrimination flickered behind Clara's stunned expression. "Excuse me?"

Before she could build up a head of steam, Callie yelled. "There is no excuse! Don't you understand? You've destroyed everything I've worked for. Quinn is telling Jamie Perkins where I am right this minute. They'll be here tomorrow to burn me out. You might as well have sent out invitations to every hooligan in the district." She shook Clara with each word. "You. Aren't. Welcome. Here."

Callie released Clara's arms and dragged her toward the cabin. "You're leaving now before you can do any more damage."

Clara's voice was weak. "But I thought you and I were going to work together, to become partners."

"That's what you get for thinking, ain't it?" Callie threw open the cabin door and hauled Clara to her trunk. "Let's be honest. Just because you might be a tom doesn't mean we can be anything together. I mean, really? Why should I settle for you just because you're the only tom I know?"

"What?" Clara sank onto the bed, her countenance one of hurt amazement.

Callie's bitter laugh belied the sharp pain that pierced Callie's heart. "You ain't what I want, okay? You and your highfalutin ways, your Boston accent. You can cook and bake like a dream, I'll give you that, but you're about worthless in everything else."

"I most certainly am not worthless!"

"Yeah? Did I mention that you can't kiss worth a damn? Besides, how the hell did Billy Quinn end up on my doorstep if you're so wise?" Clara's crestfallen look was too much to bear. Callie spun away and threw open Clara's trunk. She began to gather Clara's personal belongings from the shelf by the bed, shoving them into the trunk. "Now get your other bags out from under the bed. Daylight's wasting."

She continued to pack in silence, unwilling to see the damage she'd wrought on their friendship. Callie headed into the kitchen and rummaged around for the household items Clara had brought with her. Several minutes later, she heard the creak of the bed and the shuffle of items moving across the floor as Clara did as she was told.

Callie pushed back the tears that burned in her throat. In the back of her head, she had hoped that Clara would see through her ruse and take her to task for her insults. Callie risked a look when she brought a stack of plates to the trunk.

Clara's face was stone, her actions lacking their usual grace as she stiffly packed her things. She refused to look at or touch Callie as she inched past to collect a mixing bowl that had once been her mother's.

Again, tears threatened to expose Callie's true feelings. "I'll go get the sledge and horse ready." Callie stomped out of the cabin and slammed the door behind her.

* * *

The agonizing trip to town forced Clara to retrace the steps she'd taken earlier that morning. That time seemed like a million miles and a million years away, a time of adventure and happiness, of satisfaction and power. Now it was a horrible drudgery as she made her way in the early evening light.

They hadn't spoken since Callie had forced her to start packing. Clara had no defense against Callie's painful, biting words. Was it because they were true? Was she as worthless as Callie had so baldly stated? *Am I?* Up until her second altercation with Billy Quinn at the cabin, Clara would have argued the point until she was blue in the face. She'd done a fine job of defending herself in town, though the initial fracas had terrified her. Regardless, the truth was that Quinn had followed her from Skagway, something Callie would never have let happen. Clara's inexperience in woodcraft had allowed this danger to come to pass.

I shouldn't have gone to town. Of course, that contrition was of little value now. Callie was right; Clara had endangered both of them by her rash action. How many less-dangerous scrapes had she and her friend Emma gotten into in Boston? There, at least, Clara'd had the benefit of her father's social standing and finances to protect her from the repercussions of her shenanigans. Nothing protected her here in the wilderness, though, no one to step in and gloss over her indiscretions. *Hardly a New Woman if I must depend on a man—any man—to defend me from the backlash of my own actions.*

Smells and sound loomed ahead, the flower of a typical Skagway evening in full bloom. Callie's face was set as they entered town. The northern sun was still out and the streets still busy. If anyone recognized them or realized that the same packhorse and sledge had passed this way earlier today, no one gave indication. People were more interested in their business or hedonistic pursuits. Even the catcalls from the prostitutes on the balcony didn't invade the grave shell surrounding the two travelers.

As they neared the first hotel, Callie finally broke the silence. "Which hotel?" she asked coldly.

Clara's heart ached at the utter lack of emotion. "Not that one." She refused to even look at the establishment where she'd spent one of the longest nights of her life. Had it only been a fortnight since Callie had fled, leaving Clara to sit alone in the darkness until it was safe to return home? *Home. I have no home now.*

If Callie noted the ache in Clara's voice and face, she didn't show it as she clucked at the packhorse. Three blocks later, they arrived at Skagway's second-best hotel. "Go see if they have a room. I'll unload the sledge."

Eyes downcast, Clara nodded and entered the hotel to make the arrangements. Her silent hope that there were no vacancies was dashed, and she paid for a week.

"Any luggage?" asked the jovial-looking fellow behind the desk.

Clara's voice caught in her throat. "Yes. Outside. A trunk and four bags. My…friend…is unpacking them."

The mirthful desk clerk smothered his hospitable smile but failed to match her somberness. "I'll have my man bring them up to your room." He held out a key. "You'll find your room at the top of the stairs, third door on the right."

Clara murmured a distracted thanks. As the clerk arranged for her bags to be delivered, she blindly examined the key in her hand, at a loss. Should she go up to her room? Should she check on Callie, see if she needed help with the bags? No, Callie wouldn't thank her for that. Callie didn't want her, never had.

Hot tears stung her eyes, the lump in her throat painful as she attempted to force it away. She'd masterfully kept control of herself all day, from the moment Quinn had accosted her in town this morning. Now it seemed that her control had ebbed beyond her ability to forestall her emotions.

The choice taken from her, she fled up the stairs to her room, weeping silently for the love she'd thought she'd found, the love she knew she'd lost forever.

* * *

Callie waited outside until a big Scandinavian man with bushy blond hair arrived to retrieve Clara's luggage. The muscles of his arms popped as he picked up the trunk, hardly batting an eye as he lugged it inside. She waited until all the bags were taken and postponed her departure for several minutes. She wondered whether Clara would return to argue her point, suggest an alternative, or at least say goodbye.

She never returned.

Can't say as I blame her. Callie pulled off her hat as she leaned against the packhorse, rubbing her burning eyes. *What's done is done. At least she'll go on to have a long life. Maybe she'll decide to marry after all. She'd make a great mother.*

When she was sure she wouldn't start bawling, Callie climbed onto the horse for the ride home. Barebacking wasn't the easiest way to go, but if she wanted to make good time with nightfall coming on, she'd need to ride rather than walk.

She navigated through Skagway, avoiding the worst of the drunkards and malcontents that seemed to overrun the town when night came on. The whores hooted at her like they always did, but she ignored them, the cloud of misery around her too bitter to succumb to their innuendo. One thing did cut through her haze of wretchedness—a smug, hated voice she recognized.

"Why, Callie Glass! Did you come to town to invite me back for supper?" Billy Quinn called, his tone sly. He stood bold as could be on the side of the street.

Without thought, Callie pulled the packhorse to a halt and slid off its back. The sight of Quinn, bold as could be on the side of the street, sent her into a fury. A red haze covered her vision.

His expression faded from complacency, thumbs hooked casually into his suspenders, to fearfulness as he dropped his hands to his sides and backed up to the saloon wall at her rapid approach. "Now, wait a minute there, girl —"

Callie grabbed him by the throat with one hand, the barrel of her pistol digging into the side of his head. "Shut up." She hardly recognized her voice; she imagined Quinn didn't either.

Quinn frantically searched the growing audience for assistance. Other than a few exclamations from those nearby and a general scuffling as space was cleared around them, there didn't appear to be any help on the way.

"You scum-sucking, lily-livered little bitch." Callie pressed the pistol harder into his head. It would leave a hell of a bruise if she didn't shoot him first. "You mucked up everything. Everything! You hear me?" When he didn't immediately answer, she shook him.

He grunted assent, his face red as her grip on his throat tightened. Gurgling, he attempted a response, but couldn't get the words out.

"If I ever see you or your friends anywhere on my property, I won't hesitate to kill you. Understand?" She shook him again, ignoring his hands digging into her wrist to loosen her grip. The pain felt right and good. She didn't want to kill him though, not yet. Against her better judgment, she loosened her hold, and he gasped for air. "I asked you a question, you bastard."

He emitted a deep cough that sprayed Callie's face with phlegm.

As disgusting as the sensation was, she didn't wipe it off. Instead she pulled the hammer back on her pistol.

Quinn went very still, the whites of his eyes showing as he tried to see the gun at his temple. He swallowed, breath raspy as he focused on her. The smell of urine rose between them.

"This is your final warning, Billy Quinn, and you've had more than anybody else," Callie said, her voice deceptively soft. "Step on my land and die." When she saw that he fully comprehended her, she continued. "And that goes for Jamie Perkins and his men too."

Quinn nodded, a jerky action that seemed almost like he was having a seizure. He shook like a leaf, his foul breath coming in asthmatic wheezes.

With care, Callie released the hammer. The light of hope sparked in Quinn's eyes for the briefest of seconds before she brought the gun down on his temple. He crumpled to her feet, unconscious.

She stepped back and wiped his spittle from her face with a grimace. The murmur of conversation around her reminded her of where she was. She turned and saw twenty or more men watching, none familiar. Any one of them could be one of Perkins's men. *Hell, one of them could already be on his way to let the cat outta the bag.* It was time to go.

The witnesses scattered as she strode to her horse and clambered once more onto his back. Clucking, she urged him down the dusty street, eyes open for any immediate retaliation as she headed out of town.

CHAPTER NINETEEN

Cautiously, Callie unblocked her cabin door and stepped outside, rifle in hand. The yard appeared untouched. The taller vegetables in Clara's garden waved gentle greeting in the morning wind. The bell of a steam ship on the water made Callie's throat ache, but she swallowed the lump with pragmatism. *What's done is done. She's safe now. I can't hardly take care of myself let alone her too.*

The night had been long. Sunset had come upon her on the way home from Skagway, making the trail perilous. The packhorse had done most the work, plodding along the familiar path with his keen sense of smell and awareness of danger. Callie had put him up in the shed as soon as they'd returned. She'd then barricaded herself in the cabin in case Perkins didn't have the sense God gave a gnat. He hadn't shown up to inflict any reprisals in the darkness. No doubt he gathered his resources in town. After what Callie had done to Billy Quinn, Perkins would be out for her blood. Even if Clara had to remain in town a day or two to make travel arrangements, Callie doubted Perkins would know or care.

She recalled last night's vicious altercation, the tendons and muscles of Quinn's throat beneath her digging fingers and his bulging eyes and red face, the flash of light on metal as she pressed the barrel of her pistol to his temple. God, how she'd wanted to shoot him! But even though Skagway was a lawless town, that didn't mean she could kill with impunity. Eventually the government would send their enforcers to clean up the area—it was simply a matter of time—and all those witnesses would gladly point to her as a murderer.

This way is better. Perkins will come wanting blood and Clara will have escaped untouched.

Callie sighed with resignation. Should she go out on the trapline? Did it really matter? At the very least, she should get out there and clear the traps she'd set. No reason to leave animals to suffer if she'd never collect them. She glanced in the direction of her brother's grave, wondering what strategies she should employ to protect herself and her property.

"You're concerned he'll have his men surround the cabin. What if we put out those bear traps?"

She stood frozen, remembering Clara's words. At the time, Callie had been both shocked and wickedly delighted that the prim and proper young woman would suggest something so dastardly, but it seemed the perfect strategy at the moment.

With a grim smile, she circled the homestead in search of hiding places that attackers could utilize, marking where she should set her traps.

* * *

"As much as I'd like to say otherwise, we ain't got a cabin on an outgoing steamer for three more days."

"Three days?" Clara battled despair, not willing to lower herself to hysteria in public. She stood in the office of the Pacific Coast Steamship Company, drawstring purse clutched in her gloved hands. "Can I be assured that one of those cabins will be reserved for my return trip to Seattle?"

"Oh, ayep." The company representative shuffled through some items under the counter. He was of middle-age and clean-shaven. His dark blue suit indicated how much pride he took in his appearance. The outfit was crisply pressed and the narrow tie impeccably knotted at his throat. An emblem was sewn onto the breast, the golden thread outlining a steamship. "The *City of Topeka* will be through here day after next." He extracted a large leather-bound book and opened it. "Ayep. Here we go. We have a number of berths yet available, leaving in three days for Seattle."

"I'll take it."

The man raised a bushy eyebrow. "I ain't told you the price yet."

Clara sniffed, drawing upon years of hauteur to hurry the hated procedure along. "It shouldn't matter. I paid for my return trip when I purchased passage here." From her purse she retrieved the voucher she'd been given when she'd booked her initial trip in Seattle, the one her father had insisted upon as condition for not interfering in her choices. She'd hoped to keep it for its duration and burn it in celebration on the anniversary of her arrival. *I never wanted to use this.* The ever-present lump in her throat grew larger but she shoved it down with vicious alacrity, presenting the voucher to the representative.

He studied the document. "Everything seems in order, Miss Stapleton. I'll book you for a double cabin." He plucked a pen from its stand, and prepared to write her name in the register.

"Wait!" The last thing Clara needed was to share a cabin with another woman. It had been fine for her initial foray, her sense of adventure strong as she gossiped among the other passengers. But after…well, she simply didn't have the patience to deal with another woman constantly present. She needed the solitude in which to grieve for what wouldn't be. "I'll pay extra for a single cabin please."

Again the bushy eyebrow rose, but the man nodded. "Of course, miss." He set the pen down, grabbing up paper and a pencil, licking the pencil lead as he calculated the new charges.

A quarter hour later, Clara exited the steamship company's office with a bit less cash and feeling considerably worse. The deed was done. In three days she'd be gone from this place forever. *Forever.*

She took a deep breath to forestall more tears, and marched back to her hotel. Right now, Callie was probably on the trapline with the packhorse. Had she been home, Clara would have cleaned up after their breakfast and perhaps weeded the garden before checking her own traps. *Did Callie have anything to eat this morning? She doesn't take care of herself well enough, and she's still healing. Would she have thought to eat the cornbread leftover from our last dinner?*

Their last dinner.

Clara forced the tears back. She'd cried more than enough last night in her hotel room. It was time to buck up. Tears wouldn't fix a damned thing, and crying didn't make her feel one whit better. Instead she'd be left with an ache in her sinuses, a clogged nose and red eyes. Chin up, back straight, Clara continued along, desperately casting about in her mind for something that wouldn't trigger a bout of sobs.

"Clara?" a man called.

Overwhelming terror froze her for the briefest of moments before she recognized the voice. It wasn't Billy Quinn. She fought the urge to swoon in relief as she slowly turned to see Daryl McKenzie approaching from across the street. She plastered a gracious smile onto her face, and waited for him as she tried to calm her nerves.

McKenzie tipped his hat. His eyes darted about, probably searching for Callie. "What a pleasant surprise."

"It is, isn't it?" Clara knew McKenzie was sharper than his curmudgeonly appearance indicated. She also knew that any attempt to prevaricate or drive him away would be met with questions she didn't want to answer. Rather than incite a scene here on the street, she took one of his arms. "Will you be so kind as to escort me back to my hotel?"

"I'd be honored." They walked a bit before he spoke again. "I'm amazed to see you here. I doubted Callie would be up to traveling so soon. How is she?"

How is Callie? Clara didn't have an immediate response. How could she tell McKenzie that she'd made a supreme error in judgment that would probably send Callie on to her great reward? That she'd unwittingly betrayed the woman she loved on a lark, for no other reason than to prove herself the equal that she could never be? "Not well, I fear."

McKenzie frowned. "What can I do to help?"

"You'll have to ask her."

He gave her a sidelong look. "Are you two staying in town tonight?"

Clara sniffed, more to push away the tears than to show pique. "I'm here alone." She gestured toward the ticket office. "I was booking passage to Seattle."

"Wait. What?" McKenzie stopped, turning to stare fully into her face. "You're leaving?"

"She's thrown me out." Clara had meant to deliver the words in petulant anger. Instead they became a gateway of despair as she burst into the dreaded sobs. "She's thrown me out, Daryl! And it's all my fault!" She burrowed into his arms and succumbed to the tears again, the exact emotional whirlwind she'd expected. She imagined that these were Callie's strong arms holding her close while she bawled out her fear and sorrow.

Eventually the flood ended, as all her recent dolorous weeping did, with a mixture of relief and shame as she realized she'd made a fool of herself in public despite her best efforts. She struggled with the drawstring on her purse, and located a handkerchief that she used to wipe the tears and snot from her face. "I apologize," she murmured, voice crusty. "I don't know what came over me." She brushed at the tear stains on the lapels of his jacket with a helpless laugh. "I've made a mess of your coat."

He lightly snagged her wrist, placing her palm against his heart and patting the back of her hand as he smiled. "It needed a good cleaning. By my estimation, it's become less of a mess now." He released her and crooked his arm, smiling when she slipped her hand through it.

They strolled along in silence until Clara regained full control of her faculties. It took her some time to realize that they'd passed her hotel, not that she'd had the sense to tell McKenzie where it was. He seemed unconcerned as they walked through town with no particular destination, a cozy parade of two weaving through the streets and boardwalks, past thousands of people who didn't care.

For the first time, Clara witnessed all of Skagway, not just the parts that she'd passed on her previous visits, but also the hinterlands of this burgeoning town. In one part of Skagway, she saw corrals full of horses preparing to take on one of the two trails to the Yukon goldfields, heard the ring of hammer on anvil as furriers shod the scrawny animals. A handful of men loaded packhorses and sledges with the thousand pounds of supplies required by Canadian authorities at the Yukon boarder. Another group had already left, plodding down the trail to await their turn at the base of Chilkoot Pass. Pacific Freight wagons trundled to and fro between the mud flats and the corrals, laden with the goods that would give a man a shot at surviving the cruel winters and the even crueler will of his fellow competitors.

And here was the sour smell of unwashed humans, horse manure, and fried bacon that forced the handkerchief out of her purse and back to her nose. They strolled through what seemed like a field of tents that housed hundreds of men and their gear as they waited for their turn at the passes.

A pack of dogs fought over offal near a temporary butchery, their growls vicious and teeth snapping. Instead of turning her stomach, the smell of blood made Clara almost nostalgic for the Alaskan wilderness, the crunch through the bush, her traps, and conversation with Callie. She hastened away from the scene lest the sniveling begin again.

Farther on, tubs of water heated over outdoor fires as laundresses scrubbed and repaired clothes for the men, charging a penny a shirt or two pennies for trousers. One even offered boot polishing for a nominal fee—a foolish proposition considering the amount of mud and dirt on the unpaved streets. Clara doubted the boot black made much money here.

A line of men stood outside another tent, battered tin plates in hand as they waited to be served a breakfast of fried potatoes and eggs. The sign on the side of the tent indicated no menu, but offered breakfast, lunch, and dinner for twenty-five cents a head. *"Bring your own plate and utensils!"*

Circling back toward the established residences and businesses of Skagway, she noted boarding houses and freshly built homes, the smell of cut pine thick in the air. The sound of children's laughter startled her, and she unconsciously took the lead in their travels as she searched for the source. Three little boys played with sticks in the dirt yard of a new home, brandishing the wood like swords as they whooped and hollered. "I had no idea there were children here."

"There's some. Not many though." McKenzie nodded toward the house. "That there place belongs to a fellah who wants to open a bank here."

"A bank?" Clara marveled. "Why, next thing you'll tell me is that they'll elect a sheriff or magistrate to run things."

McKenzie laughed. "Oh, I doubt that! Not any time soon anyway. There are too many confidence men in town right now fleecing the sheep. Perhaps in a year or two."

Clara imagined Skagway in a year or two, or even five. Seeing the evolution of the town from lawlessness to a real township would be fascinating. "I'm sorry I'll miss it."

"You don't have to."

Her breath hitched as she tried to think of something to say.

McKenzie continued walking. "I know you love it here. Whenever we've talked you've been most vocal about your love of the wilderness. While I can appreciate your reasons for leaving, perhaps you should reconsider." He waved his free arm at a restaurant with another line of folks waiting outside. "It wouldn't take much to set yourself up in business, and you'd reap plenty of money to make it worth your while. I'd be glad to help in any way."

Clara suddenly realized he'd taken her on a tour of all the businesses in town that were owned and operated by women. A fond smile briefly crossed her face at his subtle attempt to dissuade her from leaving the Alaska District. She'd had similar thoughts over the first few weeks when her presence at the Glass cabin had been tenuous. McKenzie was right; it would be easy enough to set up in business here. She'd have to cancel her upgraded berth on the *City of Topeka* as well as write her father for more money, but it could be done. Callie had said that

Clara cooked like a dream—opening a restaurant wouldn't be unwarranted with her skills.

She imagined a line of rough men waiting to be fed, hiring others to serve them while she cooked in the back. And then she remembered Callie at the table in the cabin, focused intently on her food as she complimented Clara between bites. Pain shot through her heart.

If Clara remained in town, she'd have opportunity to see Callie every fortnight or so. Even if she didn't see Callie, she'd know approximately when Callie would come to town to do business. The thought of slaving away her days over a stove, mind fully occupied with thoughts of Callie—wondering if Callie would inadvertently show up at the restaurant or whether Clara had the strength of will to not chase after her—opened a trap door beneath Clara.

She stumbled against McKenzie. "No," she whispered. His arm went around her waist, holding her up as she regained her equilibrium. When her voice was stronger, she repeated herself. "No. I can't stay here. I can't afford to run into Callie, not after…not after…"

"Not after what?"

Clara looked into McKenzie's puzzled eyes. "Not after what I've done." And she explained everything.

CHAPTER TWENTY

Clara sat on the edge of her bed, gloves in hand. Her luggage waited by the door. She marveled at the vagaries of time—two days had passed, two days of mourning and fond remembrances, three nights of sleepless nightmares. The time had passed with such speed, and yet each minute had crawled out into hours. She glanced at the clock on the mantelpiece. The Pacific Coast Steamship porter was scheduled to arrive in ten minutes to retrieve her property. She'd already decided to follow him on foot, to experience Skagway one final time before she boarded the *City of Topeka*. In a week, she'd be back in Seattle. What she planned to do then hardly bore thinking upon.

The tears didn't threaten this time. She'd cried so many of them that they'd left her a desiccated husk. At this point she'd become numb, disinterested in the world. McKenzie had visited each day, escorting her on daily constitutionals and filling her head with various rumors about the township as he subtly encouraged her to remain as a businesswoman. None of it mattered to Clara, to the thick wad of cotton batting that had filled her heart and mind. She'd let him natter on, nodding where appropriate and urging him to continue with polite questions. The longer he talked the less speech was required of her. She simply couldn't dredge up the energy to hold up her end of their conversations.

Instead, she mulled over a number of things that she regretted about this venture. Not being able to meet Jasper, the man who'd asked her here and that had meant so much to Callie, was one of them. From what she gathered from both Callie and McKenzie, Jasper Glass had been a singular man. Clara had imagined a life with Callie while Jasper found someone else to marry, the four of them becoming a family of sorts. It would have been a wonderful life.

Her inability to conceive of staying here without Callie was another regret. Perhaps if she hadn't fallen so hard for Callie, she'd have been able to convince herself to follow McKenzie's suggestions, stay in town and start her own business. But her mental imagery failed to show her a vision that didn't include crushing sorrow whenever Callie came into view. Who on earth could live like that?

The biggest regret in Clara's heart was that she hadn't had the courage to see Callie one last time. Clara had no photos, no drawings of Callie. Had Clara been thinking clearly, she'd have considered taking the picture Callie owned of her and Jasper. In time Callie's face would disappear from Clara's memory. It was a natural inclination—she couldn't picture her best friend Emma Whitman in her mind after only a month's absence. Soon, Clara wouldn't remember the exact hue of Callie's golden hair, the distinct pattern of freckles across her upturned nose, or the haunted expression of Callie's eyes. It would all turn to smoke. *Just like me. I'll be smoke, drifting in the wind, with no substance.*

A hurried knock at the door shocked her from her melancholic musings. Now time chose to speed up, to truncate the remaining minutes of her folly? She noted that time hadn't distorted the other direction, that the porter was actually early for this appointment. When she opened the door surprise yanked her from the melancholy cotton.

Daryl McKenzie stood there, brown eyes wide. He held his hat in one hand, his white hair askew on his head. Before she could speak, he blurted his news. "Jamie Perkins left town about an hour ago with a dozen men. He's heading for the cabin."

"A dozen men?" Clara's hand covered the sudden beating of her heart. *Callie!*

"Yes. I'm gathering some fellahs together to go after, but I thought you should know."

"But—But I'm leaving!" Clara hated the shrill hysteria ringing in her voice. "The porter will be here any minute!"

McKenzie's face crumpled and he wiped at his beard. "Damn, pardon my language. I didn't realize…" He tugged at his beard. "For some reason, I thought you weren't going until tomorrow. I thought you'd want to know what was happening."

"Daryl?" someone called from downstairs.

"I'll be right there!" he shouted back. He took Clara's hands and gave them a squeeze. "You have a safe trip. I'll write a letter as soon as this is done. It might be a few days before it arrives in Seattle, but I'll send it via the steamship company." He shook his head, his craggy face regretful for telling her of Callie's danger. "I'm so sorry! Had I realized…" He trailed off at his apparent stupidity.

"Daryl! Come on! We gotta meet Roman at the saloon across the street."

Torn, he glanced over his shoulder and back at Clara. He hastily leaned forward and kissed her cheek, and then clattered away.

Clara followed him to the landing and stared down into the hotel foyer as he ran down the steps. Two unruly men waited there, rifles in hand. One of them was Malcolm Hansen, the butcher.

Hansen pointed out the door as McKenzie reached them. "Roman said he had three more t' the saloon."

"Let's go get them. That should be plenty enough to show Perkins we mean business." McKenzie led them out of the hotel, bowling over a young man wearing a suit.

The young man paused as the excited trio passed before approaching the desk. "I'm looking for Miss Stapleton's room. I'm to deliver her belongings to the *City of Topeka*."

It was time. She'd put Callie in mortal danger by leading Billy Quinn to the cabin. Jamie Perkins had set out to attack Callie and would probably kill her. McKenzie had rounded up a few hearty souls to stop the bloodshed. And yet it was time for Clara to exit the stage, like a pretty actress in her final scene, to a steamship headed south.

Once again, time slowed to a crawl as she considered her choices. She could forfeit her cabin on the steamship, stay and do her best to deal with the repercussions of her actions. She had enough money to cover two full months at the hotel. That allowed plenty of opportunity for her to contact her father for another ticket to Seattle. It would gall her no end to succumb to such an unconscionable action, but her father's wealth was a resource that had been tapped through most her youth. Callie was in danger. The last thing Clara could do was board a steamship and bury her head in the sand, not knowing the outcome of the confrontation.

She leaned over the banister. "Excuse me!"

Both the hotelier and the porter looked up.

"I'm canceling my cabin aboard the steamship. My apologies for the lateness of it all. No need to come upstairs." She turned to the jovial desk clerk. "I'll be extending my stay for a week, perhaps longer. I'll know more this afternoon."

"Of course." The hotel clerk opened his register to make the adjustments while the porter tipped his hat and left.

Clara whirled around and dashed to her room. She didn't have much time to prepare.

* * *

Callie sat back on her haunches as she wiped sweat from her brow with her forearm. She squatted in Clara's garden, pulling recalcitrant greenery that shouldn't be present in the neat rows of vegetables. *Weeding's harder than it looks.* She remembered all those times she'd watched Clara blithely maintain the small plot of land. Callie had never realized the truly strenuous nature of the task.

The bitter regret that had been her constant companion for the last three days reared up. She wished she'd thanked Clara for all that she'd done around the homestead. There wasn't a speck of dust or a cobweb anywhere in the cabin, Callie's clothes smelled fresh and clean, and everything just seemed neater and brighter. Clara had toiled long and hard to make the cabin a home. *One we'll never share.* Rather than dwell on what couldn't be changed, Callie scanned the yard, forcing her thoughts to other things.

She'd begun to wonder whether or not Perkins would show. Years of acquaintance had indicated he'd never been blessed with an overabundance of patience. He'd either become more mature over the years or else his plans for her didn't include invading her territory. *Or he's out there right now, watching me.* Her eyes studied the woods behind the cabin. She'd had the sensation of being watched for a day or more, but had attributed it to her justifiable concern. That feeling was stronger now. A steamship whistle echoed across the yard, its volume loud in the unnatural quiet. Alarm grew in Callie's chest as she craned her neck to take in as much of the view as she could. *I don't hear the birds.*

A shot rang out when she turned. She felt the wind of it as it passed through where her head had just been and plowed through a stalk of corn with a *zipping* sound.

At the same time, a man gave a piteous scream to her left, his agony interspersed with the sound of chains. Billy Quinn staggered over the rise, a bear trap clenching one arm as he tried to shake it off. Like all the bear traps, this one was pegged to the ground. When he ran out of slack on the dangling chain, it pulled him back, and he stumbled and cried out louder.

Without thought, except to silence him, Callie pulled her pistol and shot him in the head, silencing him forever. She burst from the garden, firing shots in random directions as she ran for the porch. She'd celebrate Quinn's demise later; right now she needed to stay alive.

Despite her cover fire, multiple rifles and pistols went off all around her. Fire streaked across her left upper arm and head as two bullets grazed her. The rest missed as she dived for cover and crouched behind the wood she'd stacked on the porch to provide a protective barrier. Near Jasper's grave, another man screamed. Callie grinned. They might have had plenty of time to surround her, but she'd had the same to leave a few surprises. She had to give Clara credit; that had been a wonderful idea to set out those traps. Callie had also placed every weapon she owned on the porch. Now she picked up her rifle and peeked over the edge of her log barrier.

The men had closed in after the first shot. She had no idea how many there were, but even one was too many. From her vantage point, she saw two huddled by the shed. Another crouched on the southern decline that led down to the point between the two inlets that flanked her land. He was the one who fired at her, and she ducked back as chunks of wood showered her head.

The graze on her head bled like a bitch, but she wiped blood from her eyes and ignored it. Instead she closed her eyes, carefully remembering where each of her immediate enemies was located. When she had their placement firmly fixed in her mind, she popped over the logs and fired.

The man in the grass was first, her shot entering his neck at the junction between his shoulder and head. The idiot hadn't even moved, apparently believing a woman couldn't shoot for shit. *Joke's on him.*

Her next four shots were at the shed. As much as she worried about the packhorse neighing in protest inside, she couldn't afford the sentimentality. She could only hope he'd survive the rain of bullets flying everywhere. She pegged the first man in the thigh, knocking him down. His partner jumped back, and used the shed as cover. Callie estimated his placement and fired through the thinner walls of the shed. She saw the soles of his boots when he collapsed, and hunkered down to avoid retaliation.

"Is that the best you can do, Jamie?" she called during a break in the gunfire. "Ain't any of you boys been hunting before?

Christ on the cross, I cain't believe none of you can shoot." She checked her rifle, and topped off the rounds.

"I can shoot well enough, Callie Glass. Just you wait and see."

She scuttled toward Perkins's voice on her right. It sounded like he was near Billy Quinn's corpse. On the opposite side of the yard she heard the pathetic moaning of another bear trap victim. "I been waiting for days. Didn't you get my invitation?"

"I hear it's fashionable to be late to parties." There was a pause. "Why don't you come on out? I promise not to shoot you. At least not at first."

A chill ran through her at the assurance in his voice. "I can't make the same promise."

"I guarantee you won't shoot me, Callie Glass. Not before I plow that field between your legs a dozen times." Rough laughter seemed to come from everywhere. "And my men have some ideas of their own. I invited them to this party, and they need their entertainment."

Though she doubted Perkins was unprotected, she popped up long enough to fire in his direction.

A volley of rounds assailed her, digging wood chips from the front wall of the cabin and the porch. She saw a flash of gunfire and shot blindly in that direction, hearing at least one grunt of pain. Before she ducked back down, a round hit her left upper arm, the force of it knocking her onto her ass.

Dazed, scared, and a little pissed that she'd been hit, she gasped as she peered at the wound. Blood dripped from it, mixing with the crimson stain from the graze. There was so much of it. The sight of it made her feel faint. The pain was excruciating at the point of entry, accompanied by a sharp ache that radiated down to her fingertips and across her shoulder and chest. *At least it's not a gusher.* Whether by luck or divine intervention, the round hadn't pierced the artery in her arm. She tore her shirt sleeve off, unable to keep from crying out at the stab of pain she caused, and used the cloth to tie up the injury.

"That sounded pretty promising, boys!" Perkins called out. He received a round of hearty agreement.

Idiots. Didn't they know that every time they spoke or laughed aloud that she could figure out their location? They might have the advantage in numbers, but this was her territory. She knew it like the back of her hand.

Thanking God that the shot hadn't injured her shooting arm, she crossed to the other side of the porch, knowing they wouldn't expect an attack there. She glanced back once to confirm that the porch post would partially block Perkins's view of her, and raised up.

Two men were crouched over and running toward her position. Their astonishment was almost comical as she opened fire, dropping them both. Agony exploded in her right shoulder. She fell back with a cry, her rifle falling from now useless fingers. Either Perkins had gotten a lucky shot or there was another shooter in his vicinity that hadn't been hindered by the cabin.

As if to punctuate that supposition, a scream heralded the discovery of another bear trap, this one from behind the cabin. That was the third one. She panted against the pain, but a vicious smile stretched across her face. That meant they were flanking the cabin now.

She grabbed up Jasper's still fully loaded rifle, ignored the torment as the tortured muscles of her left arm complained, and scooted into the cabin. She slammed the door and used a shim of wood to wedge it closed.

Keeping low, she worked her way to the rear of the cabin, in search of something to stanch the bleeding from her shoulder; each movement sent excruciating tendrils of anguish throughout her body. She used her knife, and sliced off a fair length of the sheet from her bed. She felt nauseous and weak. *Probably from the blood loss.* As she wrapped the linen over her shoulder and under her arm, she vaguely realized that despite all the running and tumbling about her ribs didn't hurt near as much. She chuckled. *Well, there's a blessing in disguise, eh?*

"Turtle's in her shell, boys!"

Perkins's hated voice was enough to return her to her task. Blood loss or not, she'd be damned if she'd let him win. Maybe they'd both die here today, but Perkins wasn't going to survive the afternoon. Once she'd bandaged herself, she peered out of a crack in the shutter. The last two she'd shot at were still down, as were the two by the shed. By her estimation, at least half her shots had hit home, whether they inflicted mortal injuries or wounded her enemies. And she'd only suffered four hits.

Only. She slumped against the wall beneath the window.

The scream and rattle of a fourth bear trap was loud on the other side of the cabin. Apparently one of the men had intended to bust through the window.

Callie chuckled. "You have an evil mind, Clara Stapleton of Boston, Massachusetts. A brilliant, evil mind." Tears spilled over her cheeks, tears of both pain and happiness. After three days of second-guessing, she finally knew she'd done the right thing by sending Clara away. She hadn't saved Jasper but she'd been able to protect Clara. That was a decent enough memorial for a woman's life, and one she was pleased to attribute to herself. "It beats a cup of laudanum, doesn't it, Jasper?"

She heard him whisper back. "It sure does, Cal. Bully for you."

Outside, the men blundered closer as they discussed what to do next and whether there were any more traps. She had nowhere else to go. If she didn't get help she'd bleed to death anyway. Either that, or her wounds would become infected like Jasper's had. Better to go out there and meet her maker on her own terms.

She staggered to her feet, leaning on the cold stove as she headed toward the door. "I'll be there in a minute, Jasper." Though unable to raise her left arm above her waist, she fumbled her pistol into it. A kick dislodged the shim at the door. "I'm coming out!"

Heart pounding, she threw open the door.

* * *

Clara heard the distant, chilling sounds of gunfire over the horse hooves. She rode behind McKenzie, clutching at his abdomen as she jounced along. Her fanny had gone numb long ago, and she had doubts she'd be able walk by the time they arrived. All such mundane thoughts fled as she listened to the intermittent fusillade ahead.

Seven other horses followed, each with a determined man on its back. One of them was the doctor that had cared for Callie in town. Clara had hoped that his presence wasn't necessary, but the sound of martial fury ahead didn't bode well for that supposition.

McKenzie pulled up well short of the homestead. The others followed suit.

"What are you doing?" Clara demanded as he slid off the horse. "We're not there yet."

His face was grim. "If they're still shooting, she's still alive. We need to come upon them unawares or we'll never take 'em. They outman us two to one."

Clara hated the truth of his words, but knew he was right. He helped her down. As expected, her legs didn't work properly. She clutched the horse's saddle as she acclimated herself to her own two feet once more. She'd changed into her trousers and coat before leaving the hotel. The pistol Callie had purchased for her hung fully loaded at her hip. Once Clara regained the use of her legs, she pulled her rifle from where McKenzie had lashed it to the saddle and joined the others.

The gunfire had quieted, but suddenly a man screamed. The sound of it echoed through the trees, a haunting wail of anguish.

"What the hell was that?" one of McKenzie's friends asked, his face pale.

Clara's thoughts were quicksilver. She clapped her hand over her mouth to keep the laughter down. The other men gave her looks of uncertainty and uneasiness. They'd argued against her presence on this venture and now wondered if she'd fallen sway to the hysterics to which all women were prone. "Bear traps," she finally whispered. "Callie must have set the bear traps around the yard."

Grudging respect flickered across many craggy faces.

"Not a bad idea."

"Smart thinking."

McKenzie interrupted their murmurs of admiration. "All right, here's what we're gonna do." He split the men into three groups, two to flank the homestead and one to approach via the main track.

As they broke away from each other, Clara added in a loud whisper, "And watch out for bear traps! She has eight, and we don't know how many have been sprung."

A couple of the men looked a little green, but everyone acknowledged her warning as they disappeared into the woods.

McKenzie and Clara stood alone. "You ready?" he asked.

Clara hefted her rifle. "Sure as shooting."

With a rueful grin at her pun and a shake of his head, McKenzie led the way down the track.

The road itself was clear of traps. McKenzie kept a slow, steady pace until a single shot came from ahead. Terror in her throat, Clara rushed forward, half running and half hobbling as her thigh muscles complained about the exertion. It took her less than two minutes to reach the edge of the yard. McKenzie caught her before she could burst from cover and dragged her to one side, using a thick pole pine as cover while they observed the yard.

Callie was on the ground at Perkins's feet, her golden hair splayed in the dirt. With blood-crusted hair and stained, torn shirt, she seemed covered with improvised bandages. A body lay nearby, no longer pumping blood from the wound in its skull. Four men stood hale and hardy in a semi-circle around the front of the cabin, and a fourth sat a few feet away, holding his gut wound.

She's still alive!

Callie struggled to sit up, one arm tight against her stomach.

Perkins hit her with his fist and knocked her back to the ground. "You know, you don't look like much, but just seeing you like this has got me harder than a diamond." He laughed as she writhed at his feet, spitting blood. He began to unfasten his pants. "I told you this would happen. Get ready for the party, you unnatural bitch."

Clara's heart squeezed as she realized what Perkins planned to do. The sick feeling she'd experienced at the hands of Billy

Quinn flashed through her so swiftly that she was never sure later that the sensation had ever been there. It fled from the icy fury that swept through her soul. She marched forward, rifle at her shoulder, easily evading McKenzie's hand as he reached out to grab her.

She pulled the trigger, and dropped one of the three remaining men with cool detachment. Startled at the interruption, everyone aimed weapons at her. McKenzie must have revealed himself behind her because Perkins's two flunkies wavered.

Perkins laughed. "Welcome to the party, Miss Stapleton! My boys will have some fun with you next." He waved carelessly at his men. "Shoot the old man."

Clara aimed at Perkins. "I'd think again if I were you, gentlemen. We didn't come alone."

"Ain't that right?" Hansen called from the eastern edge of the yard, near Jasper's gravestone. "Fancy seeing you here, Jamie. What's that you got between your legs? I can barely see it."

The attackers spun to see Hansen and two others come into view, weapons ready.

Perkins snarled at the insult, buttoning his fly with choppy movements. Before anyone realized his intentions, he pulled a large knife and grabbed Callie's hair. He hauled her semi-conscious form into a sitting position.

Clara, McKenzie, and his men all prepared to fire. "Best let her go, Jamie."

Perkins brought the blade to Callie's throat. "I ain't gonna live through this, and neither is she." He pulled back to plunge the blade into her throat.

But Callie had pulled her own knife while she squirmed in pain on the ground. Now she thrust her blade into Perkins's unprotected midriff at the same time that Clara pulled the trigger of her rifle.

Perkins barely had time to register his evisceration before the bullet in his brain put a stop to all thoughts. His knife fell from limp fingers and he collapsed to the ground.

Clara's rifle also hit the ground as she abandoned it. She ran forward, pistol slapping at her thigh as Callie slumped back, her hand dripping with blood that wasn't hers. Clara fell to her knees at Callie's side, her hands roaming Callie's body as she searched out all the injuries.

"Thought…I told you…to go."

"Shush." Clara knew her tears gave lie to her attempt at sternness. "Save your strength. The doctor will patch you right up."

Callie smiled, the blood from her mouth giving her a garish look. "Before I go—"

"You're not going anywhere, do you understand me!" Clara wiped at her tears. "And neither am I!"

The doctor arrived at their side. Between his pushing and McKenzie's hands at her shoulders, Clara was forced away. She willed Callie to survive.

Callie's gaze wandered, confused. Was it blood loss or something more serious? Clara didn't know. What she did understand were the words that Callie mouthed to her over the doctor's shoulder.

"I love you."

Unable to be strong any longer, Clara burst into tears.

CHAPTER TWENTY-ONE

In the garden, Callie carefully wiped sweat from her brow with her one good hand. She'd planted her behind in Clara's garden, pulling at the recalcitrant greenery that had invaded the neat rows of vegetables. It was about the only thing she could do that didn't earn the ire of Clara and the doctor who'd been back twice in the last week to check on her.

Her right arm was in a sling, forearm lying idle against her abdomen and getting in the way more often than not. She'd been forbidden to use it and, truth be told, it hurt too damned much to do anything anyway. The bullet that had entered her shoulder had broken the big bone, the one the doctor called a "scapula." She'd be in this sling for five weeks or more while it healed. They had to wait and see if she'd regain full motion of the arm. All things considered, she'd been lucky that it had been the most serious of the wounds she'd suffered.

She still had difficulty raising her left arm above her shoulder, and found it quite painful to carry much. She could pull weeds, feed herself and pee, but that was about the extent of her abilities. Fortunately, the damage had been to soft tissue only. It itched like mad where the doc had stitched it up. Once the stitches were out she'd be able to work on it more—the doctor thought she'd make a full recovery there.

After the firefight, McKenzie, Hansen and the men they'd brought along had loaded up the bodies and paraded them, along with the wounded, through Skagway. Most went to the coffin-maker. Of the dozen men that had attacked the homestead, only two had left the property completely unscathed. The bear traps had wounded three, and a fourth had survived the initial onslaught with a mere gunshot. The fifth, the man in her yard with the gut wound, had died on his way back. Word had spread quickly that most of them had been killed by Callie herself, giving her one hell of a reputation. She was of the opinion that the greatest improvement in her life was Jamie Perkins's death. That fact alone had eliminated the greatest physical threat to her and Clara.

Callie focused on the garden patch. She'd gotten all the weeds that had showed their heads. *Until tomorrow anyway.* She gave the yard a speculative scan, searching for something—anything—to do. *Maybe I can fire up the smoke shed.*

With half the use of one arm, she struggled to get to her feet and retrieve the bowl of weeds. She wavered as she regained equilibrium. Maybe the smoke shed could wait. She balanced the bowl in the crook of her sling as she let herself out of the garden, firmly latching the rudimentary fence. She thought of all the little things that could be done to improve the homestead. A new garden fence for one. Clara had done a good job, but Callie didn't expect this one to last much longer against the hungry deer and hare. There'd already been evidence of burrowing, and plants along the fence line had suffered the telltale nibbles of thieves. Then there was the henhouse Clara wanted to build. She was a big baker, and eggs never lasted long.

As Callie tossed the weeds to one side of the yard, she glanced at the area that Jasper had cleared months ago for his wedding cabin. *Maybe I should work on that. It'd give us a little more room. Clara's spoken about inviting her friend and brother up here.* She eyed the location speculatively. Here would be the main entry, there the kitchen. Maybe a formal dining room and parlor could be added. The task would probably take a couple of years, but they had plenty of time.

Callie heard Clara enter the yard from the main track with the horse and sledge and laid aside her daydream.

Clara tied the horse off at the porch. With a brilliant smile she embraced Callie. "How was your morning?"

"Boring as all get out," Callie groused, crooking her lips in a tiny smile. "I swear I'm gonna go crazy sitting around here on my butt all summer."

"You will not." Clara punctuated her words with a deep kiss. When they broke apart, both breathless, she said, "I'll keep you busy."

Callie cleared her throat. "I got no complaint."

Clara laughed. "I doubted you would. Come on, help me bring this into the house." She sorted through the items for things that were light enough for Callie. "What were you doing over there?"

As they unloaded the sledge, Callie told Clara about Jasper's intention to build a cabin in which the newlyweds could reside. "I'm thinking we might not be able to get started this season." She shrugged a shoulder as a reminder of her limitations. "But we should consider doing the same."

"Really? A cabin for me?"

Callie nuzzled Clara's delectable neck. "For both of us." She welcomed Clara's arms, her skin singing with the human contact.

* * *

Clara gently awoke, her eyes drifting open in the darkness. She luxuriated in the heavy warmth of multiple blankets and furs, and felt the chill January air on her exposed cheek. Her stomach grumbled and her insistent bladder marred the sleepy cloud of contentment.

The cold months of winter had brought nights that seemed to last forever, the sun setting as early as three thirty in the afternoon and not returning until well after eight o'clock in the morning. Her daily routine had slowly evolved with the longer nights; she retired to bed not long after dinner, slept until the wee hours, and then arose for a brief spate of activity around the house before taking a nap until the sun deigned to show its pallor face. It seemed an odd way to live, but she'd quickly eased into the cycle.

She continued to ignore her bodily complaints, rolling toward the radiant heat beside her. She snuggled closer to Callie, enjoying the half-awake sensation of skin against skin as Callie groggily turned toward her.

Clara drifted in and out of consciousness, listening to the steady thump of Callie's heart. Eventually her bladder became insistent, and drew her fully from sleep. With a regretful sigh, she gently extricated herself from Callie's arms and eased out of bed. The air was icy against her bare skin, and she hastened into her flannel gown and a heavy robe, putting her sock feet into her slippers at the foot of the bed.

After heeding the call of nature with the honey pot under the bed, she carefully opened the stove, stirred the banked coals back to life and added more wood. She tossed in a couple of chunks of coal for good measure. Then she lit three candles rather than wake Callie with the brighter light of a lantern. Rummaging under the counter, she pulled out potatoes to fry for an early morning snack.

As she peeled potatoes, she saw Emma's envelope lying on the other side of the table. Letters from her flighty friend were rare enough to make them special, but this one was even more so. Clara's brother had finally succumbed to Emma's charms—he'd proposed marriage last month. They'd be wed next April and on a train to the west coast soon after. Clara's dream was coming true; Bradford had graduated law school and wanted to start a practice here in the Alaska District. Clara could hardly wait to see them. Her ambition to see Bradford and Emma living on the homestead wouldn't reach fruition—he'd need to reside in town for business—but the specifics didn't matter. They'd be mere hours away, not thousands of miles.

She sliced the peeled potatoes, humming under her breath, and remembered the excitement she'd first felt...when was it? Early spring last year? That breathless discussion with Emma as she had revealed her intention of becoming a mail-order bride. Clara glanced fondly at the tousled blond hair peeking from under the covers. Things rarely went the way they were planned, but Clara wouldn't trade her life here for anything or anyone else.

She carefully placed the fry pan over the heat and added a dollop of lard to it. When she added the potatoes a few minutes later, they hissed and sizzled.

Callie pulled the covers down far enough to look at Clara, and yawned mightily. "What time is it?"

"I don't know. I didn't bother to look." Clara smiled as Callie grumbled and rubbed sleep sand from her eyes, hair askew. After checking the potatoes, she sat on the edge of the bed.

Callie pulled her down and they nestled together, the smell of potato filling the air. Clara caressed Callie's left arm, fingers sliding over the ugly mottled scar of the gunshot wound. Her lover had regained full use of that arm, but not the other. Callie toiled every day to strengthen both arms but she'd never have the full range of movement that she'd enjoyed before the firefight in the yard. The lack hadn't crippled her however. She still went out every day on the trapline. The problem came when she attempted to lift anything over her head.

Callie stared into Clara's eyes. "I love you, you know."

Clara smiled. "I believe I've heard that once or twice before." Her grin widened as Callie curled her lips in mock disgruntlement, her blue eyes sparkling with humor.

"If you don't watch it, I'll tickle you." Callie's fingers made a swift journey to Clara's ribs, causing Clara to jump.

Tensing at the feigned attack, Clara laughed. She brought her elbow in to pin Callie's hand. "I love you too, silly."

"Who's silly?" The offending fingers applied a brief amount of pressure. "You're the silly one here, Miss Stapleton."

Clara squirmed. "Silly for love. Guilty as charged."

The answer must have been the correct one. Callie left off trying to tickle her, and instead pulled her close for a kiss. Long, sumptuous moments later, Callie broke it off, and leaned her forehead against Clara's.

Clara basked in the adoration she felt both in her heart and that issued from the woman in her arms. This was where she'd always been destined to be, right here with Callie Glass.

"Clara?"

Her heart pounded at the sound of Callie's husky voice, her blood hot with the memory of the ecstasy of many winter nights just like this one. "Yes?" she asked, her voice breathless.

"I think the potatoes are burning."

Clara's eyes flew open.

Bella Books, Inc.

Women. Books. Even Better Together.

P.O. Box 10543
Tallahassee, FL 32302

Phone: 800-729-4992
www.bellabooks.com